# *COLOURS*
### *and*
# *SHADES*

*by*

*Isabella Clarke*

Published in 2008 by YouWriteOn.com

Copyright © Text Isabella Clarke
Copyright © front cover image Mandy Kasafir
Copyright © back cover image Issi Doyle

First Edition

The author asserts the moral right under the Copyright, Designs and Patents Act 1988 to be identified as
the author of this work.

All Rights reserved. No part of this publication may be reproduced, stored in a retrieval system, or
transmitted, in any form or by any means without the prior written consent of the author, nor be
otherwise circulated in any form of binding or cover other than that in which it is published and without a
similar condition being imposed on the subsequent purchaser.

Published by YouWriteOn.com

*To Colin*
*– always –*
*for encouraging me to see life*
*in brilliant colour*
*rather than in black*
*and the occasional white*

>             For frequent tears have run
> The colours from my life.
>
>         *Sonnets from the Portuguese* no. 8
>         Robert Browning

Kings' daughters were among thy honourable women: upon thy right hand did stand the queen in a vesture of gold, wrought about with divers colours.

>         Psalm 45, v. 10
>         *The Book of Common Prayer*

Glory be to God for dappled things –
   For skies of couple-colour as a brindled cow;
     For rose-moles in all stipple upon trout that swim;
Fresh-firecoal chestnut-falls; finches' wings;
   Landscape plotted and pieced – fold, fallow, and plough;
     And all trades, their gear and tackle and trim.

All things counter, original, spare, strange;
   Whatever is fickle, freckled (who knows how?)
     With swift, slow; sweet, sour; adazzle, dim;
He fathers-forth whose beauty is past change:
              Praise him.

>         *Pied Beauty*
>         Gerard Manley Hopkins

# INDEX

## COLOURS

| | |
|---|---|
| *Black* | *11* |
| *Red* | *17* |
| *Orange* | *29* |
| *Yellow* | *33* |
| *Green* | *37* |
| *Blue* | *45* |
| *Indigo* | *53* |
| *Violet* | *67* |
| *White* | *81* |

## SHADES

| | |
|---|---|
| *A Stain the Colour of Blood* | *115* |
| *Driving Gloves* | *127* |
| *Guinevere's Gift* | *135* |
| *Twitches* | *141* |
| *The Retreat* | *149* |
| *Stained Glass* | *155* |
| *Bobs and the Yo* | *165* |
| *Pike* | *177* |
| *Vince, Pete and Valerie* | *183* |
| *The Performance* | *201* |
| *The Key* | *209* |
| *The Sound of Bees* | *213* |

## *COLOURS*

# *BLACK*

They played the opening gambit a week ago but the game has been halted even more often than usual by the old man's illness. Tim's eyes rest, for a moment, on his father's knees, skeletal under the grey serge trousers. He is repeatedly surprised at how thin the old man has become. His father's white shirt, which appears to drain all colour from his pale skin, sinks into the hollow of his chest and stomach. The shoulders are sharp ridges; the hands are claws and the strong nose has developed a beak-like ferocity.

Tim wonders how long he has appeared this weak. When his father speaks – 'Get on with it, Tim!' – he realises that the strident personality has disguised the physical deterioration.

Tim is middle-aged and sandy-haired, with the look of a submissive butler. He moves his bishop and then glances up at the old man. His father's face still has the same daunting angles that made Tim tremble as a child. The irises still have that iron glint and the eyelids compress his expression, just as often as in the past, into disapproval or distaste. Tim sees in his father's features the clearest message: my son, the disappointment.

It's an expression Tim first recognised when he was six years old. He was running in the 50-yard dash on school sports day. They raced not on the forgiving grass of public school fields, but on the harsh asphalt of a city primary. Tim tripped over his own floundering plimsolls and fell heavily onto his knees. He inhaled sharply. As he tried to stand, the pain cut at him and looking down he saw blood running from his right knee to stain his school sock. He started to cry and raised his eyes to the adults by the side of the chalk-drawn track. He saw his mother in her flower-sprigged best dress push through the crowd. She ducked under a rope and her heels clicked on the tarmac.

He dropped his chin and closed his eyes, wailing in both pain and relief, waiting for her to scoop him up.

Instead, he felt a steely grip on his upper arm. He was pulled to his feet. His mother stood a few feet away, her wavering smile an apology.

'Stand up properly, Tim, and stop blubbing. You're embarrassing yourself. And me.'

His legs wouldn't take his weight, but after his father had shaken him, and then bent down to hiss *stand up* in his ear, his breath like ice on the child's skin, Tim managed to lock his knees. As the grazes moved over his kneecaps, stinging as though scraped with rock salt, Tim cried out again.

'Shut up and finish the race.'

That was when he first saw in his father's face the expression with which he later became so familiar. A look that said more through what was absent than what was present.

Tim did as he was told – though the other boys had long finished and the winners' names had been read out. Many of the parents had left the track and were applauding their successful children at the headmaster's table, but a scattered few remained. Tim could not look at them. He could not risk their pity.

His father nodded; said, 'You were last, son. Try harder next time.'

Were he a father of the 90s rather than the 40s, he'd have called it 'tough love'. As it was, whenever he had cause to criticise his son, Tim's father described it as 'making a man of you'.

Now Tim is a man. And a father. But he will always be a son.

The old man sucks at his teeth and narrows his eyes. He reaches out for his queen, stops, pulls his arm back and starts to tap his fingers on the tray table. Tim tries to stretch the stiffness from his shoulders. He would like to close his eyes, push his cool palms against their heat. That might ease his headache. He makes do with a deep breath. The air carries the scent of disinfectant, to cover the odour of age. Overlaying both is the thickly sweet smell of pot pourri.

His father moves a knight, nimbly leaping one of Tim's pawns, and then hesitates, his veined hand hovering over the pieces. He lifts his gaze from the chequered board. There's a peculiar sort of wariness in his expression.

Tim can't read it. He can't read the game either.

When he looks at the board, it means nothing. Chess has no shape for him. No strategy. He moves in response to his opponent, for something to do. He acts, yet without tactical awareness. The battle is against his nature. He is not a black and white man, not a competitor.

In his father's view, this is a character flaw. Whenever Tim made a decision of which his father disapproved – as when he turned down a promotion which would have meant a move to Dubai the year before his daughter was due to take her A Levels – the older man would describe his son as a loser. In more jovial moments Tim's father would tone down the criticism to 'one unfamiliar with the concept of success.' This would inevitably be followed by a grating laugh.

He had laughed when Tim had suggested chess as a way to fill the time on his visits to the home.

'Well, if you want to humiliate yourself, I can't see why not. Though it'll be a bore for me, winning all the time.'

Contrary to his expectations, the old man enjoyed the victories and started off by keeping a count: how many moves it took to checkmate his son. His best so far: five. Whatever the state of his lungs, his brain was still good enough.

Over time, the games take him longer to win. They are interrupted increasingly regularly by harsh coughing fits, spells where, eyes glistening with moisture, mouth and nose obscured by the oxygen mask, he is unable to do anything but concentrate on breathing between the coughs. Tim listens to the rasping breaths and feels the constriction in his own chest. He can offer no consolation. His attempts to help are ignored or met with frowns.

And yet, the old man still wins, in the end. And always the sharp light of exultation shines in his eyes as his downturned smile leaves Tim with the same old feeling of failing and a sharp pain of tension between his shoulder blades.

Tonight, though, as the winter moon rises over the black forms of the leafless trees at the end of the landscaped garden, Tim sees, in the half second it takes for an owl to hoot from the oak outside and its mate to answer, a hidden message in the static black and white figures. It is as if the pieces are highlighted. He realises that his father's move has made his queen vulnerable to attack. Tim can take her, with his black rook. And then, the king, the white king, will be trapped. It is a perfect finish.

Tim stares at the board. The squares pulse and dance. He blinks and looks again. Nothing has changed. His mind has not served up a wish disguised as fact. In two moves he can win. In just two moves he can finally beat his father.

He can feel the greasy wood under his fingers; hear the sliding tap across the board and the click of wood on wood as he knocks his father's queen off the board. He can hear his own voice say 'check' and 'check mate'. But he cannot imagine the look on his father's face.

Tim looks across and catches the old man's eye and he knows that his father, just after moving his knight and thus removing his queen's best protector, saw the same unstoppable sequence. There is a feverish flush on the blade of bone above his sunken cheeks and his expression carries less certainty.

Tim watches his hand rise. Rook. *Pick up the rook and move it.*

His father makes a guttural moan and the coughing starts.

Tim stands up and tries to help the old man pull the mask to his mouth, but is slapped away.

He sighs and is about to sit down when he sees his father's eyes glistening, bright as a consumptive's and sharp as a crow's. The old man is staring at the board, at his son's black rook and his own white king.

As the old man wheezes into his mask, all his concentration is on the battle.

Tim feels the struggle for breath, the clamp of iron around his rib cage. He has an urge to tip up the board and watch the pieces clatter to the thin carpet. Instead he turns and leaves the room. He keeps walking through the hall, passing the red-haired nurse in the corridor. He's aware of her spinning on one low-soled heel. She might be saying something. He doesn't want to speak. Once through the door, the cold air embraces him.

Tim heads for his car, gulping draughts of the chill night. He pulls the key from his pocket. A beep, a yellow flash, the door opens, the interior beckons him home. He presses his eyes closed, clenches his jaw and locks the car again.

From where he stands, he can see the old man through the bay window of the day room. Father and son have the room to themselves on their chess nights. The staff smile at Tim like accomplices at a child's surprise party as they shepherd the other old folks through to the TV room. They tell him that his father 'looks forward to the visits.'

Tim sees that he is still coughing; that his skeletal shoulders shake with the force of the battle. The red-haired nurse is kneeling by him, her pale hand on the arm of the chair.

A cloud passes, the night is black no longer.

He will return. To the end game.

But before turning back to the hospice, he walks toward the nearly frosted lawn. He steps onto silvered grass, expecting the crunch of ice but feeling turf as soft as spring.

The half moon, waxing, pours milky light over his pale hair. He feels the muscles in his upper back ease and his shoulders drop. His footsteps leave a dark trail over the damp grass and his strides lengthen. He breathes in the dew heavy air and his headache evaporates.

Tim grants himself another minute and then goes back inside, to win.

His father is no longer coughing. He says, 'Where've you been?'

'Nowhere.'

Tim sits down and they both look at the board.

'Well, go on, Tim; move before I die, will you?' His laugh is raw. It sounds rough enough to provoke another fit of coughing. He is staring at the black rook, at the black rook and then the white king.

Tim smiles. He picks up a pawn, plays it, and leans back in his seat, stretching out his back and watching as his father shuffles forward on his seat, blinking, his mouth gummily open. He has the face of a grey, wrinkled infant.

The old man picks up his queen and takes Tim's rook. As he puts the black piece down next to the board he says, 'You left yourself unprotected, son. Still, your game's improving.'

# RED

The boy lay on the grass like a toppled crucifix. Elena and Liviu stood at the window, frozen into stained glass. Elena's hair hung black as a crow's wing down to the crimson silk of her dress. When Liviu touched her hand to pull her away she flinched like a horse twitching off a fly.

    She held onto the frame and leaned out as though irresolute. *Do you follow him, Elena, or do you remain a wife?* The question she had been asking herself for months. Though it had never been so brutal as now. The moon came out from behind the clouds and, of a sudden, the boy's face shone luminous in the light engulfing darkness. Blood shone on his pale cheeks. If she had been superstitious, Elena would have seen his lips move, perhaps, or a wraith-like shape rise from his sprawled form. As it was, she sighed and stood up straight. Her husband, watching her, opened his arms and she let herself fall into his embrace.

'Are you Elena Tatarescu?'
    She twisted on heels too fiercely spiked for the toned lawn of the President of the University's lodgings and left a scar like forked lightning. Had the boy not looked as he did she might not have answered, but she could not escape his beauty and she nodded, though she held back her smile, for a while at least.
    'Mirco,' he held out a hand, 'Mirco Stefoniou. I have signed up for your class.'
    Now she did smile. A student, just a student. 'Well, I shall look forward to working with you, Mr Stefoniou. I remember your application. You sent some beautiful work. Haunting…'

His eyes were polished jet and he grinned. 'I am glad that you liked it.' Then he leaned forwards and touched her. Elena started, stepping back, but he showed her the beetle he had pulled from the scarlet wool of her jacket before throwing it into the shrubs. In his glance she imagined the hard glare of the insect's carapace and when he turned and walked away she raised her arm and almost called him back.

*Mirco.*

The first time she met him.

Four weeks into term and he was in front of her each Tuesday morning and Thursday afternoon – and in her mind constantly. Did his poetry really, obviously, refer always to her? Or did all the women in the class feel that shifting tilt in their stomach as he read? Did those jet eyes burn her only, bringing the colour to her breast, neck, face, or was each woman nurturing searing scalds under their silk and lace?

'You seem fascinated with your class this year,' said Liviu as she prepared more and more specific workshops designed to illuminate her need to know whether the boy sowed his black fire-filled soul to everyone, or just to her.

'They are talented.'

Liviu nodded slowly, 'So what is the exercise you plan for tomorrow?'

'The one about the objects? The five objects and their history?'

Again he nodded. 'And will you give objects to each of the students?'

She looked up from her papers, but before she could answer, he said, 'And you will give the snake bracelet to that boy.'

She tried to shield the look in her eyes, but she could not. Liviu had done the same thing when she had been his student seven years ago. The snake bracelet – and then he had caught, with the coils of the serpent, the knowledge he needed. He had left his wife of 17 years, his two children, and the justification for it was simple, 'Elena is my muse.'

'I thought as much,' he said.

Elena sat at her desk, silent. Still. Waiting.

Liviu said, 'So, you want a young lover? You have had enough of my old shanks, the coarse hair in my ears and the rolls on my stomach, which I can neither firm nor remove? You do not have to reply, Elena: I know. Have this boy, then. I grant you this gift.'

'I do not want a gift, a boy as a gift. You cannot grant me a person! You cannot give me someone who is not in your power, Liviu.'

'I know he is not in my power; but he is in yours.'

'Just as I was in yours?' She stood up, but did not move away from her desk. Liviu remained sitting on the leather sofa, his feet on a stool, his papers at peace on his lap.

'Were you in my power, Elena? I am not sure. Perhaps it was the other way around. I don't know. I do not know.' The age showed on his face as though a cloud had crossed in front of the sun so that the hillside lost its beauty and definition, its crags becoming not carved things, but looked instead like sagging sacks of darkness. He dropped his head briefly before looking back up to catch her eyes. 'I do not want to lose you. So, if this boy gives me more time, I will make that sacrifice.'

His permission felt like a burden.

Liviu left the room and Elena sat down again. The lesson plan, like some indiscreet love letter, lay exposing itself in front of her. She tore the page to pieces and slammed her palm onto the solid elm of her desk. Outside, in the fields, a vixen screamed – her call for a mate sounded like a child being torn at the throat.

The following day, Mirco, who was usually first into the room, was late. Elena felt a breathless ache in her lungs; her legs became stiff and words danced outside her range. She could not look the other students in the face for fear her desire gleamed from her eyes like pain. One girl was missing too. As the image of the boy's darkness and the girl's white-blond hair invaded Elena's imagination, she lost the path of her discourse and stumbled into silence. When she started to speak again, her voice had a raw edge with which she was not familiar.

The door swung open and Mirco crashed in, laughing, pulling the girl behind him. Elena, head snapping up like a puppet's when the strings are jerked, span and stepped towards them.

'I'm sorry, I'm sorry – no, we are sorry, Mrs Radacanu–' it was the first time he had used her married name '-we missed the bus from Drumul Taberei –' he spoke of the district where Elena knew the girl lived '-and then…'

She could not listen to the excuse or the story. She knew she should smile and smile and present the look of a tolerant married woman who has put all this love and sex and raw-red passion behind her, and tell them, indulgently, to sit. She should précis the first fifteen minutes of the class and tell them what the exercise involved. Instead she snapped, 'How dare you behave like this in my class! The Head of Department will hear of this. Get out, now!'

'But, Mrs Radacanu…' Mirco's jet eyes flashed.

'Mr Stefoniou, you heard what I said – get out.' The girl was hanging behind him, still holding his hand in hers. Elena read different emotions on the young woman's face – or did so in retrospect – at the time all she was aware of was the white heat of her own anger. 'And you, Miss Silivasi, you get out too!'

Elena turned back to the class, now silent. A couple of the students had flushed; one young man shook his head, frowning. Elena closed her mind to them and somehow rediscovered the track of her lesson, somehow got through an hour and ten minutes more, somehow avoided for 70 minutes the eyes of her students and the awareness that they knew.

When they left, she closed the door and sank to the floor. Her body ached as though she had been beaten and her face still held the heat of her anger, her shame. She felt a burst of nausea so intense that she tipped forwards and crawled to the bin, but she retched nothing, and, as she coughed into the grey metal, eyes smarting, she felt a hand, his hand, on the back of her neck, stroking, holding her black hair away from her face and she heard his voice telling her everything that she needed to hear. In her mind, she asked him if he was a dream; in her classroom he showed her that he was not.

Liviu had not been writing for a year or so, but when Elena started her affair with the boy, his inspiration returned. Since he had given permission for the relationship, he took some interest in it and the details of its progress. He wrote while Elena met Mirco at his dark room near the University in central Bucharest. The student accommodation was not of any quality, so in time, Elena and Mirco took to spending afternoons together at the married couple's house while Liviu was teaching. At length, they were granted whole days and even evenings as the husband wrote in his rooms at the University. Why not, after all? Why not have warmth and comfort, wine and food at hand, books to quote from and the big bed in the spare room in the attic where Elena's tongue traced rails of desire around and about Mirco's still boyish body?

After six months, Liviu had written the first draft of a novel.
    'I shall put it away now,' he told Elena, as they drank pink champagne to celebrate the completion of those 80,000 words. 'So I shall not need to spend so much time at the University.'
    She looked up from the pale bubbles in champagne that was coloured as though with a few drops of blood. 'You'll be at home more often then?'
    'Exactly.' He watched her lick her lips. 'Is that inconvenient, Elena?'
    'Well, no, not really.'
    'I am surprised. I thought that you might still require the time and the privacy.'
    'I have been reconsidering.'
    'Oh?'
    He had been so involved in his fictional world for the past few months that his interest in the real affair that his wife was conducting had faded. The reality of the situation no longer mattered greatly. The imaginary relationship that this situation had created was what held him in its clutches. For Liviu, the narrative of his novel had held a more powerful sway than the story of his married life. He was surprised that she now appeared to be so much less tied into the drama of love than the protagonist of his novel had been.

She looked up at him and felt the old camaraderie she had fallen for. 'Well, you see, he has become rather affectionate and this has changed our situation. I mean, it was his wildness and what I thought of as detachment, emotional frigidity... a sexual fire combined with emotional frigidity – that combination which made this affair desirable to me. Now it is something... other.'

Liviu nodded and she went on, 'So I think that I must extricate myself. I thought I had better wait until the academic term was finished in case it got unpleasant.'

'That is very sensible, Elena. Of course. Can I help you in any way?'

'I don't think so. I can use the fact of your increased presence to start distancing myself. No – as far as the logistics are concerned, I think I can resolve it. However, there is something else that you can do for me.'

'Oh yes?'

She went to her desk, walking swiftly. It was the first time in more than a year that he had seen her show excitement for something that he was, in part, the cause. She unlocked a drawer and pulled out a sheaf of papers. 'These,' she said, 'are "The Goodbye Letters" – a series of poems in which a woman attempts to break with her young lover.'

'Has he seen them?'

'You mean, have I started breaking it off?'

'Well, I mean, for a publisher, the poems might have even more appeal if they were also real.'

When Elena sent the first poem, Mirco responded by critiquing and praising it, seeming not to realise that the message contained in its *terza rima* verses was for him. She sent him the next, and then a further two. Meanwhile, her physical detachment to him was maintained justifiably by Liviu's presence in their home and her distaste for the dank rooms Mirco had in the centre of the city.

'I'll move, Elena. In fact, if you left him we could afford a flat together. With your salary, and me working as a waiter or barman or something outside the University...'

'Mirco, that is not going to happen.'

'But I cannot bear to see you so rarely. It hurts me. It breaks my heart.'

'Don't be so clichéd! Surely I have taught you better than that!' She smiled as she spoke and stroked his cheek

'Leni, please, I have become desperate – the emotional has complete power over the intellectual.'

'What about exercising both by considering my poetry?'

A quick look in his eye – she just caught it, like a spark of phosphorescence in a darkened sea. 'Do we have to look at them, Leni? I find them… unnerving.'

'I think you need to consider them.' Her voice was quiet, ragged at the edges.

He looked at her sharply, took her meaning, yet asked, 'What do you mean?'

'Mirco, I need you to let go. Stop fantasising about a future together. I am married. You always knew that.'

'You've had enough of me? Your little flirtation is over? Is that it? No – no, I can't believe it. I have felt more, there is more. Leni, please. You cannot do this, you cannot build me up and then crush me!'

She stared at him. She appeared as still and as fierce as the stone statue of Artemis in the corner of her sitting room. 'I thought that you could not be crushed. That is why I chose you.'

The next day Elena, having marked the end of term assignments, locked her office at the University and left – intending not to return until she started to plan for a new course in six weeks' time. As she walked down the corridor, the sun shone, beckoned, through the glass doors and she could smell, above the wax and dust of the hallway, the cut-grass scent of early summer. She shook out her hair and felt her strides become liquid and her shoulders release the tension of term-time.

She did not register the footsteps until she felt herself crushed from behind and pulled into a room. She gasped and struggled, but, knowing it was Mirco, she did not scream. Her eyes closed and she felt the desire to soften into his arms. Yet she could not. In the room, an administrative office, empty since term had ended the previous week, Mirco pushed her against the wall, running his hand over the rose coloured cotton of her summer dress, his mouth warm against hers.

Elena released one of her arms arm and, twisting his ear while stamping on his foot, forced him away from her.

'You fool, you stupid, ridiculous fool, what did you hope to achieve by this except to disgust me?'

'I do not disgust you, Leni. I can feel in your body that I do not disgust you.'

'My body is not my mind. You have made this impossible. Give it up.'

He was shaking his head, holding his hands out towards her. She slapped them away and pushed past him. His knees seemed to give way and he fell back against a desk. He started to speak but, as she looked into the black tar-pools of his eyes, she focused on their dark light and let his words slip away. Whatever he said did not matter. She was able to turn away, walk away and step into the sunshine. She got in her car and drove home. To Liviu.

'Liu? Are you here?'

The fond name, the tone of voice. He hurried from his office, wearing the black cashmere sweater she had bought him early in their relationship. He took her in his arms and let her cry. That night, they printed the remainder of 'The Goodbye Letters' and posted them the following morning to Mirco.

'Did you ever consider leaving me, Leni?' Liviu asked as they sat, late one night, in their kitchen drinking the ferocious, deep-red Feteasca Neagra, produced in the region where Elena was born.

She nodded and concentrated on the wine, deepening its crimson glow in her glass as the candles softened their flames.

'And why did you decide not to?'

'I don't know.'

Liviu drank and they sat in rare quiet. That day they had unplugged the phones. Mirco had been calling – and when the phone was not ringing it was because he was outside their iron gates, shouting at the windows of the house.

'I am so sorry,' said Elena. 'It should not have become so difficult. I am sure, at least, that he will stop soon.'

Liviu shrugged, but doubted that a man who loved Elena would give up easily.

So when the stone smashed through the window, he was not surprised. 'We must resolve this, Leni. We must speak with the boy.'

She bit her lip, but, nodded in agreement,

Liviu went down to the gate and opened it, speaking softly, trying to calm the young man, but Mirco ran past him, up to the house crying out for Elena.

'Come, sit. Let us talk.' Liviu pulled a chair out from the table, but Mirco knelt at Elena's feet, his body shaking. She held his head in her fine-boned hands. And then she raised her face to her husband, who stepped back but did not leave the room.

When Mirco's body stilled, Elena pulled him to his feet and led him to the chair. Liviu poured wine. They drank. A candle guttered and Liviu lit another, the hiss and flare of the match dramatic in the darkened room. Outside, the rain started to fall, summer rain bringing release from the sultriness of another humid day, the sound regular, soothing – like a purr, or the croon of a child.

'You have to leave us to our lives, Mirco. Elena and I have our own lives.'

The boy coughed, choking on his words before speaking. 'You let me in. Both of you. You conspired to draw me in and make me a part of your lives. You cannot just evict me!'

Elena glanced at her husband. He tipped his head slightly and she said, 'What do you expect from us? It is over. It has to be.'

'You still love me. You do still love me. Something has made you pull away. Is it him?' The boy waved a hand at Liviu – but he did not look at his rival. Liviu watched his wife, closely, and saw a flash of something in her face – regret ? He frowned.

She said, 'I had to pull away. I had to.'

The boy was focused entirely on her, his attention, like dark fire, shooting towards her. As Liviu watched them, he saw the heat rise red in her pale face and he didn't know if he could ever turn her skin back to pure alabaster without the memory of this night forever staining her.

It was the boy who moved first. He stood, and she, as though she were attached to him, rose too. They stood together like partners in a dance, in the middle of an empty stage, with nothing around them but their own drama, and Liviu felt himself pushed back as though the gravity that pulled them together had some equal and opposite force keeping him away.

Mirco took Elena's hand and they walked. He'd know his way, of course. The boy knew the house so well, and they walked through the darkness of the unlit hall to the stairs. As Liviu heard their feet on the oak steps, he, restored to mobility, rushed to follow them. He saw the ghosts of their shapes start to climb the next flight, to the attic. As he reached the first floor, they passed into the spare room, with its wide bed, quilted in scarlet shot with silver thread, and the big window overlooking the lawn.

When he reached the threshold of the room, Liviu's breath was hurting his lungs, and he could feel the weight of his confusion like a boulder. They were standing by the foot of the bed, between the bed and the window, and she was stroking his face as he spoke, and he was speaking so softly that Liviu could not hear. Though he was so close and though his breathing, which tore, raucous, through his throat, was so loud, they paid him no attention, and he felt his own absence overwhelm him. He was as absent now as he had been all those months when he wrote and they used this room for love. All those months in which he had written a story where the wife of an older man takes a lover and dies for that young lover, for that heartless young lover, with black eyes as hard as the carapace of a beetle, while the honourable husband lives on with deep, personal shame.

And was it to be enacted before him, this drama of a woman lost in dangerous love?

Elena was shaking her head and the moonlight lit the tears on her face, turning them to moving silver, molten silver, silver melted by the dark fire of the young man's eyes.

As Liviu watched, they stepped to the window, a step closer to the window, and again he was granted mobility and he went forwards as Mirco cupped his wife's face in his hands and kissed her red lips. Even as Elena's eyes closed, her tongue tasting her lover for the last time, she started to push him away. Liviu, moving forward suddenly, to tear them apart, slipped on the bedside sheepskin rug, slammed into them, and Mirco stumbled backwards, fell, crashed, shattering the glass, his blood splattering on the glass, and the glittering music of a life breaking, ended with the thud of his body landing on rain-wet grass.

Afterwards, Liviu held her, his heart half lost, and he heard her speak into his cashmere.

'You asked me why I decided not to leave you.' She didn't wait for him to respond. 'It was because I wanted to publish the poems. Those poems were about saying goodbye to the man I loved. God will damn me for placing more value on my poetry than on my lover.'

Liviu said, ' No, no,' and rocked her in his arms, inhaling the midnight scent of her hair. And yet, as they embraced, it was the chill of statuary that he felt, not the warm beat of flesh and blood.

## *ORANGE*

This morning I put on the dress I wore on the first night of our wedding. It was always my favourite. It carries the colours of my homeland's sky at sunset. It is all fire and flame, the very colour of life. This dress is what I want to return to – the me who was alive and happy and spirited. This dress is the colour of my name: Zubaida, marigold.

Over it now I drape a cloud of black silk. This represents safety. In this place, I am too afraid to show myself as I am. And more than that, it's part of me – it's my culture, my religion, my privacy. I cloak my body in the *abaya*. I cover my head with the *hijab*. My face is shielded by the *niqab*.

I open the door. Outside it is all grey. The sky, the streets, the pavements, the houses, even the faces of the people. Their eyes, too, are always grey. Whatever the colour, that blankness and neutrality can only be described as grey. I try not to hate them for Masood's sake.

My husband sees this place as our future. He says I should be glad that we are here not stuck in Gaza now that the Israelis have closed the borders. He tells me that Fayzi and Jaleela are desperate to come back to London, but they are trapped with no money in the home of Jaleela's parents. 'Am I not grateful?' he asks. *No, Masood, I am jealous.*

My husband does not understand. But then my husband learned English, while I speak Arabic and French. Something in my head prevents me remembering the ugly sounds that stumble without music or passion from the tongues of these grey people. I am stuck, like a child, with a meagre handful of words. Please. Thank you. Hello. Goodbye. And one other which these people will never let me forget.

He says I do not try; he says my hatred prevents me from helping myself; he sighs and turns from me in our bed. Even at night I am alienated from what and from he whom I love.

For him, coming to this cold, damp country was a matter of pride. He feels that his degree, earned in an English university, will count for so much more than a diploma gained in the Middle East. At least he did not wish for Harvard. I could not have gone to the United States.

Masood says I am too radical. I think that I understand politics better than him, but a woman should not be arrogant. I do not condone the bombers, but I understand their frustration. My husband does not understand this subtlety, which is strange since he is the student and I am the farmer's daughter. We both want peace, but I want the peace to be fair to our people. I want a nation my children can inherit.

Since he left for his classes this morning, I have been craving oranges. Not the pallid liquid that passes for its juice in England, nor the pale imitations in their plastic wrappings, but the fruit, fresh enough to still hold its leaves. I imagine the warmth of that small globe of sunlight in my hand and the sunshine taste of its flesh. I shall go to the Indian grocer's which is next to the Halal butcher's and opposite a shop run by an Ethiopian which sells food such as we have at home. It is too long since I have cooked a proper meal for Masood. I have been too depressed in this place. But I predict the oranges will lighten my mood.

In Gaza, I did not wear the *niqab*. Here, I would feel naked without it. The way that those neutral grey eyes stare… I would feel unclothed. Masood says I should, like him, forego our traditional dress. 'When in Rome,' he says and I want to slap him more each time. It is not easy for me. My modesty forbids such exposure. It is bad enough that he wishes me to appear unveiled before his friends from the university, but unthinkable that he should wish me to walk the streets uncovered.

My husband must learn to accept me as I am.

I have given up telling him how I feel. Instead I say, 'It is written.' Now he accuses me of being a fundamentalist as well as political radical. No, I am just a woman whose culture is part of her identity. I can no more cast off my beliefs, or my *abaya*, than I can change this tawny skin from olive to greyish white.

I walk and I think of Abasan. I think of the rows of olive trees and the bitter taste of their fruit. I think of the heat beating down as we tended the fields. I imagine figs melting on my tongue. I smell the streets. Vegetables enriching the air as they over-ripen; spices colouring the breezes with their varied perfumes and underneath the dank smell of sewers and, occasionally, the high stink of dried sweat.

I think of the orange light at dawn and dusk when the *muezzin* sings from the tall mosque tower. In some towns they replaced the man with a recording, but not in Abasan. For me the rough-edged passion of his voice was part of sunset and sunrise. Even here, where the sound of cars is all that you can hear, that and the occasional headache of music from speakers vibrating with bass, even here, when the day is born, when the day is dying, my mind brings me the call from thousands of miles away, from hundreds of years ago and I ache to be home.

My dreams carry me to the shops. From the Ethiopian, I buy *hummus bi tahina* and *baba ghanoush*. Across the road I buy lamb, eggplants, cauliflower and carrots for *maqluba*. I shall cook *musakhan* bread and we will finish our meal with *ma'amoul*.

The oranges are as I wished them to be. As I smell their puckered skin, I can sense the hot sun that formed them and the dust in which the roots found their nutrients. The colour is all glory and I feel my mood lift. I will make this work. I will be a good wife for my husband. I will stop him turning away from me at night.

On the way home, I am almost happy. My pace is lighter and I feel the tightness at my temples ease.

Ahead, a child in a red top stands in my way. He wears a hood. I smile under my *niqab*. They mock us for our veils, and then they cover themselves in cultural uniforms of their own. The smile dies out quickly. He stands in my way. He does not move. Never in Abasan did fear quicken my pulse, prick my back with sweat as it does here. My steps falter, though I try to disguise it. The gap between us is now a matter of only a few feet, and his cold grey eyes seek mine. I have tried not to catch them. My veil is here to protect me, here so that I can hide, but even under my black cloak, he seizes my gaze none the less.

'Terrorist,' he says. The word I am never allowed to forget.

He spits as I pass and I feel the weight of his disgust on the black silk. And yet, underneath, the orange dress burns, erupts, explodes into brilliant fire. I am these two things: the blackness and secrecy of the *abaya*; the glowing marigold of the dress. These two are me. I am Zubaida. This country must learn to accept me as I am.

## *YELLOW*

Pass me the butter, would you, my lover?

No, I don't need to weigh it – I've been baking cakes since afore you was born. I used to make 'em for my Robert and the boys when I was a young wife. And when the boys were grown up, I started working here.

This your holiday job, is it? Earn some money afore university? I weren't clever enough for that – cakes is my talent

So, we creams the butter with the sugar... see how frothy it is? Now the eggs. Whisk 'em together in this bowl for me, will you, dearie? That lovely orangey-yellow. Reminds me of the daffydils in church.

You go to Mass, do you? No? Course, there's not many Catholics round 'ere. Easter Service was bootiful, it was. The ladies as arrange the flowers, they picked armfuls of daffs and put 'em up in the windows. They were shining like little suns, they were, all golden and yellowy orange.

That's right – add the eggs, little by little; then sieve in the flour. That's where the magic comes in. The air makes it light as duck's down. I reckon as it's like adding a touch of the Holy Spirit, if that's not blasphemy to say so. Blasphemy! Big word for a farmer's wife, my old Dad would've said. Oh, 'e didn't hold with all that fancy-dan education.

He said Church is where God comes along to check up our tally of good deeds and bad deeds. I was scared to go as a little un in case I'd done sommat wrong. I feels differently now. Not that my dad was wrong, so much as that I sees it different. You see, my lover, for me, Church is where God looks down to give you a helping hand and forgive you your sins – but only if you're truly sorry, mind! Oh, and Church is where, sometimes, He sees fit to answer your prayers.

Grate in the lemon zest, my little maid, and some juice too. Lemon Drizzle, my John's favourite. He lives in New Zealand, you know. Not been back these four years. He writes 'is old mother every week and tells me about the country and the vineyards and 'is work on the farms. I tell 'im it's better'n that Country File on the telly, but I do still miss 'im, I do.

In Church on Sunday, I was looking at the priest and the bootiful colours of our old East Window and I was praying to Our Lady that she'd let me see my boy again afore... Well, I'll come out with it, afore I dies. Oh, don't look at me like that! It comes to all of us, in time.

What's that, my dear? Oh, it's the same as Mother 'ad, cancer.

I've not told John, though Peter knows – he's my other boy as runs the farm now, since dear Robert died backalong. And I was praying for my Peter, too, that 'e and Susan could have a little un afore I dies. They've been waiting so long to be blessed with a baby.

Now the cake's in, we make the syrup. It smells lovely, it does, so fresh.

Anyhows, I was that busy praying I didn't notice Mass was over! I knelt down and I said to Our Lady, 'Please, Holy Mother, I'm a mother like you, I've never asked owt of anyone.' And all around me there was this golden light, from the East Window and from those daffydils, and that light flashed through the church onto the statue of Our Lady and I felt it like a blessing.

I thought, 'This is a blessing, Rose, you'll have to remember this – she's listened to your prayer at least. You can't ask no more.'

But listen to this, I went home – Peter and Susan live at the farm now Robert's gone; I'm in the cottage as was stables in the old days. So I goes in and there's Peter – and his face is as bright as the East Window with the morning sun shining through it. And 'e grabs me in this big hug and he says to me, he says, 'We're having a baby!'

I cried, I don't mind telling you. I were stroking his hair and saying, 'My boy, my boy.'

Then 'e said, 'Let's tell John.' So we calls John and I leaves Peter to tell him, while I dries my eyes.

When I comes back, Peter gives me the phone and my John says, 'See you next month, Ma. I'm coming home.'

I was right overwhelmed and it took a few minutes to sort meself out. We had a nice lunch over at Peter's. Susie made a roast. I was itching for Monday though, so I could go back to church and thank Our Lady.

It were cool and clean in the church, with the library smell of the prayer books and the stony chill that always makes me think of holiness. I looked up at Her and I felt Her love, a mother's love, shining down on me and I felt so happy. I knows there's not long on this earth for me, but what there is, is precious, and my boys will make it so.

Here we are – your first cake at the Castle Café. Yes, you did make it – you helped, you added some of your magic, you did. It's that lovely bright yellow of the Church at Easter, the bright yellow of happiness. Oh, look at me, I'm weeping again – right sentimental I've got. My old mother always said, 'The best cakes are made with a woman's tears.' As for me, I'd say, 'Only if they be tears of joy.'

## *GREEN*

The tall white houses looked self-sufficient as though gardens would be redundant. Yet they all had a green spine stretching, long and narrow, behind their pristine facades. Just as the owners hired painters to keep the fronts as neat and white as royal icing; just as they paid for cleaners to polish the blond floor boards and vacuum the biscuit-coloured carpets; so they employed gardeners to tend the ribbon of grass and shrubs out back. And Lula Bryce worked on at least three of those gardens, perhaps four, Terry had never been sure.

Lula started her business *Outside Rooms* in the late nineties, and had, after the initial three months, during which all start-up companies are quiet and edgy, been tolerably busy ever since. This last year, Terry had even seen an advertisement – with a pen and ink drawing no less – in the Yellow Pages, so he assumed she had cash to splash.

The gardening sector in Brighton was fiercely competitive in those days, with turf wars fought by the postcode district. Shears, secateurs, hacksaws—the weapons were traditional, the battles were not. Terry would never forget the rearguard action Mick Fontaine came up with when the Jago brothers started their door-to-door leafleting campaign in BN4. Yes, it was a dog eat dog world, that's for sure. The Jago brothers hadn't been seen again. Terry understood they'd moved along the coast to Hove.

Lula Bryce had stepped into the market before it had developed its nasty side. The big white houses on Drew Crescent were between Terry's patch and that of an old boy known as Plum. For some reason neither of them had claimed the Crescent. It might have been a strange delicacy, still evident before the turn of the millennium, neither wishing to offend the other; or perhaps it was the cartographic oddity of the Crescent's location. It seemed to be squeezed in between two of the larger hotels, and they of course were the undisputed province of the big concerns, who concentrated on business and public space contracts. Whatever the reason, Lula had found the gap in the market and sidled in as silently as a cushion-pawed cat and as inconspicuously as a wedge-tailed wren. One week the Crescent was as sterile as a hospital waiting room; the next week jasmine blossom scented the air, and a green aura seemed to be spreading along the street. It was decidedly odd. Terry would've discussed it with Plum, had he and the old boy been on speaking terms, but they'd never exchanged a word, just the occasional nod if they met at the nursery or the tool hire shop.

Terry had the same kind of relationship with Lula who'd been operating near his regular roads and byways for nearly a decade. He'd been surprised when he'd first seen her – just a little scrap of a girl. No taller than his shoulder and slender as a willow with it. She had a mass of dark hair which billowed, around her face like an unpruned hebe. She always smiled, waved and said hello. He would respond with *the nod*, though after she'd turned away again, he'd follow her with his eyes for longer than he wanted to.

Lula Bryce. A strange name, Lula. As for the Bryce part, he didn't know of any Bryces. Was it a married name or a maiden name? He'd never noticed a ring on her finger, but why would he? He wasn't interested. And besides, she might garden without it.

Whatever the doubts about her origins or status, his views on her skills were consistent. Green fingers. Not the green fingers non-gardeners or hobby gardeners refer to. He meant green fingers as those in the business alone can judge. There's an almost magical power some people have to breathe life into a plant. A dried stick will sprout leaves; diseases will disappear; Russian vine will come under control and orchids will never die. Gardeners talk about real green fingers with awe, in hushed tones, as though harsh notes or a voice raised could break the mystery of the gift. Of course, knowledge also determines success. And there is instinct too and that a gardener will see in a mess of overgrown and tangled greenery the potential for order and beauty. But green fingers makes the difference between competence and professionalism on the one hand, and natural genius on the other.

Lula apparently had genius. Terry had never been to any of the gardens she tended, but rumours about her grew like honeysuckle, wrapping themselves around the facts and becoming local folklore. He'd heard the stories too many times to doubt that there was some truth to them.. He didn't begrudge it. He earned enough to keep himself in the style to which he had become accustomed: modest and conservative, in the bungalow his parents bought when they retired and which they left him when they died. His ex-wife Margaret had the former council house they had so carefully considered, and then bought, back in the eighties. She lived there with the man she'd left Terry for, and the garden he had planted, as well as the birch tree he'd planted far too close to the house, just before he left. He figured Margaret and Ali had a few years at most before the roots caused subsidence and destroyed their foundations, as effectively as Ali had destroyed the foundations of his happiness. For Terry had loved his wife and never suspected for a moment that his feelings were not returned. The first he knew of it was when he got home from the Stephensons' half-acre garden to find a suitcase packed in the hall and Margaret in the kitchen with a strange Asian man. When Terry came in, frowning, asking who was moving in, Margaret had said, 'You're moving out' and that was that.

All of which meant that he had far too much more time on his own than was healthy to brood about Lula's green fingers and successful business. He wasn't quite alone: his one extravagance was a pair of Norfolk Terriers who he allowed to accompany him to his gardens. The unwritten rule that the dogs were allowed to come with him had limited his uptake of new clients. His original homeowners who'd refused to have the dogs scrabbling on their lawns and peeing around the apple trees were gradually weaned of his services. He'd usually recommend Plum, sometimes Mick Fontaine, and, once or twice, Lula.

His reason was that he thought he might then be able to find an excuse to come back and discover how green the girl's fingers really were. The problem with this plan was that he was never certain whether the people had gone with his recommendations, and unless he spied on the house – or on Lula, appetising as that sometimes appeared – he'd never know. Sometimes he told himself, and the terriers, if they were listening, that it didn't matter. But in his heart, he knew it did.

On Sundays, when Terry never worked, he took the terriers out for a long walk along the coast, or through the bridle paths tattooed across the Sussex countryside. He'd set out at nine or ten in the morning and walk until lunchtime when he would enjoy a pub lunch or fish and chips before returning to do his weekly accounts.

This had been his habit for the past six years since he had bought the terriers, long enough for any change in the routine to be unthinkable. Yet, when he found out, through a throw-away comment at the garden centre, that Lula Bryce had been seen every Sunday afternoon, to be walking, alone, along the promenade and then out along the coast path, he decided on a whim to do his accounts in the mornings.

That Sunday it felt decidedly strange to be in the house as the playful breeze animated the clothes on his line, like a puppeteer without any real sense of narrative or characterisation. He found himself shaking his head at his foolishness, as the sums refused to add up and his painstakingly neat columns of figures all of a sudden rocked and jittered, more leaning towers than skyscrapers. When, at last, it was done, he felt most uncomfortable walking around the estate to his local hostelry, where the roast lunch was not what he and the terriers were used to, the beef greyer and gravy thinner than at any of the country pubs he usually frequented. He shook his head again, while the dogs, two bitches called Penny and Clemmy (after his favourite plants – the peony and the clematis) looked mournfully up at him.

The spirits of all three lifted when he put the blanket, washed and dried each Saturday, back in the car and whistled them in. He drove the short distance to the car park on the sea front, and the dogs bounded out with the same enthusiasm they'd had as pups. His hands trembled slightly as he clipped the leads onto their collars, and he had to give himself a good talking to, trying to stop his heart hammering in his chest like a trapped seagull, beating its powerful wings against the enclosing net.

As he had driven in, he had, while claiming to be seeking a space in the car park, looked out for Lula's little van. It was easy to spot: green with a rather dramatic magnolia flower and the words *Outside Rooms* in large letters followed by a mobile telephone number which Terry had stored in his phone some years back. Just in case.

He hurried to the promenade, turning left and right to see if he could make out her diminutive figure in the distance while telling himself that this was a damn fool idea, and what was a 55-year-old man doing chasing after a little chit of a thing like her.

Not seeing Lula, Terry decided his mission was destined to have failed, and he may as well take his walk on his own. The seagull inside him dropped its head and settled into a heavy depression. He turned left, away from the town, and started walking.

For some while he could not put from his mind his stupid behaviour and pathetic loneliness, and ignored the sparkling sea sizzling onto the white sand, and instead stared at the paving stones passing beneath his feet. A tern flew overhead calling, 'Lula! Lula!' and the bitches seemed to be panting with lust. Terry wanted to slap himself, punch himself, somehow punish himself for allowing hope to take root and, though starved of light, send its tender tendrils around his heart.

The terriers ran to the ends of their extending leads and tugged him lightly along as the breeze pushed him from behind. It was as though the world had decided to direct his footsteps. The regular pace of his steps had a hypnotic effect, and his mind began to empty of the chatter of self-criticism and questioning. He began to enjoy the sense of his strides, the slight strain in his thighs and the repeated in and out of his breathing. Terry almost forgot Lula. He almost felt as if it were morning again and he had a whole Sunday ahead of him – a lunch to look forward to, and his accounts to do.

A little further along and he started to take notice of his surroundings, the susurrations of the sea and the bullyboy calls of the gulls. The water shimmered like a mirage – or like a blanket of quivering lights. The sky was forget-me-not blue, with clouds bowling along like day-trippers as the sun, warm as an overbearing uncle, grinned hugely.

Just as he'd accepted that his plan to meet Lula had gone awry and that it was probably just as well, he turned a bend in the path and saw a small silhouette with an aureole of massed hair coming toward him, with the afternoon light behind her. His heart hiccupped in his chest and re-established its earlier frantic rhythm; he felt himself stand up taller, straightening the forward bend at the top of his spine; and he held his chest out with the pride of a man who has done physical work every day for the past 35 years (pushing back into a dark corner of his mind the unserendipitous realisation that 35 was exactly how old he had discovered Lula to be).

As she came closer, she waved, the wind whipping away her cheerful 'hello!' And he could see that far from being black, her hair was actually a mixture of chestnut, mahogany and the dark brown of a seal's wet head.

The terriers ahead of him were first to reach Lula and she squatted down on the path to stroke them. Clemmy and Penny leapt up, competing to lick her sun-drenched skin. Terry smiled to see her so natural and relaxed. As he approached, he heard her say,, 'Oh what sweet little people you are! And how are you on this lovely sunny day? Hmm? Happy and smiley? Yes, I can see that!'

'She really is charming,' thought Terry. Aloud, he said, 'Hello there… Miss Bryce… we've never really been introduced… Terry, Terry Donohue.'

She glanced up, the smile on her lips shrinking from Cheshire cat to dutiful niece, 'Hi .Lula, call me Lula.'

He had expected a little more, to be honest. But he assumed she must just be shy and felt more comfortable focusing her attention on the dogs.

Nothing ventured, nothing gained. Terry decided to try again. 'Six years, I've had them, affectionate little blighters. Usually we walk in the mornings on Sundays, but, well, a change is as good as a rest. And what a fortunate one, allowing us to run into you!'

'Umm…'

He had the feeling she wasn't really listening. Goodness, she was very shy! Best to try the direct approach. 'Perhaps you'd join us for an afternoon tipple at the White Horse. It's just 500 metres or so off the path.'

'What?' She looked up at him, a crease between her dark brows.

'Umm... well, I asked you if you wanted to join me for... a drink... or dinner... perhaps...'

'Oh, no! I mean, nice of you to ask, Terry, but no.'

'Not even a thank you!' he thought covering his pain with indignation as he watched her stand up, rub the hairs from her jeans, nod her head at him and walk off. His eyes followed her as his mind made spirals of accusation and counter accusation. Even as he condemned himself for a fool and her for a witch, he noticed the elegance of her walk and the bounce of her hair. The he felt the leads pull against his hands. He stumbled forwards, almost falling. The dogs were chasing after Lula, trailing at her heels like competitors at Crufts. Terry, twice stabbed by female rejection, yanked back on their leads more aggressively than he had ever done in their lives. They flew a foot or so back towards him, Penny – or perhaps it was Clemmy – yelping in shock or pain. But Terry didn't care; he set off in the opposite direction, dragging the terriers behind him. He could hear their claws scraping through the hardened turf of the path and their occasional whines. He knew that if he looked back he'd see their collars pulling their rough tan fur and little triangular ears roughly forward. He knew they'd keep trying to turn their heads to keep their eyes on Lula Bryce.

By the end of the summer, he was seldom taking the dogs to work. He picked up a couple of other jobs where dogs were not welcome, and even in the gardens where Penny and Clemmy used to be greeted with a bowl of water and half a Rich Tea biscuit each, he worked alone, muttering into the heavily pruned magnolias.

For a while, only the weeping willows really flourished under his touch, the weeping willows and the rue.

But in time, life smoothed back to boring and mostly Terry did not think of that unscheduled Sunday. He hadn't thought about it at all for days, when one morning in the nursery, waiting with a group of other early birds for the new delivery of spring bulbs, he heard them talking about Lula Bryce and her famous green fingers, and how all the plants loved her.

'Huh,' he thought, 'not just the plants – bloody dogs too. I wonder what fingers that takes? Brown, eh?'

He clicked back into the conversation, and the men were still talking about her. Frustrated, he said, 'She only seems talented. I work near her,, and I've heard she doses her gardens with chemical fertilisers and insecticides.'

The nursery silenced. It was quiet enough to hear the forest ferns curling up their delicate leaves and the autumn roses closing their buds.

For the first time, old Plum spoke. 'You're jealous, boy,' he said. Then he walked over to Terry and stood right in front of him looking slightly down his generous nose. 'I never thought I'd hear a gardener of Brighton speak like that about his rival. You've disappointed me, boy.'

He stared a moment longer and then walked away. The other five gardeners followed.

Terry wanted to retaliate, but he knew there was nothing he could say. He looked at the display pictures of bright croci, narcissi and daffodils and wondered if he would feel healed by the time they came into bloom.

# *BLUE*

Imagine this...

A girl, almost a woman. She works in a hotel. Long, dark blond hair knotted at the base of her neck. Slim legs, almost as slim as she wanted. Attractive in a strong-boned way. Arresting rather than pretty. She has taken a cream tea out to the patio where a young family sit in silence. The child, a little boy, follows with his deep-blue eyes every move, every expression on the face of his mother, who has the look of someone walking on broken glass. Her husband reads a magazine, seeming to ignore his wife and child. The girl watches through the window as the young woman pours tea, her hands shaking. She knocks the saucer, which tips, and falls with the cup, to the stone floor. Her husband leaps up, his voice is unexpectedly gentle, but even so the woman appears to weep while the child reaches forward and takes her hand.

    The waitress feels something sharp shift inside her.

    When they have left the patio, she collects the plates and cups. They have scarcely touched the scones – only one has been cut open. Her shift is over. She wraps the remaining scones in a napkin, slips out the front door of the hotel and runs across the road to the beach.

    She hears the sea suck through the pebbles on the shoreline. She hears the clattering chatter of the stones jostling with each other as the sea rushes out, and then the whoosh and hiss as it returns to kiss the land and rise up the stony beach to her feet.

    The young woman sits down a little distance back from the water. She unwraps the scones and eats as she looks out to sea. It is warm for September. The sky is the clear blue of memory. Siamese-cat's-eyes blue. The sea echoes the colour and plays with it, creating a graduating scale of blues from the almost black at the shaded base of the waves to the crenelations of nearly white foam.

Her eyes seek the horizon.

She is thinking of her parents.

\*         \*         \*

She ran home across the fields, clumsy and heavy, breath heaving into straining lungs, cheeks reddened by chill and effort. A yellow Labrador cantered ahead of her, tongue lolling out. It's one of the thrills of childhood, that self-important excitement of having something exciting to tell a parent, something they will want to hear. As she tripped over hummocks of grass, which crouched like hiding hares in the pasture, she imagined her father's pleasure, his anticipation, on hearing what she had found.

Halfway across the five-acre field, she slowed to a walk, still breathing heavily. Without stopping, she leant down to tuck her jeans more tightly into her wellies and then held her long straggling hair in a pony tail to let the cool November air touch her hot neck. The dog tracked back and jumped up, pawing muddy prints over the denim. Distracted, she reached out to stroke its golden head before breaking into a jog-trot again.

At the kitchen door, she kicked off her boots before slamming into the house and shouting, 'Daddy!' as though she were on fire.

Her father's voice answered, tired, as though predicting that her urgency was the result of nothing more interesting than a buzzard sighting or the discovery of a fox's den. She hurried through the kitchen and the long, narrow dining-room of the farmhouse into the sitting-room, where he was laying a fire.

'Daddy, you'll never guess what!'

'You're right, I won't.'

'Oh, come on, Daddy, please try!' She leaned over him, arms hanging around his neck.

'Darling, you're suffocating me.'

She unwound herself, stepped back; felt the disappointment seep through her.

He must have sensed it. He raised his head to her, gave a tense smile and said, 'All right…You found a gold mine? A unicorn? A suit of armour?' The smile became more genuine as he watched her shake her head vigorously, as he saw her obvious enjoyment in the game. 'OK, I give up, what?'

'I found a treasure trove of glass bottles!'

'Right... that sounds lovely...'

'But, Daddy, you like bottles! I know you do! When we found those ones in the hedge in the chicken run... You liked it... I thought you'd be happy and we could go on an... an... expedition.' Her voice stumbled over hummocks of unrealised pleasure.

Her father looked up at her. He was kneeling on one leg, resting his elbow on the other thigh. He reached out and stroked her flushed cheek. 'Yes, let's do that. Not today – I have to make dinner for Mummy – you know she's not feeling well.'

The child nodded. She'd spent much of the day out in the fields after another tense morning. Her parents had been up most of the night. She had managed to sleep at some stage, having fled upstairs, while her mother stood fierce, breathless and tear-stained in the kitchen as her father rested his head on his hands and closed his eyes against the argument.

The girl had not been surprised that her mother had not got out of bed the next day. She was no longer innocent; she shared her parents' pain.

'Saffira?'

The child looked up from her father, turned to the stairs.

'Go on, Saffira, go up and see Mummy.'

In her parents' room, the air was stale. Her mother was sitting up in bed, wearing a cotton nightdress decorated with sprigs of little blue flowers; her dressing gown was draped around her shoulders. She had her glasses on and, when she looked over to her daughter, her eyes were magnified, owl-like behind the thick lenses. She smiled and her left eye closed in the nervous tic, which seemed more like a fragile form of wink.

Saffira ran to the bed and dived into her mother's embrace. The argument had scared her. Her own anger at seeing her father hurt had scared her. Her distaste for her mother terrified her. But here was the mother she knew, a tender woman, nestling in her bed, surrounded by the aura of her own grief and confusion, surrounded by love for her daughter.

'What have you been doing, my little chicken?'

'I took Blizzard through to the Reddaways' fields and I explored the woods and I found a badger's house and I found a whole treasure trove of ancient bottles!'

'How exciting! You're a real adventurer, aren't you?'

The child nodded, her face still pressed against her mother's breast. She said, 'Will you tell me an Arabella story?'

'I'm not sure I've got one just now.'

'Oh please!'

'Well, let me think.'

Mother and daughter stayed holding each other as the light outside darkened and the room turned from dull to dimpsy. They listened to the sounds of the man downstairs chopping kindling and filling the coal scuttle from the box next to the fireplace.

'Once upon a time,' said the mother, 'there was a little girl called Arabella Louise Jones, and Arabella was not what you'd call a pretty little girl…' Saffira snuggled closer against her mother and closed her eyes. It was a childish pleasure, to have a simple story told to her in a warm bed on a chilly evening, but childish pleasures are comforting and after the restless night and the upsetting sight of her father injured, and her mother furious, it was what she needed.

Her father carried her to bed an hour later. In his arms, she mumbled, 'Promise we can look for the bottles tomorrow, Daddy?'

'Yes,' he said, kissing her head. 'I promise.'

The following morning, Saffira went down to the kitchen in her dressing gown, hearing the sound of the radio and the noise of kettle, tea pot, grill tray. Her mother was up, smiling as though nothing had happened. Saffira gave a half-smile – almost shy, faced with a new woman, a different woman from the tender owl-eyed mother in her sick bed. This mother was bright, determinedly breezy, desperately, it seemed, trying to conceal the pain of the memory of betrayal.

'Daddy said he'd come to the bottle place with me today.'

'I'm sure he will. Tea? There's toast under the grill.'

Saffira sidled over, then hurried, seeing smoke. Her mother always burned the toast. She took the less charred pieces and started to spread butter and jam on them.

'Where is Daddy?'

'Finish your mouthful first.'

'Where's Daddy?' Having to repeat the question made her nervous. She imagined blood; she remembered the sight of steel flashing; she recalled a grunt of pain. Saffira trembled, shook herself, looked up into her mother's face and saw, as the woman smiled, that tender tic, that half-wink. The child wished that she could heal her mother. She wished that she could heal her father too. She wished that she could make the family whole.

The back door opened and her father came in, with the post and the fresh air of early winter.

They left at mid morning. Her father carried a bucket and a couple of trowels; Saffira skipped at his side and the dog, Blizzard, led the way. At the corner of the five-acre field, the girl showed her father where she had scrambled through the hedge. He followed, with more difficulty. They were in scrappy woodland, with mud, brambles and saplings amongst the occasional mature oak and beech. A path made by foxes, badgers, or perhaps deer, wound through the trees. Blizzard caught the scent of rabbits and set off at a sprint; father and daughter ignored the dog.

'This is where I saw the feathers, Daddy,' said the child.

Her father turned to her, confused. She gave him the impatient look children reserve for inattentive parents and continued, 'I was following the fox last week when he took our hen and I came this way. I liked this place, so that's why I came back yesterday. I thought I'd find the foxy's hole-'

'Den.'

'Yes, but it's a badger's one I think because of the fur.'

'What fur?'

'On the roots that stick into the hole.'

He nodded, as though he followed her conversation. *As though I care.* Then he struck out that thought and took her hand – a silent apology for a crime of which she was not aware. She looked up at him, her eyes a radiant blue, echoing his own, with a smile of such brilliance, that he felt the muscles in around his heart tighten. The child trotted onwards, pulling him behind her.

They came out into a clearing, where a stream cut through the soft ground. On the other side of the water, the bank climbed steeply upwards. Saffira pulled herself up, gracelessly. Her father followed more easily. They crossed the corner of a field where cattle looked up from their grazing, curious, until the man and child came within a couple of feet; then the cows, heads lowered, leapt back in sharp shock, their soft eyes rolling, showing the whites. After climbing a five-barred gate and passing through a patch of scattered trees, they entered a more established piece of woodland and there, under a fallen beech, was the badger's den.

'Look!' Saffira pointed at a shard of green glass.

'Well done, darling.'

'Come on, let's start digging!' She pulled out a trowel and set to.

'Gently! Glass is very delicate! Calm down, Saffira – more haste, less speed, remember.'

She smiled and frowned at the same time. Her impatience reminded him of his own – his own desire to forge ahead, to find something new, to feel excitement. He repressed the thoughts and concentrated on unearthing bottles.

They found four plain white bottles, one had Boots embossed on the side. Only one was modern enough to have once had a screw cap – that one they rejected. He found a deep green bottle, with ridges on its flanks.

Saffira held it reverently, 'Oh it's such a pretty colour. I wish I'd found that.'

'Well, you can have it.'

'But it's not the same as if I found it.'

'Never mind, Saffy; it doesn't really matter, does it?' These conversations with her frustrated him. He had spent much of her childhood working abroad. The way a child thinks. The way a child reacts. It was alien territory to him.

She pouted, but started to dig again. They worked in silence for a while. He considered telling her it was time to go back for lunch, but before he could speak she cried out and called him over. He followed her gaze and watched her scrabble with muddy fingers around a subtle shape. Her fingertips slipped on the glass. He offered to help and gently loosened the earth around a bottle that was the most delicate shade of sky blue, powder blue, the serene blue of a September sea shining in the landlocked fields of mid-Devon in mid-November.

He pulled the bottle from the greedy earth, which sucked it back, loth to release its treasure. As it came into the light, they both inhaled. So perfect. The man turned it in his hands and then Saffira said, 'Look, Daddy, there's another one underneath!'

Together they extracted the second bottle. It was the same fragile blue, but smaller than the first, and this one was completed by a glass stopper in the same pure blue.

'It's like you and me! A daddy and a daughter bottle!'

He smiled at her, brushing mud and grit from the glass. 'Come on, then, Saffy, let's get these home and wash them.'

The lights were on in the kitchen, even though it was the middle of the day. It gave a Christmassy feel, a celebratory tone, to the occasion. Saffira was cold. She looked through the windows into the warmth. Her father turned on the outdoor hose and started to clean the bottles.

She watched, 'Be careful, Daddy.'

'I am being careful.'

'Especially with those blue ones.'

He forced the water, using his thumb to create a powerful jet, into one of the clear glass bottles, but could feel his daughter's eyes on him. 'Go and put the kettle on, Saffy.'

She left him and went inside.

Her mother smiled sunshine at her and said, 'I'll make the tea, Saffira. Ask your father if he wants a cooked lunch. But I'd prefer to just have sandwiches and cook later.'

Saffira turned back through the kitchen door and watched her father as he bent over the trough and emptied muddy water from the clean, clear bottle. She went to him and started dunking the one made of green grass, shaking the dark contents and then emptying it out. When it was as clean as she could get it, she held it up to the sky and watched the clouds mass behind its forest depths.

Her father picked up one of the precious blue bottles; Saffira lifted the other. They began to wash them together; he using the hose; she, the water in the granite trough.

When the glass smashed, there was silence. Sky blue shards glittered on the cobbles. Man and girl stared down at something perfect lost forever. Trust broken; a childhood sullied; innocence scarred; a blue bottle lost.

Their eyes met, matched, clicked together in blue fire.

'I'm sorry,' he said.

The child nodded, just once. She closed her eyes and when she reopened them, smiled. 'It's all right, Daddy. I forgive you.'

\*    \*    \*

Blue is the colour of memories; the colour of innocence; the colour of forgiveness.

The young woman pulls from her pocket a velvet bag. Inside the bag is the glass stopper from the smashed blue bottle. She had found it that day, under the curved base of the trough, where her father had left it. She holds it up to the sky, up to the clear September sky, and the past rises towards her, with the waves.

## *INDIGO*

Each year started with a rush of students coming to the library every day or so to demonstrate commitment to their course. After a few weeks, attendance tailed off until the run up to end-of-year exams. This was the period when dedicated students spent most of their lives within the breeze-block walls of the cuboid Faculty Building; normal students accelerated their learning, functioning on a revision timetable rather than a hap-hazard one; and those who had wasted their three terms – or three years –believed, in desperation, that the aura of the library, the scent of dust and paper would, through breathing the air as much as studying the texts, fill their minds with wisdom.

Alexander Greystone, Zander to his friends, and therefore Zander to all who knew him, had spent less time than most, though more than some, in the library during his two years and a term at St Thomas's.

The English Faculty Library opened at eight in the morning and closed at ten at night. Evelyn Russell worked, usually, on the late shift, from midday until ten, with a break for dinner at six. She had read English at Oxford and couldn't seem to leave. She had been one of those students who spent most of her time studying, and the majority of her study time in the library, so a post as librarian would appear to be ideal. From arriving at the University at the age of 18 until she met Zander, some 20 years later, very little had changed in her life. Indeed, if one were to examine those two decades, nothing much would stand out apart from the death of her mother, and the purchase of a kitten from a gypsy.

Evelyn, whom no one, yet, called Eve, was inclined not to pay much attention to the students. She felt that it was her job to tend the books rather than the borrowers. She would have preferred a job at the

Bodleian, but felt that her knowledge of English Literature, from Beowulf to Tom Wolfe and beyond, gave her a particular responsibility to remain at the Faculty. The books were as friends. Or perhaps children. Or perhaps, instead, lovers. She stroked creased spines as though to offer relief; she sniffed the glue and pristine paper of new volumes; she repaired torn covers; she identified, labelled, placed.

When a student brought a pile of books to the front desk, Evelyn, recording each volume, saw in her mind the gap in the shelf where that text belonged, and longed to return it, to fill the hole, to leave the whole complete.

The only thing she noticed about individual students was they way they dealt with the books; whether they flung them down; whether they brought them back violated or damaged; whether they stole or secreted; whether they clasped them lovingly or possessively; whether their eyes were filled with the desire to explore deep within them. When her colleagues mentioned someone by name or by description, Evelyn could seldom place them. And yet she never, ever, forgot the face of one who sullied, injured or purloined a volume. The destruction, she could not forget. The thefts, however, she could, with shame, both understand and forgive.

This was how she came to notice Zander.

In the first weeks of his First Year, Zander had, like all his peers, been set the daunting task of reading and assimilating the whole canons of Charles Dickens and George Eliot. Thirty odd novels – many of which boasted 400 odd pages – as well as short stories and poetry. In addition to the texts, students would be expected to have a working knowledge of the period, the social and political conditions, gender politics, biography and, of course, the wealth of texts written by esteemed literary critics. They had about three weeks for these novelists, before moving on to more demanding topics.

One night in the College bar, a knee-weakeningly pretty Third-Year student had told Zander that George Eliot's *Middlemarch* was her all-time favourite – and the young man, keen to become an all time favourite himself, decided to put extra energy into reading and responding to that one particular text. Eliot's prose threatened to beat him. He persevered. He had torn through *Silas Marner* and *Daniel Deronda* but this intense focus on one large novel was a step too far... though he would not admit it. Valiantly, he spent autumn afternoons studying Dorothea's heart... yet after 15 pages of prose, he'd inevitably fall into a 15-minute snooze. But how could he accept defeat? Returning the book would be proof that love, far from being a many splendoured thing, simply was not enough. So he kept it, out of what he then called love but later, when in love, described as an adolescent crush.

As he did not use the library often during the following two years, his theft was seldom recalled, for only when he passed his card through the electronic reader did the message flash up on the Duty Librarian's screen, 'Missing Text: *Middlemarch*. Theft status: student questioned and denied charge.'

It so happened that *Middlemarch* was a work Evelyn had studied in detail and remembered with special fondness – not so much through having enjoyed the novel itself, but because she had written an essay which her tutor, Dr. Ketcher, had described as 'insightful and original.' It was among the highest accolades he gave and Evelyn blushed at the memory of his dark, earnest gaze as he looked at her, as though for the first time, when handing back her manuscript. She still had the handwritten pages in a drawer of her desk at home. His curling script, in red biro, alongside the neat lines of her small, fountain-penned theories. At the end, circled, Alpha minus. She had equalled and bettered that often over her three years, but it was the comments that touched her. She seldom felt insightful, and never original.

That essay, though, had encouraged her to dream, and she had written her Third-Year theses with optimism and eagerness. So confident had she been of their merit that she had sent one on Feminism to her mother, a travel writer who spent much of her life in unprepossessing locations such as the back streets of Dusseldorf, the cement jungles of Cincinnati and the oil fields of Saudi Arabia, where, despite the seeming lack of material, she wrote books which consistently sold well and received critical acclaim. After two months she wrote back to Evelyn saying that she felt 'duty-bound by maternity' to give an honest opinion. That opinion was that the work was bunkum and that Evelyn was so hung-up on the fashionable French theorists that she failed to see the wood for the trees.

When marked formally, Evelyn's thesis had been granted a low Alpha helping her achieve her First, yet she had lost faith, utterly, in her perspicacity.

This conviction, that she lacked insight and original ideas, dissuaded her from committing to a PhD and convinced her to study not to become an academic, but instead to become a custodian of academia.

Even so, even many years after she had made her choice, those words, insightful and original, and *Middlemarch*, haunted her. Evelyn tried not to assess whether her life was satisfying or even satisfactory, but increasingly she had the uncomfortable feeling, as when your sock ruckles down and off your foot inside your shoe, that all was not as it should be. At night, sometimes, when the Oxford sky was dark inky-blue spangled with neon, as she read the literary magazines she borrowed from the Faculty, or watched an arthouse film on the portable television she allowed herself, she felt a stirring of desire to experience more than cataloguing and bibliographical indexes. But what? She was approaching middle age and knew nothing of anything much outside Oxford, English Literature and what she had taken to describing, with a mental downward tilt of her lips, as spinsterhood.

Solitude, Evelyn had always believed, became her. And now it had become her life. She, and the cat, now 14, lived in a terraced house in Jericho. Since she had bought her home in what was then a cheap and undesirable neighbourhood, Jericho had become first fashionable and lately exclusive. Were she to sell the house and buy a flat somewhere on the outskirts of town, Evelyn expected she would have enough money to fund worldwide travel every year and as many adventures as her spirit could contain.

'I'll never do it, though, will I, Casaubon?' she asked the cat, as he eyed her sceptically from the back of the armchair across the room from her ascetic's sofa. 'You and I are too well settled now to move.' He blinked, the green flames dowsed and reignited, then yawned vastly. Even the cat did not take her demurrals seriously.

The most potent reminder of her lost options was the thought of Dr. Ketcher's words, which could so easily pierce the protective sheath Evelyn had attempted to create around herself. She would feel the abyss yawning beside her and, staring into its darkness, would wonder what lives she had relinquished, what loves she had failed to experience.

As the years passed, she felt her ability to pull herself clear of the drop into depression weakening. In the early days, its depths had claimed her only passingly; but as she watched her face become less the smooth mask of youth, and more the personal proof of her individuality, she found herself abandoned to its darkness for days and sometimes weeks.

Evelyn was frequently preoccupied by her untaken paths by the time Zander was a student at St. Tom's.

When he walked into the English Faculty Library late on a cold February day in his Third Year, and his card, passing through the scanner, flashed its message on the screen, she felt the thin carapace of her protection crack. *Middlemarch*: she was not the only person to hold it too tightly in her heart. She looked up, half expecting to see a girl with Emily Bronte locks, but instead saw Zander. Tall Zander, with his curling dark chocolate hair. Zander, with his fine-grey eyes sweetened already by laughter lines. Zander, tanned still from a skiing holiday over the Christmas vacation, his wide mouth always ready to smile.

He caught the librarian's eye and he did smile, his teeth flashing another message, which Evelyn could not yet read.

Of course, no woman's life is so protected as to leave her completely free of disquieting carnal memories. Evelyn had the recollection, for example, of Stuart Striding's dry proddings one full-moonlit night in her Second Year.

The experience became emotionally as well as physically damaging when she overheard Striding describing her to a fellow student in the College bar as 'less responsive than a plank of wood'.

After that, sex had been absent from her existence, apart from the occasional onanistic investigation, which left her shamed and sleepless, until less than a year before she first saw Zander.

Like her dead dreams of scholarly ambition, her experience of sex was centred on the unexpected figure of Dr. Ketcher.

He walked through library doorway one summer's evening, after, as she knew later from examining his timetable, his lecture on 'The Genesis and Development of the Novel'. He recognised her with delicate, scholarly surprise, claiming not to have been in the Faculty Library's concrete cube more than twice since Evelyn started working there nearly two decades previously.

'Well, there's the Bodleian. And I do have my own modest resources,' he explained.

Evelyn imagined brown leather chairs and oriental carpets, dark wooden shelves and the pleasures of privacy.

He asked her why she had refused his advice to continue her studies. She explained her conviction in her own limitations.

'I'm sure you are far more thrilling than you allow yourself to believe.'

She blushed, but, with rare courage, it being her dinner break, asked if he'd care to accompany her to the canteen. He accepted, with a curious smile.

As they sat at a Formica table, with tea in thick, white institutional china, Dr. Ketcher ('Call me John') reaffirmed his praise of her abilities and Evelyn felt the warmth of his words touch the very core of her.

He invited her to dine with him and his wife at their home. Evelyn hid the disappointment that bloomed in her heart when he said the word 'wife' and agreed to a night the following week.

She spent the next few days considering her wardrobe. Dinner invitations were rare. Dinner invitations with a long-lost mentor who had seen her secret depths were, until then, non-existent. She bought, from a boutique in a narrow road in North Oxford, a dress of clinging indigo jersey that flattered her lean, boyish figure. In front of the pewter-framed mirror her mother had given her, she undid the long plaits that she wore bound into buns and fiercely pinned to her head. With the hair flowing freely, like happiness, or like tears, around her head, Evelyn's features were transformed into something approaching grace. The straight-lipped mouth was framed and given a certain sensuality; the strong nose became regal; and the deep, dark eyes earned a lustre that was usually absent. She applied mascara and lipstick. She looked at a woman she scarcely knew; she looked at a woman capable of allure. A woman of mystery. A woman who could have adventures. She looked at a woman who made things happen.

A woman rather like her mother.

Yes, as she stared into sharp grey eyes, Evelyn noticed how like her mother she had become. Perhaps she had inherited the wilderness spirit of the lone traveller? Her mother had been a true feminist, she supposed. Not one to spout 'we are the sea, we are the wind' like the lipstick-wearing, mink-coated French academics Evelyn had written about, but a woman totally equal to a man. A woman of independent will. It crossed Evelyn's mind that her mother had been objecting to the content and philosophy of that long ago thesis, rather than the construction of the academic argument. Yet the comments still nagged.

She replaited her hair and pinned it back up.

Evelyn walked to the Ketchers' Regency terrace and knocked first quietly, and then with some force, on the Royal-blue door. She stepped back, preparing a smile for her former tutor's wife. But Dr. Ketcher answered and roused as much pleasure as perturbation by saying that his wife wasn't present. Apparently she'd been called away unexpectedly to visit her aging mother in Reading.

He and Evelyn were to eat alone. He had cooked lamb, slick still with red juices, and fresh vegetables, baby potatoes and home-made mint sauce. That was followed by an apple pie – 'I've always been a good pastry chef' – and organic ice cream. Evelyn had not eaten so well for weeks. Nor had she drunk so much fine red wine.

When they had finished eating, Dr. Ketcher showed Evelyn his library and she touched the leather bindings of first editions with the lustful tenderness of a lover. He used the same combination of caution and desire when he first stroked the soft skin of her cheek. She gasped and seemed unable to move away as his mouth met hers. He had been speaking of recataloguing his books, and she had been imagining long evenings surrounded by editions that spanned the centuries – from calfskin and gold leaf, to glossy-coloured paperbacks with raised print.

In her fantasy, an intimacy grew gradually. In reality, a sexual relationship flowered that very night: Evelyn, astonished by the role of the tongue; Dr. Ketcher, glad that he had not judged the book by its spinsterish cover.

The affair lasted eight months. It took Evelyn two before she could remember to call him John rather than Dr. Ketcher. It ended when he suggested that his wife would like to get involved. Evelyn, feeling a fool to have hoped that he might leave his marriage for her, realised that far from betraying his wife, Dr. Ketcher was in fact titillating her.

She spurned him frostily. He accepted her rejection graciously. She cried like she had never cried before and took only her third day off work in 19 years. Casaubon flashed his green gaze at her without sympathy as she cut into pieces the indigo dress she had bought for the dinner and the fine lace nightdress Dr. Ketcher had given her for Christmas just a matter of weeks before the relationship ended.

As well as the expansion of her sexual lexicon, the relationship brought one profound benefit: she realised that allowing a man to dictate the course of a love affair was an unwise policy which was destined to failure.

This was the sum of Evelyn Russell's knowledge of love before she met Alexander Greystone.

His experience was as broad as hers was narrow and as happy as hers was disappointing. Zander had no shortage of options and little inclination to limit his enjoyment. 'If you can't be good, be safe' was the motto he loved by and he'd had no cause to regret it. He had lost his virginity to the Head Girl at the school where he was to be Head Boy two years later. His first real relationship was with a friend, albeit a much younger friend, of his mother's. In his Gap Year, he had travelled the world and left Cleo in Melbourne, Sasha in Auckland, Bibi in Buenos Aires, Tia in Rio and Cindy in Los Angeles. He could not pronounce the name of the girl in Tokyo – though he remembered her tiny frame with a special fondness matched only by his tumescent memories of Cindy – a blonde nearing her 40s yet toned as a teenager by daily surfing.

Zander claimed he had never hurt anyone – saying that every woman he 'had fun with knew the score'. A brief survey of the females in question would have proven him wrong, yet a real, or perhaps a deliberate, ignorance allowed him to enjoy the illusion of pain-free love. It was certainly pain-free for him. His ability to look onwards and forwards as soon as the thrill became habit (which, in those early days, happened, with Zander, fairly swiftly) was a reliable anaesthetic.

When he caught the questioning eyes of the librarian and saw, like Dr. Ketcher, something intriguing despite the cream blouse and cameo brooch, Zander felt the whirring buzz of anticipation. He gave her a crooked smile, his grey eyes merry, and then half halted – stopping his mind after his body had reacted. This librarian? With a plain woollen skirt, flat shoes and hair in a bun?

He turned away, masking a frown as he sleeked back his dark curls, and strode between the rows of book-filled shelves. Hidden from her, he stopped and, though he knew she could not see, plucked out a text and pretended to examine it. He addressed the rush of blood and the physical reaction; he considered his mental image of the woman who initiated it. He walked, almost on tiptoes, to the end of the row and peered around at the front desk, ready to jump back if she was looking his way.

A long neck, angled to the screen of her computer. Tendrils of hair, brown yet with the flash of occasional grey. The look of being neat, lean, well kept under her clothes…

He shot back behind the books, heart thudding, feeling the plastic-coated cover slick in his sweating hand. Zander glanced down and registered that it was *Middlemarch* before it slipped from his grasp. He stared down at the volume, a Penguin Classic, in its neat black and red livery.

Footsteps, and her voice, 'Are you all right? Mr. Greystone, isn't it?'

His eyes lifted to meet her intent gaze, and then escaped back to the floor.

'Let me pick it-' she gasped and their eyes met again. '*Middlemarch*?'

Zander felt guilt rise red up his throat and saw the echo of his blush form on her cheeks.

Their hands met over the book as each sought release from the tension by bending. Evelyn pulled hers away and stood up – but she did not leave and instead met his eyes again when he straightened.

'Do you still have, in your possession, a library copy of this?'

He nodded.

'I thought as much.' When she smiled, the light of grace shone on her features, and Zander realised what he had recognised when he walked past her desk.

She turned to leave him, but hesitated before slowly facing him again. Zander, staring into her face, stepped back between the shelves and Evelyn followed. She put her hand to his cheek, and when he did not move away, let out her breath in a half gasp, half sigh.

Zander opened his mouth, but before he could speak, Evelyn took a step forward, rose on her toes and kissed him, once, on the mouth. And then the librarian, quiet by habit in the hushed world of the Faculty Library, returned to her desk with hurried steps, the straight skirt curbing the length of her strides.

She sat at her chair and spun around to face the screen. Of a sudden, upon returning to her seat, Evelyn felt as though she were awakening from a dream. But it was not a dream. She had acted!

The exultation of action was short-lived. She stared at the words and numbers. They made no sense: they might as well have been unfamiliar constellations in a distant galaxy. With the hairs at the back of her neck, she could feel Zander behind her, somewhere amongst the books. His scent clung in her mind, like dew caught in a cobweb, except that no amount of shaking seemed to release it. Her body carried the memory of his skin and she shivered in the central heating. *A fool!* She thought, *I am the consummate fool.*

'Excuse me?... Hello?... Ring, ring, hello!'

She started and turned. A young woman was at the counter. The man with her, overweight in the rugby player's style, said, 'Thought we'd never get your attention. Look, I need to get a text about the Metaphysicals–'

'Have you looked for it?'

The young man sneered, just a touch of the gesture, but enough for Evelyn to notice. 'Umm, do you think you might consider helping me find it instead of quizzing me about it?'

Evelyn was about to retort, but stopped herself. She closed her eyes, held her hands to her face, for a moment, then exhaled slowly, relaxed her features and said, 'I'm so sorry, forgive me. I had something on my mind... a headache, I'm getting a migraine.' She gave a tight smile. 'What is the title, Mr?'

'Reuben, name's Reuben...'

When she had found the book and apologised again, Evelyn asked her assistant to cover the desk and walked to the staff room, where she sat, with her palms to her eyes, for ten minutes, trying to control her breathing. If she pushed hard enough, she thought, his image would be imprinted on her eyelids.

Zander was wondering why her image had not already been fixed in his mind before tonight. How had he failed to notice her in these three years? But, of course, why should he have looked at a librarian? Tutors, lecturers, students, waitresses – all of them had attracted him over the course of his time at Oxford, but librarians? The caricature closed his eyes to them – and the uniform she wore kept her anonymous.

So unexpected. For the past weeks since he had been coming to the library every two or three days, to work, to breathe the peaceful paper scented air, he'd had no wish to start a new liaison. He was seeing a German graduate student, Rosa, whose long, long blonde hair he could wind around his wrist so that her head, as she liked it, was held motionless as they made love. Instead of considering some as yet unseen other, when his thoughts drifted from his revision, he would return to the previous night and her open lips and closed eyes beneath him.

He shook himself and walked through the shelves to the Shakespeare section. The Late Plays. Zander wanted to discover a new way of seeing, an original dynamic. Concentrate. Focus. The only way to evict Miss Russell – Miss E. Russell (*What did that E. stand for?*) from his consciousness was to study.

In the staff room, Evelyn sat up straight and frowned. For so many years, she had held herself tight, turning herself into wood. And yet these feelings were not the feelings of a statue: the warmth between her thighs when she kissed him; the heart like a clenched fist punching her ribcage from within and the shooting-star synapses of her brain creating a narrative for them, for him and her. She recognised not the will to be swept along, as she had been by 'Call-me-John', but the desire to do the sweeping herself. Her mind showed her a flowing-haired woman who made things happen. The sort of woman who could travel to Svalbard alone at 78 and die there in her sleep from nothing more exotic than a stroke. Did she have the courage to become that kind of woman at last?

She rose and returned to work.

At 7 p.m., Zander stretched and closed his books. He put the volumes back and decided to take out a critical analysis of *The Winter's Tale* and *Pericles*, which addressed inter-generational sexual tension.

As he walked to the desk, Evelyn turned in her chair and faced him. Their eyes snapped together. Zander handed her the book and his card. He spoke to her with his gaze rather than with words.

She looked away through long years of habit, trying not to understand. Her voice was hoarse, 'You want to take this out?'

'Yes, and I want…' He turned, scanned the room: no one was near him. 'I want to take you out.'

'What?' Her face opened, and then slammed shut.

'You heard. I want to see you.'

She licked dry lips; stamped the book; handed it back; waved him to pass on.

'When do you finish work?'

She shook her head, but he could see the light in her eyes, he could see that look of grace returning to rest on her features.

He leaned forwards, whispered, 'Miss E. Russell, please, I want to take you out.'

A smile was forming at the corners of her lips, 'I don't think so.'

'Why not?'

'Because I don't want to be taken: I'd prefer to do the taking.'
'Sorry?' He frowned, stepped back.

Evelyn shrugged. She could see him considering, and she turned away, afraid. Would the free-flowing woman be afraid, though? No. Evelyn raised her face slowly, and her breath came out in a sudden, relieved gasp as she saw him grin, a cheeky schoolboy grin.

He said, 'Tell me what time you finish.'

She almost smiled and said, 'Ten.'

'I'll be there.' He pointed through the glass doors.

Evelyn watched him leave. She watched the movement of his body under jumper and jeans. She watched the way the halogen strip lights illuminated the rich chocolate curls. She felt a jolt within her. Her emotions swung between vertigo and the thrill of a safe landing.

At 10:10 p.m., the feeling had shifted to pure vertigo. Her assistant and the two juniors had already left. Evelyn's fingers stumbled over the keyboard as she logged off the computer; she dropped her car keys and felt herself blush as she patted her bound hair. She looked into the darkness beyond the glass. Out there her hopes waited. To be fulfilled? Or to be dashed?

She stopped. Realised that he, if he was outside, could see her, and turned. She could not go through. She was a fool! An old fool! Of course, he would never be there. She pressed the switch that bolted and deadlocked the doors and hurried through the half-lit building to the back exit.

As she passed between the shelves, she could feel the books pressing in on her. She felt sandwiched between the thoughts of all those writers: so many dead, a few still living. All these years surrounded by all the insight and originality the world of literature could offer.

And how had it affected her?

She stopped.

It had left her awestruck.

Instead of feeling the claustrophobia of living in a mausoleum, she had been glad to be as static as these texts; to be picked up, once, by Dr. Ketcher, and misinterpreted. She had read and responded, but had never written a narrative of her own.

If it was plot she wanted, she had the chance to start writing it tonight. If it was plot she wanted, she had the perfect hero, perhaps, waiting outside. And if he was not waiting? Well, if he was not waiting that would start a different narrative. Tonight, yes, tonight, some story would begin. The tension in her chest was now freed, and she breathed deeply. Oxygen rushed like wine into her bloodstream.

Evelyn retraced her footsteps through the texts, which now receded, backing away like extras deferring to the protagonist. She unlocked the door and set the timer. As she walked into the night, she pulled out her hairpins, which glistened in the moonlight and tinkled as they fell to the ground. As she walked into the deep-blue night, she thought, 'I am Eve: tempter, not tempted.'

## *VIOLET*

I have been sitting here with the curtains closed since Beth left. He seemed to want to sleep and I thought the sunlight was disturbing him. He's been sleeping a lot lately, of course, but I'm glad he woke up when Beth was here. Touched her hand, gave her that special smile he reserves for her. The very same smile he gave the first time he saw her. No, I never had any doubts about him after that.

    The colour of the light squeezing between the panels of taupe linen tells me the sun is low now, and preparing to sink, red, orange, gold, into the Chilterns. That's why we chose this as the master bedroom – though it's not the biggest room – because he loves to watch the sun set. Every night, he said, it was different, sometimes subtly so, dramatically so, after days of storms, when the sky starts to clear just as the day ends and the sun's display is at its most glorious.

    Me, I humoured him. I loved to watch him soak in the colours with his eyes. The next day, when he sat down to work, I knew that the brilliance of the sunset would shed light on those complex sums that I never understood. Theoretical mathematics. Some kind of genius, he is. I never made sense of what he said when he tried to explain. The earnest look on his face as he struggled to pare it down to simplicity. Vectors I just about grasped; two dimensions, three – that was all right; but when the concept of $x$ dimensions came in, I was lost.

    'Don't shake your head, Violet!' he said. 'I know you could understand it if you really wanted to.'

    But I never did. Of course, now I wish I had.

    Let me open the curtains for him.

    There. I was right. The sun is already deep orange, that flaming ball. How many times I have watched it sink and change in his eyes. And then he would turn to me and say, 'The glory of it, Vie.' Vie, he calls me – like the French, *la vie*, not Vi, as people always had before. I looked at him askance when he first used to say it but he would just smile and say, 'You are my life, Vie. *Tu es ma vie.*' Part of me wanted to laugh, I was embarrassed, but he looked so solemn, solemn yet smiling. Dear Tristen. No one else had the tenderness to get through to me. I truly believe that. No one could have made a family of Beth and I except this man laying here, his eyes closed in the sunset light.

When we met – Beth laughs when I tell this story, she says she remembers the night, though she was so small – when we met I had no intention at all of having a relationship with a man. How could I trust them? I shuddered at the thought of being alone with one. I don't think I'd been out more than twice since Beth was born – and probably only a few times before I had her… after it happened.

Even to think of those days makes my heart start to clatter like a runaway horse.

But that night: let me get back to a happier memory. My sister came to look after Beth and she sat on my bed tickling the little girl while I got ready. I was only going to the cinema with my friend Sheila, that was all, but as I said, I hadn't been out for a long time. I had been too ashamed and frankly too afraid… or was it more anger than fear? I don't know. I don't like to dwell on it. And, on a shallow level, I was self-conscious. I'd always been a pretty girl, I suppose, and I was vain, like all pretty girls.

Laura teased me kindly – bless her, she was a good sister to me, especially in those days when my parents' shame kept them away – and I piled my hair up, then thought that was too formal; so I tucked it into a chignon and then thought that too severe. In the end I just wrapped a little scarf around like an Alice Band. And then the eye make-up – kohl it was in those days – and thick black mascara.

Laura was saying to Beth, 'Isn't Mummy funny! Look how much fuss she's making about a trip to the flicks!'

I think I made a sharp reply but she gave me that wry look, her lips pressed together, the generous smile still visible and I had to giggle at myself – and that set Beth off. She was always a happy little girl.

And so I went to the cinema and we watched *Far From the Madding Crowd* with Julie Christie, Alan Bates and Terence Stamp. I'll never forget the part about Sergeant Troy and the poor girl he betrayed – oh that hurt me and I nearly walked out. 'I should have known!' I was saying, because I'd read the book. But Sheila held my hand and shushed me. She reminded me that it ends happily, and so I stayed, though I think my eyes were moist and then glazed for ten or so minutes. At the end, we remained sitting as the titles ran. Sheila loved films and always had to watch every last thing.

When the lights came up, she turned to me and shook her head ruefully, 'Oh, Vi, your make-up's all run, you look like a panda. We'd best get you to the Ladies.'

She was pulling me along while still managing to rifle around in her shiny little bag for eyeliner and powder to sort me out, so she wasn't looking where she was going and as I pulled back, she dragged me forward and we ran headlong into the man stepping from the Gents'. Not a romantic location, I know, but the rest of the story makes up for it.

He put out his hands to steady us and caught, as though by reflex, my arms just above the elbow and he looked into my eyes and he said, he just said, 'Oh.' That's it, 'Oh.' But in that 'Oh' and in his eyes was something I had never known in the features or voice of a man. Complete kindness, utter tenderness. And there was a connection at once. Sheila saw it. She took a pace back; she said as if she was intruding.

I was just standing there. It was the first time a man had touched me since it happened. Sheila knew and she was afraid that I would scream or try to run away. Yet I just stood there looking into this man's face and he said, 'My name's Tristen. I'm going to take you out. Tomorrow night? Friday? Saturday? All of them?'

And I remember smiling at him. It was as though a huge tension had been released. I nodded and he asked my number. I had to look at Sheila – I didn't know my own number or at least, at that moment, I couldn't recall it. And she said, 'Belsize Park 611.' He nodded; he didn't need to write it down. I didn't know then, but he could have remembered a string of digits a foot long, a yard long.

I wonder if, as he's been laying here over the past days, I wonder if the numbers still kept him company, filing through his mind, dancing their quadrilles and strip the willows. They have the colours of the sunset, he says, reds, oranges, yellows, most of them, and then they stretch away through the greens to blues and indigo and then there's violet. Infinity, he said. Violet, in his mind, meant infinity.

I told him my name, after he took my telephone number, and he said, 'Ah yes. Violet.' As though he had known already.

After he left us, Sheila said, 'Golly, Vi, he was taken with you! Never seen a man look at a girl like that! He might be a few years older than you, but he's a nice looking man. Bit quiet, but that suits you, doesn't it, Vi?'

I couldn't speak. I turned to her and she said, 'Oh yes! You're as taken by him! Wedding bells for you, young lady!' And she took my arm and marched me out of the cinema and along the road to the Tube, giggling about new hats and bridesmaids' dresses. I could sense her relief. Sheila worried about my refusal to leave the flat, my refusal to socialise. She must have seen that meeting with Tristen as a moment of magic, as, I suppose, it was.

The sun is deeper, richer. What number is it now? What combination of digits and symbols? He used to paint: abstracts, the colours of the numbers haunting him at a particular time. The paintings helped him resolve the questions that puzzled him in his work. He would be stuck on a theory, trying to prove that you can describe the world in numbers, and he would get out his oils and an easel and create a picture of what was happening with the figures in his head. They could be curves and swirls, waves, sine and cosine; they could be lines and angles, planes. Some suggested the infinite dimensions; some suggested a surface of millions of numbers. And after he had finished the painting, the equation or formula he had been working on would be resolved in his head. He could come, through colours, to an elegant conclusion.

It was when the painting stopped that his illness started. That's how it seems to me. It was nearly three years ago, or so, looking back. He was getting bad headaches – not that he ever complained. No, he just got quieter and smiled valiantly when I asked what was wrong.

His moods changed too. Some days he seemed irritable. He never snapped at me, but I'd see him tear his papers; crumple them, with an impatience he had not shown in all the years we had been together. A few days later, he would be lethargic, almost languid, staying in his dressing gown throughout the day. I suppose I assumed that it was part of the process of aging. His work, I thought, must be getting more urgent, more pressured. His job was a Government post. He dealt with codes and secrets, probabilities and predictions. The Official Secrets Act, that sort of thing.

When I realised there was something dreadfully wrong, it would have been two, two and a half years ago, I was convinced they were poisoning him. Oh I called the number he had for emergencies – this was when he was first taken into hospital and they'd sent me home. Beth was with him. I was meant to be resting. But I called the number and I cried out to the man who answered. He knew who I was. They knew it was me calling them. I don't mind saying that it scared me. I accused them of trying to kill my Tristen; I told them they were destroying our lives. How could I live without him?

I calmed down a bit after awhile because the man sounded genuinely concerned. I think they must have spoken to the hospital already.

It took a few days before I found out what was happening to Tristen. The diagnosis was not poison. It was a brain tumour. And it was too late to operate. Sometimes I still suspect them. Sometimes I think they have stopped his beautiful brain for some reason, even though the man said, 'Why would we want to?' Even though I cannot answer that question. At least they have looked after us. Tristen, when he was able to take in what was happening, told me that I would never have to worry about money. No, nor Beth either.

But all I want, all we want, is him.

Last year, talking started to become hard for him. Words seemed to have lost their meaning, though I am certain that the numbers swan around his mind as graceful, as pure as ever. He had always used the sign $\infty$ , which means infinity, instead of my name on notes or cards, our private language. One day some months ago I came home from the supermarket to find him covering pages with the symbol. Page after page in his neat, precise hand. An infinity of ∞ . An infinity of me. When I interrupted him, he looked up at me and gave me that wide smile, that look so full of love, the look that had made me gasp on our first night of courting in 1967. I cried then. Though I tried not to let him see.

'It comforts him, Mum,' Beth said. 'It comforts him – the repetition of the symbol – the symbol that means you.'

Of course, Beth has comforted him too. He loved her from the moment he saw her – and I think it was returned, if not then at least within a few meetings.

Tristen and I had been out a couple of times before I had the courage to be honest with him.

Initially, I was unwilling to speak about it. I didn't want to bring the memories into the forefront of my mind; they were damaging enough in the background. We had been out for a meal in a little French restaurant in Soho and had spent an afternoon at the Tate where I was surprised by Tristen's knowledge. I became afraid that, like my parents, he would be ashamed, and disgusted, by what had happened to me. The late 60s might have been the start of the permissive society, but that knowledge had passed my parents by. When they discovered that I was pregnant, they said I should marry him. Marry the man who forced himself upon me. They chose to believe his story – that I had been willing – rather than my version, the truth, that I had not, and instead had been afraid, in tears. Although I detested their values, their snobbery, their chilly practicality, I still thought, fearful as I was, that Tristen would react in the same way.

It was Laura who brought me to reason – as she had so often before. My sweet, kind sister had stayed loyal to me despite my parents' threats. She had convinced my father to pay for a place for me to live as my condition became obvious. And it was she who negotiated the rent on my first-floor flat in Belsize Park, where I lived from the few months before Beth was born until Tristen and I married. She had met Tristen when he came to pick me up for the dinner in Soho. Beth was asleep in her box room. Laura and I were drinking tea in the kitchen, trying to calm my nerves when he knocked on the door.

'Oh, I can't go, Laura! I need to go to the loo again, I have to redo my hair! Oh, Laura, do I look ok?'

'You stupid! You look ridiculously good. I'll get the door.'

When I came back, they were sitting in the lounge, Laura telling Tristen about her disastrous boyfriends. He was laughing with her, and I watched from the doorway for a few moments, taking note of him again, seeing how he compared to my memories first impressions of him.

She didn't spend long with him, but it was enough for my sister to form an opinion – and she was seldom wrong, unless the view concerned her prospective partners, when all sense deserted her. So as I fretted over whether to tell him and how to word it, Laura just took my hand and said, 'Tell him the truth, straightforward and honest, then introduce him to Beth. Your new man will love her as he loves you.'

'Love! Come on, Laurie, that's a big word.'

She shrugged, 'Whatever you say, Vi, but you either tell him or live a lie – and I don't think you can do that. And what's more I don't think that's fair.'

I traced the lines on her palm, raised my eyes to her face and said, 'What about you, Laurie, have you met anyone nice?'

Laura laughed, 'Not as nice as your Tristen, that's for sure.' She saw the look on my face. 'No, Vi, don't feel bad – gracious, you deserve a bit of luck. So, when are you seeing him next?'

'He's going to call me tonight.'

'All right then, here's the plan. Arrange to meet him at Il Trattore – you know, the one down the road here on the right? – and tell him early on, when you get there, so's Beth's not up too long. Then bring him here – I'll be with Beth and we'll see what he says.'

'Are you sure it's not too early to tell him?'

'I don't know, Vi; only you know how you feel. Do you want to hide your past from him?' I shook my head and she squeezed my hand. 'Well, that's decided then.'

So that's how we planned it, and Tristen agreed to meet me at Il Trattore two nights later. On the phone he said, 'I can't wait to see you, Vie.'

'Vie?' I asked. 'Everyone calls me-'

'I know they call you Vi, but to me, you're Vie. Like the French, *ma vie*.'

My throat constricted and I felt the heat on my face washing down my neck, spreading across my breasts. I gulped.

He said, 'I'm sorry, have I offended you?'

'No, I'm... I'm just... I'm looking forward to seeing you, Tristen.'

I heard the smile in his voice when he said goodnight.

At Il Trattore, I was already waiting when he came in, with the tissue wrung into a rope in my hands. I stood up to greet him, jarring my thighs against the table. He kissed me lightly and I saw the expression that flitted across his face.

'Vie, what is it?'

'Sit down Tristen; let's get some wine. I'll tell you.'

We ordered a bottle of Valpolicella and Tristen clinked glasses with me, his clear-caramel eyes looking into mine. I dropped my gaze to the checked tablecloth and caught my courage before it fled.

I had planned the order of my disclosures carefully, talking it through with Laura earlier in the day. But when it came to it, sitting opposite Tristen at the hidden table at the back of the restaurant, the words came out in their own fashion.

'I was raped. Five years ago. He was my boyfriend. I let him kiss me and... touch... He wanted more. I said no. But... but he didn't stop. My parents... they thought it was my fault and they were angry... They only knew because I was pregnant and they wanted me to marry him and I said no and they made me move out of home into a flat. You've seen my flat; it's nice, but I... and I have a daughter. She's four. Beth. Elizabeth. I have a daughter.'

He had, at some point, risen from his seat opposite me and he was holding me, he was kneeling next to me, holding me, and I felt anchored by the kindness of his eyes. He said, 'Shall we go and see Beth?'

And I nodded. It was as though he had known.

Tristen spoke to the waiter and we took the wine and he held me as we walked back to the flat, his arm holding me against his long, lean body. I unlocked the door and we went in. Laura stood and smiled. Beth ran toward me and then stopped, seeing a stranger. That was when I turned to Tristen and I saw the light in his eyes, the warmth in his expression. He squatted down and nodded to Beth. She walked to him and I watched as she touched his face. She touched his face as though she were a blind child learning his features. Her small fingers followed the curve of his smile. I knew then that I could trust him. I knew then that he was the one man I could love.

    I look at him now in the red light of the dying sun and his face is still as gentle. Never once in the 40 years that we have known each other and loved each other had he forced me, pushed me, pressured me. His touch had always been tender. His expectations had always been modest. He had always been pleased by whatever I had given, whatever I had allowed. It all took time. So much time. He had infinite patience. When I was crying in his arms once, one night after we had been married for a year or so and I still felt the fear freeze me at times, I asked him how he could put up with the uncertainties of me, the hesitations, the backing off from intimacy, time and again. His reply, as ever in that soft, gentle voice, was simple, so simple. It was the only answer possible.

    'I love you.'

    Oh how I love you, how I have loved you, Tristen. I stroke the skin of his cheek, touch the delicate folds of his eyelids and run my fingers through the grey hair – once jet, but still thick.

    Back when we met, Tristen was still living with his mother. I laughed when he first told me, stopping when I saw the flash of pain in his eyes.

    'I'm sorry – but it must have been hard, having girlfriends.' He is ten years older than I; I had assumed ten years, at least, of courting.

    'I have not really had girlfriends.'

    He saw the surprise, the shock, in my face. On one level, I was astonished that a man so good-looking had evaded the clutches of a woman; on another level I was concerned by his innocence.

    He flushed, a delicate coloration, perhaps only I would have noticed. 'At university, I did… but then I got engrossed in work. My father was ill for some years and I helped my mother to nurse him. He died a year or so ago. I have not…'

'I'm sorry,' I leaned toward him, reaching for his hand. 'I didn't mean… Well, why me? What did you see in me?'

His expression changed and before he spoke I felt my throat tighten with emotion. He said, 'I saw you and I knew, Vie. *Tu as bouleverse ma vie.* You have turned my life upside down and inside out. *Tu es ma vie, ma vie infinie.*'

He often spoke in French when his emotions were strong. It was the language of his childhood. His father was a French Jew. The family had left Paris in the late 30s when Tristen was very young. They had come straight to London where his mother had family and his father – a philosopher – had been offered a post at a university.

My parents agreed to see me again when Laura told them I was to marry a wealthy civil servant. They were astonished at my good fortune, but still did little to endear themselves to me. They objected to Tristen's age, his French roots, and his half-Jewish ancestry. I did not want them to attend the service, but Tristen and Laura suggested I give them one more chance. We were never close, never, but at least Beth knew her English grandparents as well as her new *Grandmere*. My mother and father could not resist Beth even if they still showed me little affection – and certainly no apology.

Our wedding. It was tiny. Just the parents and a very few friends. I suppose Tristen was never very sociable. He was a quiet man, a man engrossed by his work and by us – and that seemed to be enough for him. So the marriage was not a grand occasion. What was special, for me, or perhaps I should say what was particularly special, for the whole day was wonderful, was that Tristen surprised me with the flowers. He had insisted on ordering them all himself, and he chose irises, violets and lilac for the bouquet and the church decorations.

'Violet is the colour of infinity, Vie. This is for ever. We are for ever.'

Beth wore a little violet organdie dress and made a beautiful bridesmaid. My sister Laura and my closest friend Sheila wore violet silk frocks and walked with me up the aisle. The one line I had drawn was that I would not have my father giving me away. The priest baulked at this breach of tradition, but I stood firm.

The best man was a bearded mathematician from Tristen's department, Jamie, a gentle Scot baffled by much of the world outside his cage of equations. He, rather than Tristen, seemed to be the one who needed encouragement. When I came into the church, my husband-to-be turned and smiled at me – at us, Beth and me. He was stating publicly his love for us both. I felt my own smile widen and I stepped towards him as though pulled by the force that had dragged us together in the cinema.

'I take thee, Tristen David Zusman...'

His names. Tristen for the Wagner opera his Jewish father loved, despite abhorring the political overtones it carried; David meaning 'beloved' and Zusman, the family name, which meant 'sweet man'. Was ever a man better named?

When the priest said 'You may kiss the bride', Tristen took my face in his hands as though it were the most precious thing in the world. He kissed me deeply, his clear eyes looking into mine. When he moved his lips away he whispered, '*Ma* Vie' and I felt the tears rise. He grinned and wiped under my eyes with his thumbs.

'Don't cry, Vie, today is the start of the best part of our lives. Our life together starts here. For you and Beth and me.' We turned to the scant congregation and I took my little daughter in my arms; Tristen clasped us both in his wider embrace and I heard Laura and Mme Zusman crying. My own mother's eyes were dry.

I cried at Beth's wedding. She looked so beautiful and Tristen so proud as he gave her away. Her husband, Daniel, is a good, kind man. I only regret that they will never have children. It was Tristen who wept when Beth told us that. He wept, even though – or perhaps because – he has no child of his own. He wept although Beth does not carry his line, his blood, his genes. For several nights, in this room, ten, twelve years back, in the long summer evenings, he watched the sun set and the tears left trails of light on his still handsome face. I did not delve into the reasons.

Tristen is all love, but he had his core of privacy. I waited for him to speak. Perhaps it was cowardice. I was afraid that he regretted our decision not to try for a child. We decided that we were complete, the three of us, a neat triangle of a family. We decided? Or was it just me? An after shock of what had happened to me? Had I somehow betrayed this man who healed me? Now I wonder if I should, perhaps, have pried into his distress. Instead, I held his head against my breast and stroked his hair, seeing with him the light change from gold, to red and then to the bruised purple of evening.

That bruised purple light is coming now. Please, hold back, for a moment, for a while at least. Leave me some more time, some more minutes with him before the day dies into night.

The shadows are thickening around him, wrapping him in their soft darkness.

These last years have been hard. I have missed his voice. I have missed the words of love, of consolation for every little disappointment in life. Every little frustration where my changeable moods darkened, he used to meet with his infinite tenderness, his grace.

*Tristen, how I have missed your voice.*

And yet I would not have lost these years. I would not have lost the chance I have had to show him my gentleness and my devotion. As I have nursed him, each act has felt like… how can I explain… an act of prayer, for that is what prayer should be – gratitude and love.

Beth has never changed in her behaviour towards him, this father who was not her father, but was more than so many fathers can ever be. She has never used the raised voice which young people (she's in her 40s, but to me is young still) use to their aged relations. She has never patronised, never held back from kissing his hollowing cheek or holding his dry hands.

The light goes. I am alone now with this bruise of darkness. Just violet now, no life; no Vie, just Violet.

I cannot hold my composure longer. Without the colours, without the sunset colours, I sense all that I have lost. All that I can never regain. And I weep. For a time that I cannot count, I weep.

When the tears have left me bereft, I cry out, 'How could you! How could you leave me like this!'

The words come back to me, through time, through love, and I hear him say, '*Ma vie infinie* – this is for ever: Violet means for ever.'

*My Tristen... something of you, of us... surely something must last?*

I open my eyes to see the deep, the unendingly deep, violet of the evening sky and a sort of peace does come.

## *WHITE*

There's a flutter of snow on a summer's day; confetti carried on an azure breeze; I am driving through water meadows on a country road. Then, around the corner, its down angelic, the smashed body of a swan. I am dreaming this.

A lurch. A moment where eternity opens its jaws. They close, the feeling disappears. I fall and collide with wakefulness, my dream fragmenting into feathers. Turbulence. I sit up, stiff; I pull the eye mask from my face. I am lucky to have this row of seats to myself, but their contours and the seat belts have dug into my sides, my hips. I feel like a road traffic accident; I feel like I've been run over by a train – and, oh my God, how can it still have the force to crash back into my consciousness and surprise me after all these weeks? At least now I can push it some distance away.

Far enough away to register the clatter and citrus scent of the trolley – breakfast. I have spent so long on planes in the past ten weeks that I am familiar with their schedules. Breakfast – so we are little more than an hour from landing. I am going home.

I back away from this thought too. Planes – yes, I allow the irritation, the outrage to well up. They feed you as soon as you get on; take the trays; turn off the lights. They want you asleep. I wouldn't be surprised if they drugged us. No need to drug me, I drug myself. Wine and the pills. If I have enough space, I'll sleep. I'm used to it now.

The first plane on this trip, I got on like a holiday-maker – no, of course not, I was half crazy, I was light-headed with grief – but I didn't know the techniques back then. Now I can almost guarantee spare seats around me. Smiles, Internet check-in, bribery, tears, one way or the other, I get my way. Or else I move when we're in the air.

That's the last ditch attempt. But that was all I had in my locker for the first flight.

I was in a row of three with a young couple. Honeymooners. All the way to Tokyo from London. I was sitting down already; they walked up, looking at all the numbers, close together, that tenderness in their voices still. I felt the cynicism like a serpent in my gut. I was in the aisle seat, so I stood up – with my pen, notebook, novel, book of crosswords, bottle of water, and the little bag with my facemask, earplugs, the pills. It was like a military manoeuvre. They slid in; they were overweight, with black clothes, long, tangled hair, piercings, and an air of peculiarly incongruent gentleness.

We made the chit chat, commented on the limited space, didn't bother with names.

Then he came up the aisle – dark, fit, you know the type – the type I used to like. That fire in the eyes – electric. He put a guitar in the overhead compartment and sat in the empty row in front. No one joined him. He spread out. He had a camouflage blanket and a book about the Royal Parachute Regiment. A soldier? Sailor? Candlestick maker? I didn't care. He had spare seats. The plane took off. I landed next to him. The smile, 'Hope you don't mind.' He did, of course; he was good at the techniques, that kid – had got three seats on a full flight. Female check-in staff; his eyes of gentian. He cheered up though, when he knew me better.

A few of those little bottles of red wine and he was telling me his life story. In the Paras, going out with a nurse, not sure about it. I've got charm when I'm in that half-mad state. I've got the fire in my eyes; I'm electric. He tells me – emotional – about the bond of loyalty between parachuting assassins and the exhilaration of moments of danger – moments near death… and I wonder did she feel that? The exhilaration of near death, just before her death… He looks at me as though I am the first person he can talk to. I'm used to that.

People always tell me, when they first meet me, that I'm so easy to talk to. They tell me that from the first conversation it feels like they have known me for years. They look at me as though they are specially blessed with a gift of friendship. I took it for granted – I usually just switched on that magnetism for fun; I knew that within months, sometimes weeks, they'd think I was a bitch, a selfish witch, cold, ungrateful, unpleasant. Whatever. Of course, it's best to look as enthralled and surprised as my new friend. Oh, what a connection! What resonance! What a beautiful moment of communion! Sometimes I even managed not to be nauseated by the sentimentality of it all.

He told me that his father worked in finance and had been transferred to Tokyo. He said that his mother was desperately lonely and hated the city. She'd been brought up on the Yorkshire Moors and missed the space, the fresh air. He was visiting to celebrate her $50^{th}$ birthday. I don't know if I believed it – if I even believed he jumped out of planes for a living. What was he doing staying in this plane when he should have gone, he should have jumped; done the gentlemanly thing and protected me from myself?

Instead, I ratcheted my level of risk up higher. This man – what was his name? He was an adventurer, so he said – and I was too – alone on that flight, alone in my flight, totally! I was so excited; I had him in my hand. And I did exactly that – I took him in my hand, there on the plane on the evening we first met, us two, on our three seats, under the camouflage blanket and he experienced a new moment of flight at 30,000 feet.

At once, I was exultant and disgusted. I pretended to sleep, moved away from his hands. I felt the fever of the mania – and the cold blade of my self-awareness. And now, more than a month later, the same heat and cold – of shame now and self-hatred – sweep me on another plane, in other seats.

That was how my journey started – and now it's ending. Another hour and it will be ending.

The air steward turns to me with a tray and a smile – the emotion as pre-packaged as the food. I take it; ask for two orange juices and a coffee. He raises his eyebrows. I hold my face blank. Wait for the little glasses; drink one as he pours the other, hold the empty one out for a refill. Now I smile – and his smile broadens and becomes real. He gives me the coffee too – waits with the jug extended to see if I swig that as well. We share a moment – a much smaller moment, a more honest moment than any of the time I spent with the parachute man.

Afterwards, I knew that Davey would never forgive me. I just hope he'll give me a chance to explain. I hadn't replied to his texts, or answered his calls in the week before I left. In Tokyo the phone didn't work. I left it there. I put it on a bench in a park and then walked away and sat on the grass trying to experience yogic calm for a few hours. I wanted to see if the Japanese were as honest as they're painted to be. A few people sat next to it, as the koi carp in the pool next to me drifted like patterns on a screen saver. The people registered the presence of the phone, left it. Then someone took it. I followed, trying to be subtle, as only a tall, female, vest top wearing Caucasian with spiky hair can be in Tokyo. He took the phone to the administration office and handed it in. I left, went to a bar. Drank sake and tried to avoid the feeling of loneliness. But all that was later.

Forget the parachute man– it was nothing. I pushed him aside with the ease for which I have become detested. I escaped to the hotel I'd booked a few days earlier, cheap enough for Tokyo, expensive by the standards of anywhere else. The room was as small as a bathroom back home, and smelt of stale smoke. I lit up as I got in to freshen the atmosphere. The bath was deep and so short it was almost square. I looked at it and then decided to run – to stretch myself, rid myself of the sick air of the cabin.

In the street, the exultation returned. It was dusk. People were going home from work, hurrying in grey and black suits, their briefcases swinging. They half-ran, with a forward bending urgency – all of them, so much on the move! So fast. I strained to overtake men in shoes as shiny as the plastic food displays in restaurant windows, as black as the evening sky behind the vast city's electric glow and the day's residual light. My blood pounded, thick and resistant at first, and then as light as my feet. It was humid; I felt the sweat on my back and breasts immediately, and my hair sank from its crested height down to my brow. The rhythm suddenly became me. Or, I suddenly became nothing more than the rhythm, as I ducked through gaps between pedestrians, hovered at road crossings and sprinted to make the lights. The speed changed, the rhythm didn't. I felt strong. I felt alive.

One day in, and I'm better! That's what I thought, how I felt. And Tokyo, like the uber-polite Japanese would never say no, never disagree.

I spent a week doing the tourist stuff. The Meiji Temple, where the monks beat a drum so huge and resounding that I felt the reverberations in my soul and wept, standing there, thinking of my sister. I lit the incense at the Sensoji and bathed my face in its smoke, cleansing myself with incense and water and trying to hide my guilt under rituals. I travelled to Kyoto, to stare at gardens of raked gravel and white sand, to watch women in strange geisha clothes bow and smile under white make-up.

In the evenings, I ate at little local bars, struggling with the language and the food. I didn't like the food. I didn't want to be rude. I made up for what I couldn't eat with what I could drink. I was on my own and the neon blared around me like the bass from over-loud karaoke bars. I was on my own in the biggest city in the world.

I thought I was coping well and then I met Sukie. She was as blonde as I am dark. Her hair hung like a sheet of plate gold and her face shone with questions. I caught her eye the moment I walked into Inferno – one of Tokyo's themed drinking holes: the upper rooms are smoky, black and grey, the floor crunching beneath your feet like charcoal, debris, ash. Then, downstairs, it's all flames and fires – and the music is mixed with the roar of fire and screams. They like that kind of thing there.

She was talking to a Japanese guy who had his hand on her hip, sneaking it round to her buttocks. She looked like an escort. It turned out she was a dancer. ('Strictly no touching!' I didn't believe her.) When our eyes met, she grinned over the man's head. I asked her a question with my eyebrows and my smile. She nodded once, with subtlety.

I strode over to her and pushed the Japanese man away, forcing Sukie to step backwards against the bar. The length of my body ran alongside hers and I whispered into her ear, 'Is that enough or do I have to kiss you too?'

She laughed like wind chimes, 'Kiss me, why don't you.'

I did. Women's mouths are softer than men's. I had forgotten. And sweeter too. I pulled away then, embarrassed, disgusted. But she raised her hand into a high five. As we touched palms, my mood span again, and the gesture was tender, somehow, rather than triumphant.

'I'm Sukie,' she said. 'And who are you, my knightess in shining denim?'

'I am sometimes Alannah.'

'And the other times?'

'Nobody.'

She tilted her head, her eyes narrowed slightly. I relaxed my face and smiled at her more naturally. I said, 'I'm struggling with the jet-lag.'

The lie appeased her. 'A drink?'

'I'm not sure I can afford to return the favour at these prices.'

'One for the road, in that case, and I'll take you to a dive where the menu might suit your pocket rather better.'

I think she was shy too. We covered the awkwardness with bravado. I told her about the parachute guy on the plane. She laughed so much that she snorted, and the couple next to us turned round to look, eyes wide, affronted. She was the first person I'd spoken to in days who shared a first language. Just that was a relief.

'So, why have you come here? Land of the Rising Sun and all that?' We were drinking gin. The fresh scent of the juniper and the cut lime formed an aromatic aura around us – it felt as though we had a shield of fluorescent green and silver.

I said, 'Just fancied a change.'

'Oh yeah?'

She was cute enough to see there was more, delicate enough – then – not to push.

'Well,' she said, seeing I was unlikely to expand, 'I came out here to escape my ex who said he'd kill me if he ever saw me again.'

'Christ, what had you done?'

'Me? What makes you think I did anything wrong?'

I raised my eyebrows, she giggled and said, 'OK then, I alerted the police to a couple of things he'd have preferred they hadn't known.

But still, his reaction was extreme. I heard that dancers got paid well out here so I came.'

'You were a dancer at home?'

'Always have been. Started as a student, to pay the fees. Liked it more than Chemistry. Yes, I know, I don't look much like a scientist.'

She had been a serious young girl – long plaits and A-line skirts for her A Levels. Never the hint of a boyfriend. She was drawn to the chemicals and compounds; the flame on the Bunsen burner made her burn; the fizz of sodium, lithium, potassium was her excitement. Now the flare of strobes and the stink of alcohol and smoke defined her – so far from the methodical logic of a lab.

What catalyst had transformed the schoolgirl into this?

She intrigued me, I suppose. We went on to the other bar. It was a good night. We drank a lot. Teased the men who tried to chat us up – who am I kidding? – who tried to chat her up – by touching each other. I felt more turned on with that girl than I had been on the plane by the parachute guy. But I'm not into women. Really, I'm not. It was just that girl, that time. Partly she was slight and slim. In retrospect I recognise that she was as slight as my spun glass sister. That same fragility of bones, as though by touching her too hard you could make her shatter into diamonded fragments. And that glint in her eyes too, the flash of shared feeling when our gaze clicked together. A lightning strike: to meet Sukie at that time was a lightning strike.

She liked my Zippo; she leaned forward over the bar grinding the wheel against the flint so the flame whooshed up like dawn in the unknown hours of the night. She liked the warmth of the metal, 'Where do you keep it, Lannah? Why's it so warm?'

I felt the twitch and lurch inside me as her lips formed a feline curve of complacence.

The omelette is strangely satisfying. Mushroom and cheese. Salty. There are fried potatoes, a tomato. Then a small muffin, fruit and a bread roll with marmalade. I eat it all and I'm still hungry. The flashing map shows us flying over Europe, not far now—46 minutes, it says, 46 minutes to touch down.

I wonder if there will be anyone to meet me. I sent emails saying what flight, what time. Part of me hopes and part of me dreads. I remember now that in my swan dream, my sister was in the passenger seat and she said, 'That's me, Alannah! That's me!' Thank God for the turbulence that threw me into wakefulness, yanking me out of my dream: otherwise my brain might have created the image.

She was run over by a train.

There it is. The bald statement of the fact.

I did not push her. I was not there. I did not trip or trick her into it. I loved her. I did what I could.

Ha! I could not have said that ten weeks ago, even five. Three weeks ago, even then, I still held the residual belief that it was my fault. And yet I still find it hard to blame her – I find it hard to say this, 'She jumped.'

Inside my gut twists and turns, the omelette rolls and coils around the potato and chewed orange pieces. I have to leave my seat.

Sukie took me back to her flat. Not that night, a few days later on an evening when she wasn't working.

I had been to see her dance. I had watched the men watch her and had felt what they felt. It interested me. I didn't think I wanted anything more, but I was fascinated by my reaction. It was an experiment. Chemistry.

After work, she'd been taking me to bars where we would sit, drinking, smoking, while she told me her story. It was as sad as I had feared. It was as lonely as a dog chained to a post in an empty yard. The need howled from her to the moon and was flung back twice as hard. I don't know what she saw in me, but I know what she wanted: safety – and in the end, isn't that what we all crave?

As for me … I had broken, fractured, fallen utterly apart. I kidded myself that I had glued myself together. But in reality, I was nothing, nothing that she could rely on.

We moved my stuff from the hotel, considered doing a runner until I realised they had my passport behind the desk.

Her apartment was in the same miniscule scale as the hotel bedroom. A matter of ten paces from kitchen to bedroom, passing the sitting room on the way. The walls were painted dragon's-blood red. It was like being inside a heart. She had the one bed. I gestured to the sofa; she lured me into her room, the crooked finger, the silk dress sliding down her body.

'I'm not...'

'Me neither,' she said, and kissed me. I felt like men did when I did this to them. In the same vein, I wanted to reassert my control – I wanted to pin her back and hurt her – and the shock of my desire confused her into tears. I licked the salt from her face, kissed her again and we both tasted the moment – like the blade of a knife.

'So, Alannah, you going to tell me why you've come to Tokyo?'

I nearly did. Her eyes were blue enough to trust – but the gleam of her need put me off. That glimmer in her eyes might turn diamond sharp and cut me into scraps.

Instead I said, 'I wanted to see the cherry blossoms.'

'You've come the wrong time of year then.' She turned away, pushed a fist under her pillow and feigned sleep. I looked at her hair, glowing in the neon light that cut through the curtains. As if irradiated. I wondered if she was dangerous or damaged. I wondered the same of me.

I put my hand on the curve that ran from her rib cage to her hip and held her gently, moving close until my lips brushed the silk of her hair. Through my fingertips I felt the progress of her tears. I imagined them gleaming blue then magenta in the light, leaving a fallen star trail behind them on her cheeks.

My sister was hurt in a different way. She was older than me, and so, I suppose, there is a gap in my knowledge of what really happened. She did tell stories of our father's friends looking at her knickers. My mother – who was not her mother – said she was a little flirt. The different versions plague me, but I do not think there was anything to compare with what Sukie's stepfather did to her. My sister, Isolde, was simply, they said, 'too sensitive'. A euphemism for her condition.

The last time I saw her healthy she had just come out of hospital after being treated for anorexia. I'd just finished my A Levels and she came to stay at our house – she had a husband – a second husband – and a home of her own back then, but she came to us. She had started by refusing food; then she had not left her house for six weeks; she washed her hands 26 times a day. They had taken her to Holdenby Road and kept her in until she'd eat, at least, one green apple ('So fresh! So juicy!') and one floury bap ('So fluffy and filling!') a day. She was released into her stepmother's care – our father was working abroad and Isolde's husband and compassion were no longer spoken of together.

On the second day of her stay at our house, my mother left us together. I forget where she went. I hadn't spoken to my sister for five years, not since she had accused my parents of 'mental cruelty' and 'psychological abuse'. She was a stranger – stranger than a stranger – the familiar almost-aunt crazily transformed into an almost-child. I took her riding. I rode the big brown mare; she rode my fizzing pony. Isolde was the right size for the animal I had outgrown in my teens.

I remember us tacking up in the farmyard; above us, the swallows were pirouetting in the sky, chattering like school children and dive-bombing the cats. Her fingers hadn't lost the memories of leather and buckles. The horses stood as patient as hillsides, with the sun warming their rich coats, their tails the only part of them alive, flicking away the flies, moving the breeze into currents and eddies around us.

We went onto the moor, up the track to Taw Marsh where the river spreads out in the valley, wide enough to ride along, two abreast. The thunder of the horses' strides, beating the rocks in the river bed, churning the water into meringues, throwing up the brilliant drops around us – and my spun-glass sister, drenched to her thin thighs with Dartmoor's sweet water, laughing, her voice high, unaccustomed to happiness..

That cut-crystal laughter. It touched me so much that I forgave her the cruel lies about Mum and Dad, the years of silence and the recent months of torment my parents had endured watching her become as delicate and transparent as glass, as she starved herself and punished them. Us.

That was nearly ten years ago. And since then I have done more than forgive. I have given her time and money; I've called and I've visited; I've listened and advised; at times I've even understood. Until the last week, when I left her to it.

How could I give Sukie what I had withheld from Isolde. Her hair was a lattice of gold, which I plaited into filigree. I held her in my cold embrace when she asked – and she didn't notice the ice. I kissed her too. My lips were snow falling on her sun-drenched skin. She thought that she could melt me.

One night, I was watching one of Sukie's numbers. She danced with a white feather boa draped around her, teasing the men at nearby tables with the ticklish feathers. One of the customers caught hold of the end and started to pull. I saw Sukie's eyes widen – her balance was delicate and the tension in the boa discomfited her for a moment. Her pout re-established, she tried to jerk it back towards her – but the man held on. She jumped down and stood, before improvising, moving towards him, swinging her narrow hips, until her stilletoed feet were at the edge of the stage. She put the sole of one foot on his chest and pulled, hard. He held on and the feathers started to come loose in her hands, floating down around her like a flutter of snow, like confetti…

I left the club, unable to watch any more. My imagination took over and I saw limbs stained red. I heard brakes squealing. The heat of Tokyo struck me like a blow.

I rationalised my departure. The alcohol was expensive there and though I was saving money staying with Sukie, I was already planning to move on and didn't want to lessen my resources. I took the metro from Shinjuko to Rappongi where there was a jazz bar I liked, and there I met a group of English men. They were celebrating something. And something in me celebrated to see Caucasian men, men who stung the core of me with lust. The saccharine sweetness of nights with Sukie was nauseating me and I craved something else.

It turned out – as much as I gathered during my few hours with them – that three of them had come to Tokyo to visit the fourth. They used to be in a band together: one now worked in banking there; one was a teacher; one had a bar in Coventry and the fourth was still playing guitar – bass, I think – with a group from Sheffield. He was the one I went for. He had that thing I liked back then, still do, I suppose – the frisson, the edge. I joined them for a round of shots. They accepted me with charm, with ease, letting me enter the conversation and the atmosphere as naturally as raindrops enter a pool.

'Two weeks, you've been here? Wow – so what would you recommend?'

'Two temples and 200 bars.'

'We might only have time for the one temple.'

'So long as you get to all the good bars.'

The guitarist was running his hands over me – mentally – I could feel it, and I played up to the attention. Each pose struck consciously, lips wet, head thrown up, throat exposed. Men aren't into subtlety: if you don't overdo it, they don't notice. With Sukie it had been so different.

When I went to the bar to order another round, he was there and we kissed. He had a tongue-stud and the warm, solid smoothness of metal embedded in his tender flesh struck me as absurdly erotic.

I am not proud of myself. I do not feel any satisfaction that I, exerted such power – such pointless power really. It never made me happy, of course. And perhaps it was worse for them. I look back and wonder what I sought – what connection was missing – and I think it's to do with Isolde. I'm sure it's to do with Isolde.

When I get back to my seat, the breakfast tray has gone; but the steward has left a glass of orange juice. I have brushed my teeth, but it seems ungrateful not to drink it. I have washed the flush of sweat from my brow and the nausea has passed.

My sister threw herself in front of the *08:34* from London Euston to Rugby. She used to run in the fields alongside the railway line in Northampton where she still lived, in what had been her marital home. Her husband had left her while she was recovering from anorexia. They'd never had children.

For two weeks she had been threatening to come off the medication. I still don't know for sure if she did. But she had threatened so much and for so long. She drove, once, to Beachy Head, stopping at every service station to call us and say she was going to jump. My father had told me not to worry; my father said he knew her. I looked into the pained depths of his sea-storm eyes and realised that he held back so much. It was why he had those unexpected weeks away. It was why my mother tended him so carefully.

'Your father can't take too much excitement.'

'He needs his sleep.'

'I'll deal with it.'

My mother was his nurse as much as his wife, and I don't think she felt able to take care of a daughter along with a father. At some point in my 20s, the responsibility for Isolde was passed, without my agreement, to me.

And I failed her. At the end, I failed her.

She wanted a baby but she could not adopt, of course. Her record was too flawed. We gave her a kitten one Christmas, which quietened the urge for a few years, but twelve months ago, it returned with the force of a hurricane. She'd spend hours going through baby names.

'I think Imogen, or Isabella. What do you say, Lann? I'd like her to have the same initials as me. Immy is ever so sweet. Imogen Maisie.'

'But, darling …'

How could I go on when I saw the whites of her eyes flashing with fear – the fear that nothing, not one thing, in her life would turn out as she had dreamed.

She used to say, 'It never crossed my mind when I was little that life would be like this. I always though I'd be married, with children, living in the country. I never thought I'd end up mad as a juniper bush in a shitty little dark house in a dog end town at the arse hole end of the universe!'

'Life never turns out how we expect.'

The look she gave me, like a razor at my throat. 'But it's not quite so bad for you, is it, Lanny.'

I had a good job. I had a nice flat in London. I could pick and choose who to be with – and usually I chose not to bother. *I worked for it*, I'd think, trying not to glare at her. *And I still have my faculties.*

*How much better off than Isolde am I now?* I wondered. I am better off, of course, but after she died, when I went to Tokyo, I took her demons with me. They just reacted differently inside me. They turned me into a weapon to damage the world; for Isolde the weapons damaged – mostly – her.

The little flashing plane on the screen is relentless. This plane is taking me home. I cannot stop it now. I cannot slow its passage. Am I ready? Am I ready to come back?

The tongue-stud guy and I finally got the round and returned to his mates. I was hungry for more and they saw the excitement in my eyes. The conversation opened up to include allure, intrigue, flesh and I told them – I had no honour – I told them about Sukie. I told them about the tiny flat, the one bed and the dance club. I offered her to the other three as payment for the stud guy. That's how I thought of it. In my heart, I thought of her as just that – a thing, with which to pay; a thing to exchange. Or perhaps I am being too harsh on myself – though I doubt it. All I felt then was the flight – the flight from Isolde. And the intense need for a distraction; that's what I sought most fiercely.

She saw me come in. I led the way – the doorman knew me. Her eyes glowed forget-me-not blue under lights that turned her body to gold. Sukie was on stage and I was proud of her as though she were my creation, and my sacrifice, my Iphigenia.

We sat at a table by the stage. It took all my efforts to keep tongue-stud's attention focused on me. Resentment and jealousy started to replace the nascent clamourings of conscience. I knew Sukie was working until four in the morning. I figured I had three hours and one bed. We left his friends at the club – he must have told them, because they told her, eventually – and went back to her blood red flat.

'You live with her? I mean, you two?'

'Not quite – I'm leaving soon. LA next.' I was undressing, he was watching, then coming closer, touching.

He said, 'Yeah, but, are you two an item? I mean, it's every bloke's fantasy, of course ...'

'You want her here too? The little lip-stick lesbian?' My anger was growing bigger than the room. 'She's not into men; I am. Do you want to, or not?'

At the time I thought he was interested in Sukie too – but now, looking back, remembering his eyes, I think he was concerned about trespassing. He didn't approve of cheating.

I saw indecision flare, like the flame of my Zippo, and I took control of myself, feeling my rage like a Rottweiler at the end of a leash, calming it, pulling it back to heel, while at the same time turning the doe-eyes onto him with apologies and my hands in all the right places.

My body felt relief with him. If I had another life to lead, I would find him at the right time, in the right place. I had recognised the type – the eyes and the way his arms hung so loose from his shoulders; his neck always holding his head tall, his back so straight and behind that gleam of excitement, a depth of something genuine. When we were together in Sukie's unclean bed, I wept at the aftershocks of sex and he held me, all five foot eight of me, like a child and I wanted to tell him that I had lost someone. I wanted to tell him that I had lost someone I loved and that I would give anything God asked of me to have done right by her in that last week.

'Hey, are you ok?'

I couldn't speak. Just nodded, smiled.

He held me as if he cared and I almost think he did. I do believe even now that he would have listened; he would have stroked my hair, my face and listened. And I believe he was strong enough to take the force of it. A storm break, he felt like a storm break. He was the first person whom I sensed had the courage to stand by me if I fell apart. We were still entwined like vines when Sukie came home an hour earlier than I'd expected.

A few weeks after I left Tokyo, I read about a dancer, a Western woman, a Brit, who was found dead in her bath, buried in sand. I dream occasionally of Sukie, her skin and hair as gold as the sand covering her, a neat slice in her throat, or a ring of dark bruises.

She would not reply to my emails. When I phoned, she hung up at once. I can't blame her. She felt – I know, because she told me that night – that I betrayed her trust and our love. When I told her that 'our love' was 'her fabrication' she slapped me. He had already gone. She had screamed after him as he ran down the stairs, and I laughed, yes, laughed.

And what of him? After it happened, it was him I yearned for – part of me still yearns for him. That finally drove me to contact Davey; to admit that it was over- as if he needed telling. It gave him the chance to tell me that he never wanted to see me again and that Isolde's death could not justify every selfish act I felt like committing. At least I gave him the pleasure of telling me exactly what he thought of me.

This happened when I was in LA, staying at my cousin's house. She was at work when I spoke to Davey and I spent the rest of the day in bed, only getting up in time to try to lessen the swelling of my eyes before she got home.

After Sukie stopped screaming and swinging her fists at me, I packed. She fell to her knees and begged me to stay. She said she was afraid of being alone. She said that she felt something bad was going to happen to her – like her stepfather, like her ex-boyfriend who had raped her with two of his friends when he came home drunk after a football match.

I held her shoulders, forced her to look in my eyes and told her to listen, 'Sukie, surely you can see that I am not the answer you are looking for. I've hurt you this much in less than one week. I'm not a good bet, Sukie. This is wrong for you – and you can see that it's wrong for me.'

She argued – but I kept repeating this mantra, until she lost her temper and told me to go, to get out and have nothing more to do with her. So I never told her about Isolde. I'm not sure it would have made any difference. Perhaps she would have understood – though, as Davey said, it did not excuse.

I went straight to Narita, the airport. I looked at the flights and heard the costs. I slept on the clean marble floor and then boarded a plane for LA– and family.

My homeward-bound flight is approaching the Channel. I hope my mother will be there when I land. I know that my father will not. Mum says he's finding it hard to forgive me. And why should he forgive? He's gone through losing two daughters, not just the one. Isolde died, and a month later I disappeared. No one knew where I had gone. My mother told me they discovered that I'd sorted out my money – and then the hotel in Tokyo came up. Of course, I wasn't there long. They'd been chasing a paper trail around the world – paper, like swan's down, like confetti, floating in the aircraft's contrail.

I long to see her. The reassurance of the body I came from. The solidity of her flesh. She still plays tennis twice a week; she walks the Pennine Way once a year. If she'd been Isolde's natural mother, perhaps… but look, I can hardly commend my own sanity. Although now, I hope, it's different. Something happens and switches the course of a life. I hope I can keep it like this. I feel that a blessing was bestowed upon me and I hold it as you hold water in cupped hands. Eventually it seeps away. But the memory, in this case, please may the memory be enough to keep my life facing the right direction.

In LA, I was haunted by a 17-year-old Isolde. I was six when we lived there. My father was teaching Literature at the University of California. We lived in a hacienda-style house on an exclusive island for the year of his tenure. My playground was the beach of the Pacific Ocean. For Isolde, it was at times heaven, at times hideous. She spent a lot of time with me – teaching me to swim, playing with my plastic horses, reading me stories and taking me for walks. She must have been desperately lonely to give her life to a child.

I used to hear her arguing with Mum. Dad was seldom around. It was the three of us women. My mother hated to see Isolde 'mooching about'. She thought company would be good for her – company her own age. I remember being scared in case I'd lose my best friend. I also remember being unable to comfort my sister. I remember shuffling out of her room, dragging Goldy Teddy behind me, while she sobbed 'Leave me alone! Can't you leave me alone?'

A few days later, her tears would be forgotten. Isolde might spend a week going to the cinema, being driven about by boys and girls we knew, going out sailing. My mother would say how glad she was to see Isolde making friends; my sister would laugh. 'They're not friends. They're just people to play with.' None of them knew her well enough to stop her spinning into disaster.

In time, always the speed would intensify – she would be out later and later; her laughter would grow more frequent, louder, changing from contralto to soprano and her eyes moved too fast to follow. She'd start asking for money; a few times she stole. Inevitably, one night she would come back with the demons spiralling around her, stinging her like wasps. I saw her tear the clothes she was wearing; I saw tears shoot like bullets from her eyes.

In between the highs and the lows, she met Scott. A blond surfer, tanned golden by the Californian sun which had also – along with the marijuana – frazzled his brain. They had that in common, I suppose. After dating for six weeks, they announced they were getting married. My parents tried to change Isolde's mind, but that was always impossible. She said that he was all the medication she needed; she claimed he balanced her out. He did seem dopily calm; perhaps she was right.

It was a barefoot wedding on the beach. Isolde sported the little flannel hot-pants she wore for sunbathing on the roof, a bikini top and a pair of angel's wings made of ostrich feathers. Scott was in board shorts. His parents had moved to Florida and didn't return for the wedding, but his sister came. She stood, hand on hip, blowing pink bubbles and twirling her white gold hair in her fingers. My mother refused to bow to the dress code and turned up like a Surrey matron in Laura Ashley, complete with hat and matching suede court shoes. Dad made a disastrous compromise – Jesus sandals under his suit trousers, shirt worn without a tie. As for me, I don't think anyone worried about what I was wearing that day. I know I was barefoot, because I trod on the dog-end of the joint, which Scott's best man threw onto the sand, and hobbled for the rest of the day.

We ate pizza at the 'reception'. I'll never forget the smell of pepperoni and Coca-Cola. It sums up my life in California. It sums up Isolde's wedding. There was no champagne – she and Scott were too young to drink.

They were happy for four months. Then he ran his truck off the road and was killed. We went back to England soon afterwards. Isolde couldn't bear to see the Pacific: her memories of Scott crashed in with the waves.

As I walked the LA streets, Isolde kept me company. Sukie too. Davey, the tongue- -stud guy – even the paratrooper. And I felt as dark as English December in the Californian midsummer.

One night, after a day of aimless wandering, I was watching some dreadful chat show when my cousin, Tess, came in from work. She looked at me with her appraising hazel eyes and, having made her decision, went to the wine rack and opened a bottle of Malbec.

'Argentinian,' she said. 'It's got the tango spirit in it – might be good for you.'

I smiled, half convincingly, as we clinked glasses and the wine glowed like the walls of Sukie's flat. I squeezed my eyes shut to hold my own demons at bay.

'Do you want to talk about it?'

'About Isolde?'

Her shoulders rose slightly – too gentle to be a shrug – and she spread her arms, 'Start where it feels right.'

'I'm hurting people.'

She nodded. My cousin is a research scientist; she's working on cancer treatments. And I have never known her to pronounce judgement on anyone. She said, 'Are you taking it out on them?'

'No, I don't think it's that. But I failed Isolde. How can I not fail everyone else?' Tess turned off the television. I carried on. 'She needed me and I let her down.'

'Tell me.'

'I haven't told anyone.'

That slight movement of her shoulders; the generosity of hazel eyes.

I said, 'She kept talking about coming off the pills; said they were making her fat. She said the depression was like looking through a glass window. She could *see* her emotions, but not feel them. I said, "Surely that's better?" But she said it terrified her – she felt vertigo. I was really busy at work – we had a new client, a big one and I was in charge of the pitch and the presentation and it was all too much – and then with Isolde as well. She was calling me every hour. I told her to call Dad – then Mum said he was struggling to cope.'

Tess refilled my wine glass and brought me tissues. She sat there, quiet, not trying to embrace me or contain me; not trying to rush me; not embarrassed by my emotion. I remembered that when I was a child in LA and Isolde had first been diagnosed, Tess used to baby-sit me. Her calm and strength all those years back swept around me now.

'So I told her to hang on to keep it together until the weekend. She said, "Make sure you're here on Friday night! Please be here on Friday night …"'

I can't go on remembering. I'm too close to home to let all this come to the surface again. And yet, perhaps that is the point – to expel it all for good in the foul air of this cooped up cage in the sky. Get rid of it now, and then return to the land, free.

I thought I had burnt it out of me on Newport Beach; I thought I had frozen it out of me on my trip to the south. I thought I had run fast enough to lose it. But perhaps if the feelings go entirely, I will lose Isolde too.

And now, when I see her slight figure, back toward me, looking out over the farmland where we used to walk when I visited her in Northampton, instead of imagining the blood of her passing or the despair of her last days, what I feel mainly is my love for her. And my loss.

'But I couldn't make it on the Friday. Work was late, the meetings dragged on. And at nine, I just didn't feel like the journey, so I called her, said I'd get an early train the next day. She was tearful, but she seemed to understand. She seemed to be holding together.'

Tess stayed silent, calm, letting me speak. The only sound was the humming of the refrigerator in the kitchen. I sat back on the sofa, encircled by the silken, velvet and brocaded cushions that my cousin loved. In the spare room, there were so many pillows and cushions on my bed that I could create two imaginary bed buddies from them – but I wanted none, real or imaginary. I had sickened myself. I had seen myself at my worst and I was ashamed.

'She threw herself under the train she thought I would take.'

I had driven, in the end. I left London at nine and sang as I accelerated onto the motorway. The roadworks at Luton were clear of traffic; there were no accidents; no hold ups. I cut across the northwest section of the town and saw, as I crossed the railway line and the meadows alongside the Nene, a train stationary and the flashing lights of emergency services.

Isolde's house was empty, even the cat, Tristram, was out. I let myself in and made coffee. She didn't have any milk. There was scarcely any food at all, some hard bread and a scraping of butter. The only thing on her kitchen table – which was usually covered in pads, books, pens, leaflets – the signs of her latest fad – all that was there was a train timetable. The whole house was tidier than usual. She occasionally became anxious about cleanliness, so I wasn't concerned at first. I thought she was out jogging. Or perhaps she'd gone to the supermarket – although usually she would apologetically ask me to go with her and have me pay.

After half an hour, I began to get restless.

I wondered upstairs. The bedroom was the scene of some strange battle she'd fought against peace… the duvet was on the floor, the sheets coiled like snakes at the foot of the bed and one pillow had burst, the feathers, like a covering of snow on the floor.

I stood as cold as an ice sculpture. The room told me her mood as clearly as writing on the pages of a book. Guilt put its chill hands around my heart.

I started making calls, the calls my parents and I knew that one day we would have to make: to her Community Practice Nurse, to the Crisis Team, to the police and the hospitals.

Tess held me as she had done when I was a child. She stroked my hair. That night I slept well and deeply. The next day, Tess took me to her little beach hut on the coast, a private place looking out over the vastness of the Pacific.

'You know, Alannah,' she said as she drove, 'I told your dad as soon as you contacted me.'

I nodded.

Tess turned to me, and I saw a new expression in her eyes now – a sharpness which hadn't been there before. 'It was cruel of you, Alannah. Your father did not deserve that. I expected more of you.'

I spun to face her, 'For God's sake, I told you what Isolde did! She showed the world that it was my fault! She made it look as if I killed her! Of course I wasn't thinking about anyone else.'

'Well, you should have; it was wrong of you.'

'I'm not sure I want to make this trip now, Tess.'

'Don't be childish. Accept the blame you deserve and shelve that which you don't. The only wrongs you've done have been since Isolde died.'

'But she believed it was my fault!'

'No, Alannah, she was angry and felt alone – she struck out at you. But she was not being rational. How can you think that what she did was rational?'

'It seemed well thought out to me. The train timetable right there for me to find; the choice of train. I'd taken that train, time and again, I would have taken that train.'

'It was carefully thought out, but that doesn't mean it was rational. You got there as soon as you-'

'No! I could have driven up that night! But I'd been drinking. I could have got a train. I just couldn't be bothered because they take so long at that time of night. I should-'

'Alannah, she was an adult. You did what you could.'

'No!'

She shook her head. 'You have to get over this, Alannah. You have to live your life. And you have to stop punishing other people. You think you're shouldering all this blame for Isolde's death. But you know what? You're using it as an excuse to hurt others. Malcolm, Davey, that girl in Tokyo. Don't think for a moment you can strike out at me.'

Our eyes met. Fire met fire. And I knew she had won. I was too weak to take on her reason and her justice.

Tess and I cooked together, that evening, in the small kitchen of her cottage. At first it was awkward. Our conversation stuttered over the risotto. I chopped onions and garlic, feeling tears start in my eyes, rubbing them away, my back turned to my cousin. She was making stock, humming along to the music she'd put on to ease the atmosphere. I put the onions in melted butter and stirred them. She opened a bottle of sauvignon blanc and handed me a glass. I nodded thanks.

'Come on, Alannah, you know I'm right. You're a smart cookie.'

'Don't push it, Tess. Please. Leave me.'

She added the rice to the pan and I watched the grains absorb the butter and slowly become transparent. We stood in silence. She stirred, then added her glass of wine to the pan. It sizzled and bubbled.

'Pour me another, will you?' said Tess. 'If we're going to row, I'd rather be drunk.'

I snorted. As I was pouring the wine for her, she put her arm around my shoulder. 'I love you, Alannah. I feel for you. I just want you to get on with your life, to get rid of the guilt that's turning you into someone angry and vicious and selfish.' I was pulling away, but she held on. Though smaller than I, she was strong, and determined. 'You are none of those things. I know you, remember. I've known you since you were a little kid. And I know that inside this bitter shell is a hurt and loving girl. Let her come out. I'll look after her just like I did when you were little and lonely and scared.'

We had to start the risotto again, later, in a new saucepan. The tension in my shoulders had eased. I realised that I had been rigid with anger; now I was starting to soften. Tess felt that I had to forgive Isolde before I could grieve. She was right; I just wished Isolde had given herself time to forgive me.

England is below me now. If I sit up tall, crane my neck, I can see beyond the other passengers and through the little porthole windows. There, below, is the green patchwork quilt of my homeland. Down there, I'm sure, my mother waits.

    Isolde too waits for me and I try, as I look at the minutes ticking down to landing, I try to recall the peace I found on my journey, the peace Tess helped me to find, the peace I need if I'm to live.

We stayed at the beach hut for three nights. During the day, we walked along the white sand watching the restive Pacific attack the land. The sky, each day, was like a swathe of pale denim, with frayed white cotton contrails.

    Tess told me about her most recent partner. She had never married – nor, as far as I knew, ever lived with anyone. Yet there was always a man wanting to marry her, move in with her, be with her. She never wanted that level of commitment. I wondered if she feared letting others down – or being let down herself. This man was working with her on shark research. Sharks don't usually get cancer so she hoped to find out what protected them from the disease and then apply it to humans. Tess was passionate about her work – and her sharks.

    'Their skin is like sandpaper. You can stroke the heads of the little ones. They poke their snouts out of the water when the technicians who feed them walk into the area. They have scarcely changed for millions of years. It's as though they were created perfect and didn't need to evolve. They were already at the peak of their evolution when we were nothing.'

    I thought of the indigo depths of the sea and the voracious sharks circling for millennia… it make me shiver.

The only message Isolde had left was the train timetable. It was a message of blame for me. How could I ever get beyond that?

On the last evening, we sat on the small patio, looking out at the sun slowly sinking into the red-painted sea.

Tess broke the silence, 'Is there anything you have always wanted to do?'

'What do you mean?'

'Some ambition – something you've thought of, but never done, dreamed of?'

'Riding across the Andes? Writing a novel? Going to the Antarctic-'

'What?'

'The Antarctic – I know a couple of people who went on those cruises, said it was indescribable, incredible, blah de blah – I'd like to see…'

'I might be able to help…' She was frowning slightly. Then she pulled her phone from her bag, started scrolling through the contacts.

'What do you mean, Tess?'

'Colleagues – ex-colleagues, I mean – more lucrative doing the eco-tourism thing than research… Have I got Bryan's number… it's early in the season, but you never know…'

She got me on the trip. All the money which I thought would last me another year away from home, covering my mortgage and my costs, all of that money I blew getting from LA to Tierra del Fuego and paying for the cruise.

It was a pseudo-scientific trip, with the expedition leaders giving talks on the wildlife, the birds, taking photographs of icebergs and surviving in minus 60. I listened. I even made notes, in the new books I'd bought in one of the interminable stopovers. But what I was really doing was feeling… the motion of the ship gave me a peculiar calm. I suppose I was lucky: the sea was bouncy, but not furious, and to me the movement, the gentle rocking, was comforting as a cradle. I watched my green-faced co-travellers with sympathy.

Strange. I felt, already, closer to Isolde. It wasn't until I was in Buenos Aires, toasting my absent cousin with more Argentinian Malbec, that I remembered how my sister had dreamed of going south.

'It's the colours, Lanny! People think it's all just white, but they're so wrong-'

'They're not right about the white?'
'Stop it! Don't tease me! Listen-'
'I'm listening, Iz, get on with it!'
'I will if you'll stop-' she hit me on the arm '-bloody-' and another jab '-interrupting! Right... where was I?'
'Wrong! It's NOT white!'

I smiled at the memory, recalling Isolde laughing too much to continue. She had read everything she could find about Shackleton and Scott; she had a library of other accounts of Antarctic journeys and photographs of icebergs, penguins and seals. This obsession had lasted for a couple of years, drifting out of her mind only when overtaken by her desire for a child.

I wondered if I could have saved her if I had spent this money five years back and brought her here. The grey sea reeled and churned below me, flecked with white froth, which feathered the surface... The stiff breeze dried the tears before they dropped down to add, infinitesimally, to the salty waves. Above me, the sea birds wheeled and spun – albatross, petrel, prion – their wings flashing even in the dull light of an Antarctic spring day.

Later, I watched a humpback whale, and smelt the rankness of its breath as it exhaled water, air and debris from its blowhole. A school of dolphins played around our bows.

There's more to life than grief, I thought; more to life than guilt for what I could not control.

The pilot says we are starting our descent. It's not just the change in air pressure that makes me swallow. I am afraid of what I am returning to. The last weeks helped me, but the closer I get to home, the more I fear the loss of this delicate equilibrium.

I bring to mind my memories of the cold southern seas: the wind scouring my self-indulgence; the chill preventing my mind from turning its destructive analysis; the beauty opening my heart to something other than pain. I think of all the colours – not just white – the turquoise, indigo, azure; the very occasional rust, carnelian, peach; the infinite gradations of grey. The sheer cliffs of ice. The ability of the water to reflect perfection perfectly.

And the cold! The purifying, lung-searing, frost-biting cold!

I inhale, and it's not this stale plane I smell, but the scent of brine and ice; the stink of penguins and the one-off aroma of a whale exhaling.

My eyes sting – not with tears – but with the spray carried on a southern wind. My heart aches – and it's the south I miss, as much as my sister.

It took us 50 hours from Ushuaia in Tierra de Fuego to get to the Antarctic coast. The first time I saw an iceberg, I was awestruck. I thought of the Titanic; I thought of clichés. And it was the tip… a few days later we passed an iceberg graveyard, a shallow bay where large icebergs grounded and gradually melted. It was more dramatic than modern art – a natural sculpture park, with shapes, weird and intricate. The icebergs are carved by lapping waves and harsh winds, then lose their balance and topple over, to be recarved… with their eroded underbellies exposed. The glaciologist explained that white ones are the youngest, blue ones are about 15,000 years old, and clear ones even older. Tens of thousands of years of erosion. Ancient ice. My own world seemed so small, my time so short.

Cut-crystal icebergs, glistening in pellucid light… reminding me of something I longed to forget.

When I saw the colonies of penguins, I felt like I was back in Tokyo or LA: instead of humanity, an avian crush.

We took the Zodiac and went ashore. So many layers of clothes and yet the cold so intense that if a flap of fleece so much as moved I felt my flesh start to freeze. When we stepped onto land, I felt it move under my feet. The noise, the smell, it was overpowering. My co-travellers got out cameras, notebooks, binoculars. I walked around, my legs uncertain, a dizziness in my head like drugs.

And then the not-all-white world – briefly – went black…

I was lying in the snow and penguin shit. The smell was like nothing on earth and my breath stung my lungs. It was like breathing ice. Above me the sky was a pure blue I had never seen before, never even imagined… a gentian blue that perhaps only exists there and in poetry.

As I lay there, the cold and the stink surrounded me and, though both were unpleasant, I was curiously fascinated. I wondered if Isolde's depression had chilled and polluted the air around her; I wondered if her depression had had the same alluring and dangerous fascination for her as this seascape, all beauty, freeze and stink, had for me now. From what she had said to me, I think it did.

I felt her close. I felt her, for the first time since she died, near to me. I almost resented the people who helped pull me to my feet and the enforced rush back to the ship to see the expedition doctor. I baulked at the door of his office – he looked too young to help anyone, let alone me, with my weight of guilt and grief that made me feel older than Methuselah.

'So, was it the cold?' he said, as he tested my blood pressure.

I shook my head, 'I'm fine, really. There's no need to fuss.'

'Well, humour me. Any strange pains? Light-headedness? Tingling?'

'Nothing.'

'Headaches?'

'No, please, there's nothing wrong with me.'

'Do you take any medication?'

'For God's sake, this is absurd!'

The pleasant face turned hard – I remembered he was an ex-Army doctor – he said, 'Please don't accuse me of scare mongering.— Ms…?'

'Drayton, Alannah Drayton. And I'm not accusing you of anything, I'm just telling you that I am fine!'

'Ms Drayton. Please try to look at it from our point of view. All these people have paid a lot of money to come to the back of beyond. You get ill, there ain't no hospital here. We'd have to organise a costly and difficult transfer – and that could affect the enjoyment of your fellow passengers. So, let me do my tests, and please help by answering my questions.'

I bowed my head, flushing. He continued to ask about my state of health, the chance of pregnancy, any recent upsets…

'My sister died three months ago.'

He glanced up and caught the look in my eyes, 'Yes?'

'She killed herself.'

He nodded, 'Go on.'

I told him. Like a rush – like melting ice in the southern spring – it all came out. I even told him about the angel wings brooch, which the police had shown me to identify her. 'The body was too much destroyed. All there was to show that it had been Isolde was the brooch. I kept saying it wasn't her, it wasn't her! But when I saw that… she would never have been separated from the brooch… a cut glass trinket I gave her as the "something old" for her second wedding – so she had the wings again, the angel wings – it was kitsch really, but she loved it…'

I was weeping. And then I was standing up, shouting, 'I'll never get over this! I'll never escape this! She will haunt me forever and it's all my fault and that's what she was telling me when she died.'

He caught hold of my shoulders, shook me, not hard, but not gently either. 'Listen to me. Ms Drayton, listen to me. Alannah! Good. Why do you think it's your fault?'

'I wasn't there!'

'You couldn't be there. It was her decision.'

'She was telling me she blamed me!'

'How?'

'Oh come on! She threw herself in front of my train!'

'Had you said you'd be on that train?'

'No, but it makes sense that I'd get there around that time…'

He was looking straight into my eyes. The direct gaze hypnotised me. He said, 'You're wrong, Alannah. She jumped under the last possible train. She'd been putting it off. She'd been delaying it. It was premeditated – people often tidy, sort before they take their lives – she was determined, but she still couldn't quite do it – so she had that tantrum in her bedroom and then finally went for the last possible train before you arrived to stop her. She had decided.'

'But she asked me to come on the Friday!'

'And you couldn't.'

'But if I had! If I had she wouldn't have done it!'

He sighed, and gave me a slight squeeze. 'It is hard, it is painful, it is horrible. But you cannot live your life through that *if*

'She left me a message – the train timetable! It was a message.'

'No,' he held my shoulders and again his eyes locked on mine. 'No, the message was the brooch. The angel wings. She was saying that she loved you. She was saying it wasn't your fault.'

I wanted to believe it. It was like a temptation, a prize, just out of reach.

He said, 'I truly don't believe she meant to punish you. I didn't know her, but I am sure that if you think about this, you'll agree. She was in despair and she didn't want you to stop her.'

'I would have stopped her if-'

'Alannah!' He shook me again, 'Look at me. You have to take control or you may as well jump into this freezing sea. And if you do, dive down – it is better to drown than to freeze. At least you get the chance of brief euphoria with asphyxia; hypothermia is just cold.'

I hiccupped and sniffed, startled by his words, and then I saw his smile. He went on, 'This may sound pat and airy-fairy, but this place can help you, if you let it.' He paused for a moment and then said, 'Come with me.'

I followed him up the stairs and onto the deck, pulling on my coat and doing up the zip as the cold hit me. I had to half run, skip to keep up – he was walking fast, turning back over his shoulder to check I was following.

'Right,' he had stopped at the rails and was pointing at a vast white shape in the distance. It was so white that it hurt my eyes and the sky was the blue of an angel's eyes. 'See that glacier?' I nodded. 'And that black thing there? What do you think it is?'

He had pointed out a small dark shape in the sea.

I peered into the distance, squinting against the glare. The air was so clear, you could see forever.

'Come on,' he said, 'what do you think it is?'

'A seal? I can't tell from here – something small – maybe a penguin's head?'

'That is a supply ship.'

Suddenly the glacier was transformed from skyscraper height to gargantuan. I stepped back: the scale made me dizzy.

'It's a lesson in perspective,' said the doctor. 'Think about it.' He turned to me. His face had softened into youth again. 'You've had a raw deal, with your sister. Don't let it destroy your life.'

He patted my shoulder, gave me a half smile, a smile full of understanding – something shared, and left me. I stood looking at the glacier and the ship until I was too cold to stay outside any longer. And even then, as clouds started to gather, I stayed longer – because the sun was setting on that Antarctic spring day. It was a sky of such bewildering beauty that one would have thought it only possible in some post-apocalyptic future.

I spoke to my sister; and asked her forgiveness; I spoke to my sister and I forgave her. Under the feathery cirrus and the snow-laden cumulo-nimbus, I saw Isolde's features soften and I felt the pain in my heart start to ease.

I don't believe that a country, a journey, can cure you. But perhaps, as Frankenstein had to travel to the north to fight his monster, I had to make that trip south to deal with mine. I don't know if I inherited Isolde's demons, or if my own fed on the guilt and the pain of her death. Now, as I fly home, I feel that I can assert some kind of control of them. I will not lash out again as I did those months ago when I left.

The beauty of the place – I'm bringing it with me, as much as I can. I remember image upon image of a world that isn't just white. And where it is white – when the snow is not coloured by sunrise or sunset, or by the indigo of night –that white is a white you never see anywhere else; a white even heaven cannot contain. Whiter, even, than the wings of angels. My photos won't record it, no camera can capture such transcendence – but my memory can. And I can translate these visual images on my camera into some version of their reality.

That, in the end, is what I have to do with Isolde. I have to translate despair, grief and anger into love. And I have to learn to accept where I did fail. As a full-time sister, I still missed the crucial moment. For the rest, I have been a part-time daughter and a part-time lover. As we circle London, I imagine the tender, involuntary half wink of my mother's left eye when she smiles. And I imagine too the electricity of the tongue stud guy. I do have another life to lead and I will meet him again at the right time, in the right place. I will learn to be full-time at last.

The plane descends, flashing white against England's cloud darkened skies, graceful as a swan coming to land on the water meadows alongside the Nene where my sister once used to run.

# SHADES

## *A STAIN THE COLOUR OF BLOOD*

The sun was nearly hidden behind Cawsand Beacon, only the last rays sneaked over the horizon, shedding an orange light over the bracken. Within half an hour, it would be dark, and the lengthening shadows were ready to steal over the turf to shield the moor from Martin Redland's eyes.

He ground the gears of his Land Rover and cursed, turning the wheel sharply to avoid a granite boulder in his way. He'd driven off the track, hoping that in this deep valley he'd get a sighting of his herd. Farms on Dartmoor had traditional grazing rights over the common land of the National Park. The Redland family, with their farm on the edge of the moorland village of Belstone, had exercised this right satisfactorily for untold generations. But over the last couple of months, roaming free on the heather-covered hills, his herd seemed, strangely, to be shrinking. Martin always expected to lose some sheep to foxes, bogs, age and cold – not to mention the problem of tourists driving too fast over the moor's unfenced roads and crashing into his prime ewes.

Things were different these days. Instead of losing the odd five percent, at the last count there seemed to be a fifth of the herd missing.

Martin felt the off road tyres struggle for grip on the steep slope. He changed tack, zigzagging up the hill with the Land Rover in four-wheel drive mode. He switched the headlights on. It was dimpsy already; darkness would soon follow. Though the lights allowed him more chance of seeing sharp stones held in the land's earthy embrace, they made it less likely for him to spot sheep outside the range of the beams.

'Where are you at, you little buggers?' he said, spinning his head, his unrestrained curls still shining in what light remained. 'You can't all have disappeared... They've never wondered further west. I reckon as tomorrow, we'll go south, shall we, boy?'

The collie next to him wagged his silky tail and shuffled closer along the seat so that his wet nose pressed against the farmer's jeans.

Martin looked down with a grin, strong white teeth flashing; he rubbed the dog's head and accelerated now that the ground was levelling out. 'We'll go home, get ourselves some dinner, shall we? Yes, I know it's past your dinner time... Wait a minute!'

He braked abruptly, one strong hand stopping the collie from sliding from the seat to the muddy foot-well of the Land Rover.

'Come on, Fin!' he said, opening the door and getting out, swiftly followed by the dog, slinking blackness tipped in white. Four long strides and Martin was standing over the pale shape of a sheep's body. She looked as if she'd been a fox's breakfast and was soon to be its dinner. Her eyes had been plucked out by the crows. Martin couldn't help himself touching her white head in silent blessing. He didn't think about what he did – it was his instinctive response to death.

The dog sniffed around the corpse, then barked, and jumped back, legs rigid, looking up at Martin and barking again.

'What is it, Fin?' Martin went back to his vehicle and got his torch from the glove compartment. He switched it on. 'Well, what have we here, then?' He leant down, looking carefully at the body, then knelt, with the torch on the ground, and turned the sheep over, disturbing a buzzing melee of flies. He sat back on his heels, staring down at the painted stain on the fleece. He stood up, picked up the sheep by its stiff back legs and carried it to the Land Rover. He dropped the body in the back, got in the cab with the dog, and started the engine. It was loud in the quiet emptiness of the moor and the headlights, when they came on, shut Martin and the dog in their own enclosed cone of illumination.

Redland Farm was a Devon longhouse; a beautiful old building made of granite and cob. Martin's mother, brought up in a town rather than on a farm, had exposed the stonework around the inglenook fireplace and installed modern bathrooms and kitchens.

When Martin drove home, the Land Rover lit up a farmyard in which the gravel was clear of weeds and where the barn doors were carefully creosoted. The house itself was freshly painted (during two baking-hot days the previous summer) and over the door of the one occupied stable, a bay mare's head appeared, ears pricked. She whinnied at the returning car and nodded her head, kicking the wood with an impatient hoof.

Martin parked by the barn he used for the sheep during lambing and carried the body inside. He stood looking at it, undecided; then shrugged and left it, uncovered. He gave the mare her bran and oats before going inside and feeding the dog and the two cats, that he'd found as kittens, abandoned by the roadside. They'd been brought up in the kitchen and were unwilling to make the full transition into barn cats. He humoured them, amused at their decision to retain a life of feline luxury.

On the fridge door, attached with a magnet shaped like the island of Corfu that his mother had bought on her one foreign trip, was the shopping list he'd forgotten. Inside the fridge was milk, cheese, a wrinkled tomato and an open can of corned beef. There was bread in the freezer. He made cheese on toast, which he ate while he shuffled through some papers at the back of the grey metal filing cabinet in his office. He pulled out a document from the Dartmoor National Park Authority relating to grazing rights. It had an addendum about the marks used by the various mid moor farms to identify their sheep.

His second piece of toast cooled and hardened on top of the filing cabinet.

The next morning he got up early. By 6.30, he'd fed the indoor animals, the mare and the chickens in their pen behind the barn. The birds eyed him, heads cocked, clucking speculatively as though querying his changed schedule. He felt underneath soft-feathered bodies for their smooth, warm eggs. All his creatures became too tame, he thought, as the hens made their gentle cooing noises, undisturbed by his hands.

Before going inside to get some toast for himself, he went into the barn where the sheep's body lay in the early morning light. She was a Cheviot. He was one of the few farmers around who'd opted for a breed other than Scottish Blackface. He didn't have any doubts that she was one of the ewes he'd pulled, wet and slimy, from her mother's womb; and from whom, in turn, he had helped to release a lamb or perhaps twins this spring past. Again, he stroked the fine hard white hair on her head.

On her right shoulder, was a red mark. A large circle of red paint, the colour of blood that's been sitting for some minutes, but not yet started to clot. That she was marked in red on her right shoulder, and was a Cheviot, all that could be an unlikely coincidence. But in the daylight, he was certain that beneath the red circle he could see the shadow of a red R, the mark of the Redlands. He'd read last evening that the red circle, on the same leg as his stain, was the identifying sign of the Luxton family, which had been registered just five months ago. They hadn't previously run sheep, having instead a large dairy farm on the fringes of the moor, too far away to have grazing rights, he'd thought. He knelt looking down at her and wondering how her lamb would fare without her, but by now it should be fully weaned. He knew, from the calls of the sheep, how much mutual affection – he couldn't describe it as anything else – existed between ewes and their lambs.

He did the urgent jobs he had to do around the farm and then went into town as soon as the shops were open. He was back and ready to leave for the moor by 9.30. He attached the horsebox to the Land Rover, loaded up the mare and drove out as far as he could into the open moorland where his herd usually grazed. Sheep don't usually range far from their lear, so it had been increasingly odd not to see them. It had been three days now and this time it didn't seem an issue of the loss of ten of twenty, but the disappearance of the whole lot.

Martin tacked up the mare and packed some food and water into his saddlebag. The dog lay, head on his crossed paws, in the passenger seat until Martin was ready. When he whistled, Fin jumped through the window onto the springy turf and they set off southwards, the mare snorting with pleasure to be out in the bracken scented air.

For an hour or so, Martin relaxed into enjoyment. The dog ran ahead of him, close to the ground and quick, black as an eel in the moorland streams. Under him, the mare felt light-footed and eager; he spoke to her through the reins and through his legs; she responded through her pace and her ears. It felt like telepathy. He stopped at the ford over the Taw, so the horse could drink. Her neck was warm, but she wasn't even sweating, her breathing gentle and even. He patted her neck and she twisted so that he could give her a mint from his pocket.

The dog barked sharply and turned, ears pricked towards the south. Martin sat up straight in the saddle, and then squeezed the mare's sides. She bounded across the river, churning the water into foam and crystal spray. Her hooves slid on the stones beneath and then she was out, on the sandy shore and building up speed as the track wound uphill. Leaning forward, so that his weight was off her back, he concentrated on the ground, careful to avoid any rabbit holes or stones – she was sure-footed, but he was a conscientious rider. The dog ran ahead, tail a black banner streaming out behind him. They climbed to the top of a tor and as the horse's metal shoes clattered over some exposed rock, Martin pulled her up.

In the valley below, a hundred head of white faced sheep were being shepherded along by a pair of collies and a thin figure in loose trousers. Martin turned the mare sharply, whistling low to the dog, so they were hidden behind the pile of granite boulders at the top of the tor. The woman, he knew it was a woman, couldn't have walked from her farm. The vehicle must be somewhere. He decided to circle the herd, out of sight, and try to find it.

It didn't take long. A scruffy little pick-up, baler cord and feed sacks in the back. In the front, cassettes of music from the 60s, a couple of hair ties, with broken strands of fine blond hair coiled round the elastic, an empty lemonade bottle and keys in the ignition. Martin pulled out the keys and put them in his pocket before leaping onto the mare and heading back to the tor. He couldn't condemn her for foolishness in leaving the keys – his too were in his vehicle. He was more afraid of losing them on the open heathland than having the Land Rover stolen.

The sheep hadn't gone far. He watched from the top of the hill, knowing that eventually her dogs would notice him. He wondered how much time she'd had to spend up here, stopping the herd from returning to their lear. Fin whined, wanting to work the sheep, and Martin spoke softly to the dog.

From this distance, he couldn't see enough to make out her features or even her age. Even so, he would have bet his whole herd that it was her – his one time fiancée, Joanna Luxton. He had broken it off with her one autumn night, with a raw wind blowing and a bitter rain which fell like recriminations.

As Martin watched her stealing his sheep, he thought about her paltry revenge and the injustice of it.

The wind must have changed; one of the collies raised its pointed nose to the tor and barked a warning. The girl span round, and Martin knew that all she could see was his silhouette on the horizon. His big bay mare snorted. He watched her shoulders sink. The dogs, waiting for her command, lay down among the flaming bracken; the sheep, swiftly forgetting their fear, started to graze.

He sat there, feeling the mare's impatience, hearing the dog whine at her heels. And he didn't know what to do. In part, he wanted to lose her keys and leave her there until he came back later for the herd. Then he felt the fatigue of this feud and thought, 'Have the bloody sheep, just leave off your hatred.' His third option was the one he took. He kicked his heels and the mare sprang forward, cantering crab-like down the slope, he sitting deep in the saddle and leaning back to keep their balance, Fin as their sleek black shadow.

The girl, still as the granite standing stones on the hillsides above her, waited.

As he came closer, he saw the fine hair blowing loose around her head; he saw a sharp nose and thin lips; and her body was the fragile slenderness he'd imagined from the top of the tor. She wasn't a beauty, and the bitterness of her expression made her less so. He slowed the mare to a high stepping trot and then, dramatically pulled the horse up. The girl, to her credit, did not back off or even blink.

'I'm taking what's rightfully mine!' she said.

'You're stealing. You're rustling.'

She shrugged up at him, 'You want to take then back to your lear? Fine. But I'll be back. You can't guard them.'

'What makes you feel you have the right?'

'You destroyed my life.'

He looked down at her, the pale blue eyes and small features, the angry red flush on her sharp cheekbones. 'Do you really believe that, Joanna?'

She didn't bother to answer. Finn whined, eager now to take over his sheep. Martin turned away from the girl, 'Let them graze, boy, let them rest.' He jumped off the mare, put up the stirrups and loosened her girth.

'What are you doing?'

'I'm preparing for a long conversation with you.'

'I don't want to talk to you.'

'I had to disconnect my phone to stop you trying to talk to me. What's changed now?'

'That was only at the beginning. I wanted to understand.'

'But I told you. I couldn't have been clearer. You didn't care at all about what I thought, or what I wanted. I realised you were a selfish little bitch and my life would be miserable if I married you.'

She slapped him. He had expected that, and just looked down at her without turning away. Under his gaze, she seemed to shrink. Her face crumpled like a used handkerchief and she started to cry. Had she been anyone else, he would have stepped forward and tried to comfort her. But because she was who she was he left her, instead stroking the mare's strong, smooth neck as she grazed the moorland grass. He didn't pay Joanna any attention until she started to speak.

'Martin, I loved you and I was so happy and we were going to be married and I know Mum and I did all the arrangements, but we were paying and you never seemed that interested. Is that really enough reason to break my heart?'

'It wasn't quite like that, was it, Jo?'

'Yes it was!'

'No, Joanna, you wouldn't let me invite anyone I wanted to; I told you I didn't want to wear one of those stupid suits, but you insisted; I didn't want a huge do, but you insisted. It wasn't what I wanted at all. But that – and you know this – that was just the start of it. Do I really need to remind you?'

'Do you mean the pitchfork?'

When he told her that he couldn't marry her, she'd driven over to his farm. He'd been mucking out the mare's stall. They argued again, Martin trying to keep himself from shouting as she leant towards him, her plain face made ugly by anger. At last, he turned and walked away. She picked up the pitchfork and swung it at him. The prongs hadn't pierced his skin, but the blow had surprising force considering her build. Even now, when Martin smelt the ammonia smell of the wet straw in the horse's stable, he was reminded of the pain of that strike.

'No, Jo, that angered me – but it wasn't that. I can't believe you need me to tell you.' He didn't want to go over this ground again. He didn't want to be talking to her at all.

She said, 'You don't mean that stupid conversation about your mother?'

He pushed the mare a couple of steps forward, and said, 'I'm warning you, don't speak about my mother.'

The force of his emotion flung him back in time to his childhood. He had last seen his mother when she went into hospital, wrapped in a bloody dressing gown. He was just ten. His father, Robert, was weighed down by grief and by the angry disappointment of his invalid father, old Mr Redland, who gave up speaking, and spent his time dreaming of the scent of heather and lanolin smell and wiry wool of the hardy sheep he bred. He sat for long days in a bath chair in his bedroom looking with desperate love at the sage coloured moors and stroking the seal like head of his arthritic black labrador Taw

The old man had outlived his son. Martin was orphaned at seventeen, but, unlike his father, was hardened to the bruises of loss. He turned the business around and gave his grandfather a few years of pleasure seeing the farm brought back from the brink of bankruptcy.

He looked at Joanna out of the corner of his eyes. She wasn't crying. She was beaten, for the moment. He pulled a couple of bars of chocolate out of his saddlebag and offered her one. She shook her head at first and then, when he nodded his head to her, still holding it out, took it and ate it quickly. Martin broke off a piece and gave it to Fin.

'Chocolate's no good for dogs,' she said.

He forced a grin, 'Try telling Fin that!'

There was hope in her eyes again and that seemed to soften her expression, reminding him of the time when he had liked her enough to consider her as a wife. They'd met at Young Farmers. Martin had been leaning against the wall, talking to his friend John, when a girl had walked passed them with hair as fine as wishes and a body as slim as the withies down by the stream at the back of Redland Farm. They'd watched her, thinking her delicacy made her beautiful in a room where so many of the women were ruddy cheeked and strong thighed with dark eyes and wicked smiles. As though feeling the warmth of their approval, Joanna Luxton had turned around and Martin saw at once that she'd be his if he wanted her.

Since he was a boy, friends and family – even strangers – had told Martin he was handsome, beautiful, stunning – whatever words they used, it was nothing to him. He wanted to be a great rider and fantastic dog-handler, he wanted to care for livestock – he wanted to excel as a farmer; his looks were irrelevant. That night at the Young Farmers' disco, for the first time, those looks had value. He grinned at John, stepped to Joanna and led her outside, where he kissed her fine white skin.

As well as being a handsome brute, as his grandfather had described him, Martin was also desirable for his farm. The only son and already running the business on his own – repairing the damage done by his mother's expensive enthusiasms and his father's inability to focus on much beyond his beautiful, raven-haired wife. Old Mr Redland, full of knowledge yet too arthritic to work, had been his welcome back seat driver. The old man had passed away a few years' back. Martin, now in his 30s had proven to be an astute businessman as well as a good stockman, and was top of the list for every mother of unmarried daughters. The Luxtons had celebrated their Joanna's new relationship by buying their daughter a car so that she could more easily make the journey to her fiancé's farm.

'Martin, please, let's try again. There's been no one else for me, and everyone says you've been on your own.'

'I don't want to try again. You showed your true self in that fight we had, Joanna. It's like with the animals – this mare, when we have a falling out, the worst she'll do is buck or threaten to nip. If she truly meant to hurt me, even in a temper, I couldn't love her.'

'You do love that bloody horse more than you ever loved me!'

'I don't believe I ever really did love you.' He didn't intend to be brutal, just factual.

She stared at him, and he saw that she wanted to cry and at the same time to slap him again, and yet also to deny what he said.

'Joanna, leave my sheep alone. Our relationship is over. I don't need to marry. I'm happy as I am.'

'Bet your father wished he'd stayed happy as he was and never married that madwoman.'

Even as she said the words, he saw her flinch, her muscles tensing as though she expected him to hit her. Perhaps the strength of the feelings showed in his face and scared her. He felt his fists clench and the dog, sensing his mood, came close to his heels and stood next to him, ears cocked. When he spoke, his voice was low, 'You spoke like this about my mother before, and I told you then I wouldn't stand it. Yet you dare to talk of her again.'

She straightened her back, resolute, 'I'm only telling the truth. Can't you accept the truth? She was mad, Martin Redland, and you know it. That's why your dad hung himself and why you're so afraid of having a relationship, because you saw what marrying her did to him.' She carried on talking though Martin was running down the stirrup leathers, tightening the girth and remounting the mare. 'If it hadn't been for her, he'd still be alive and you'd be a normal man, not an emotionally crippled fool, running scared of love and of living and...'

He wheeled the horse and his charged energy made the mare spin and stand under him, yet he held her still then and looked down at Joanna, whose face was turned up to his. He didn't know what to say to her, how to answer.

She said, 'You know I'm right, don't you?' Her eyes now had a pale blue fire about them, and her face a sort of hunger, 'I thought taking the sheep would hurt you most, but now I see I was wrong! I'm so glad you came to find me, Martin. Go on, then, take your herd home.'

He obeyed, his heart pounding like the mare's hooves on the hollow sounding turf. He whistled to his dog and they moved off, the ewes bleating as lambs, still young enough to run, skipped ahead of them. They only played at leaving though, those lambs, all were still bound to their mothers.

They climbed the tor. At the top he looked back at Joanna. She was still watching him, her two collies crouching at her feet, an aura of satisfaction about her, as though she felt she'd had her revenge. He lifted an arm and she, a stick figure below, hesitated before raising hers in response. He held his hand back and then threw it forward, the keys spinning in the clean air before clattering amongst the rocks of the tor.

## *DRIVING GLOVES*

I have this thing about cleaning and tidying. It's not that I'm OCD or anything, it's just it seems such a great idea to sort things out – like a kind of psychological laxative, if you know what I mean. Anyway, I often have the desire to go through my stuff, but, well, you know what it's like, sometimes the mind's willing but the body can't be bothered. And then there's the bleak fear that rather than clearing you out, what you find could mess you up instead. Even so, every so often, I do get down to it. Like today – I've been looking through a couple of boxes and I've found these: red gloves. They're leather on the underneath and faded sort of netting on top. Driving gloves. I sniff inside the stiffened kidskin and scratchy webbing and inhale an aromatic mnemonic: talc, lavender and Chanel. No.5… my mother… but there's more – my greedy nose draws in the residue of Algeria: sand, sweat and oranges.

I've been on the phone to Sylvie for an hour or so. My sister's not been well this past year. Actually, she's not been well for a decade. Anyway, it's bad this week and we talk about the pain and the worry; about the recent, disturbing, hallucination of a flood in the bathroom (global warming working on a microcosmic scale) and the fact she's not seen her third grandchild yet.

    I'm listening and sympathising, and thinking, 'There but for the grace of God go I.' We're both bi-polar, though I'm more highly-strung than psychotic.

    When she feels she's said enough, I haul her back from her goodbye and chaparral her into what's been preoccupying me since I found the red gloves: my mother's big drive across North Africa with a four year old (me), a Cortina (blue) and a caravan. I can't remember a great deal about it but figure my sister can help. She was 24 at the time – with two, or maybe three, babies, and a husband.

'Oh, before you go,' I say, 'you know when Mum drove to Algeria?'

'Yes?' There's a sort of hesitation in her voice – the unnerved note she reserves for when the subject of our mother comes up. They didn't get on. As a relationship, it was more *Kramer vs. Kramer* than *The Brady Bunch*. Sylvie says our mother was always rewriting the past and it drove her mad – literally. She couldn't keep quiet when Mum claimed that she went to Cambridge University, even though she didn't, or talked about 'Grandmamma the Baroness', who was actually just a Mrs.

'Well, where did we sail from? And where did we land?' I lack some very basic information.

'It was Southampton, because Trevor drove the caravan to South-'

'Why did Trevor drive?' He's my sister's ex-husband.

'Oh, Mum didn't want to tow the caravan there.'

'What? She was going to drive across North Africa but she wouldn't drive to Southampton?' I don't know why I'm surprised. This is the woman who decided to farm, and thought it perfectly reasonable that having bought the calves (Sage, Tarragon and Parsley) she should whiz off to Paris to discuss the launch of another misguided scheme, leaving her thirteen year old daughter (me) in charge of the stock for a week. Her unwillingness to get behind the wheel, despite the natty gloves, rather explains her unexpected decision to allow a young Moroccan guy she met on the ferry – I do remember this – to drive us from... wherever we landed... to... wherever his village was. I'll get the details later, I'm thinking, as my sister continues:

'And she almost didn't get to the ferry, at all – she'd forgotten her passport and had to turn around and go back. And so when we got to Southampton Docks, we had no idea where she was.'

That, too, was true to type. She was always late, my Mum. Yet, despite the false start and the fear of towing the caravan to the docks, I'm amazed at my mother's bravura. I mean, how many 1970s housewives would have come up with and then actually carried out such a crazy weeklong journey? I fancy writing it up as some kind of semi-autobiographical travelogue thing to send to some magazine or other.

My father provides a trickle of further facts, namely that we travelled by boat from Portsmouth to Lisbon, stayed on board overnight and then crossed to Tangiers where we disembarked. We drove from there along the coast – not as far as Casablanca – then headed down to Fez where we spent the night. The next day we drove to Oujda before crossing the border at Tlemcen and going on to Oran where my father was waiting at the St George Hotel.

The names don't bring back any memories.

He tells me to look at a map.

'Do you remember what the Moroccan boy was called?'

'No.' Like my sister (who's actually my half-sister – not my father's daughter), my father keeps a special tone of voice for conversations about my mother. Like my sister, my father didn't always have the best of relationships with my mother – more *Kramer vs. Kramer* et cetera. He told me once that when I was just two he started carrying a hosepipe around in the back of his car so he could gas himself if my mother's mood swings swung him completely off kilter. (I imagine him as a homunculus on a wooden swing flying beyond the point where the chains have tension… Clang!) I can't remember being two, but I can remember the three of us jumping off sand dunes in Saudi Arabia, hand-in-hand, when I was eight. Seemed happy enough then.

'Make up an Islamic name for him.'

'Hmm… I rather like the idea of a sort of self-consciousness in my narrative. I might call him "the Nameless Boy".'

He doesn't respond to that but instead tells me that in the pile of mock-leather photograph albums in my kitchen dresser I have a file of pictures from this trip.

Once I put the phone down I'm disturbed by two things: firstly that he mentioned the journey from 'Portsmouth' to Lisbon, whereas my sister said 'Southampton', and secondly his claim that the road trip element might just have lasted two days. I'm struck by the instability of the factual world and at the same time by its horrible tendency to demystify and de-romanticise memory.

When I look at a map, the route doesn't make much sense either. Why did we go west to Casablanca when Algeria is east of Morocco? Why did we go all the way south to Fez? The maps don't show main roads so I suppose that might explain the peculiarities.

I still haven't found the photographs and wonder if they exist.

Here's what I do remember. Sunlight on the sea. Water sparkling blue and the noise of engines and metal chains. My mother, glamorous, black-haired, her photographer's model smile still effective at 46. She introduced me to 'nice Mr. Nameless Boy' and explained that he would drive us part of the way to see Daddy. Of the Moroccan boy, I recall only curly hair and a wide white smile.

Then, as I sit down, with my pen and my notebook, more comes back, in the silent, juddering images of cine-film. We're driving in the blue Cortina along a track, with grass growing in the middle and sugar-cane – I think – as tall as the caravan, it seems, on either side.

Telling this story, years later, my mother used to say, 'I was wondering if Nameless Boy planned to cut our throats in the fields and drive away, leaving me and poor little Lelly dead!'

Far from it. He took us to his home. A circular daub and wattle type of structure with a cylindrical roof made of more sugar canes. It was the shape of a witch's hat and inside we sat on maroon and gold cushions with his mother and sisters, drinking sweet mint tea from tiny glasses.

They told my mother that in an Islamic country, a woman should not be driving a car. They told her to be careful. I remember soft French voices, the minty clinks of little cups and kindness.

That night, I think… or perhaps it was the previous night… we stayed in Fez. And the next day – or the same day as the village and the sisters – we, my mother and I, headed to Tlemcen. And this is where her story, like a horse granted wings, moves from narrative donkey to mythic Pegasus. Please, give me wings: let me follow…

At the border, the Algerian customs officers were suspicious. A Western woman, on her own, with a small child – and a caravan which had previously never been further south than Mevagissey in Cornwall – was strange indeed. At that time too, the political situation in Morocco was colourful, as, in the mid-70s, the country was busy annexing most of Western Sahara. So, it's perhaps not surprising that they questioned us closely – and searched us too.

I had a beloved toy: a brown rabbit in a long orange dress who held in her embrace a little rabbit. Mummy Rabbit and Baby Rabbit. The customs officers took a long needle and began to poke it into their soft bodies. I started to cry. They were untouched by infidel tears and continued to probe.

Then a man came in. He held in one hand a sub machine gun. He wore combat colours and he had the look of a born predator and the heavy-featured charisma of the powerful – and the dangerous. The guards turned to him the way a pack turns to its leader. My mother spun to face him, as she held me, still weeping, against her body. She told me afterwards that she felt real fear and tried to shush me. But I was untouched by maternal reason.

'Why is she crying?' he asked, in English, his voice deep as a growling dog's.

'Because they're sticking a pin in her rabbit.'

His face broke into a smile and he waved the guards to stop, 'It is the child's little friend, eh?' and he leaned forwards to stroke my hair. I looked up at him, my blue eyes wet and huge, cheeks flushed with emotion. He said, 'Let them go.'

My mother thanked him and we drove into Algeria.

Twenty years later, when Carlos the Jackal was charged with the Paris murders of two policemen, tried, found guilty and sentenced to life imprisonment, she recognised the face and bearing of the man who'd saved Mummy Rabbit and this story became the centrepiece of the drive across North Africa.

I suppose it's possible. This would have been during the period when he was involved in planning for the attack on the OPEC headquarters in Vienna in December of that year, 1975. He was believed to be in Beirut – but Wikipedia assures me that he had strong connections in Algeria.

For me, it's the centrepiece of the journey for another reason. It's complete fabrication, surely. My mother wanted something exciting to have happened. She wanted to turn the journey into a story. Now I look back at that narrative and I wonder what, if anything, is true.

I have been feeling unnerved by the whole North Africa thing. My sense of self is starting to unravel. In bed, I can feel the loose strands pulling away from me as I toss and turn. My mind is considering itself, wondering which parts are manifestations of the peculiar fictions my family have told me and which parts are based on real experience. Would I be as disturbed as my spun glass sister if I were all real? Would I have the vibrant photographer's model confidence of my mother if I let the myths take over?

I don't get up until midday when someone knocks on the door wanting to sell me household products – sponges, dusters, Marigold rubber gloves and the like. I buy a few cloths and some Marigolds, as I feel sorry for the boy and besides, the drains have started to smell. I imagine snaking my arm through the black-stuff in the U-bend.

Of course, I don't plan to tackle the task straight away and so I search out a square inch of space in the kitchen to store my purchases. I open the stiff drawer which I thought contained Egyptian cotton napkins and cork placemats. Inside, of course, is the file of Algeria photos. Well, file is an exaggeration: there are two pictures. One shows my mother and I on the ferry. She clasps me to her hip as she does that 'one foot forward' pose which showed off best her hourglass figure. I look into eyes, which I know were fractured rain cloud grey – I don't need image or story to remind me of that. I see the slight squint of her right eye as she looks at the camera, a tender tic showing the vulnerability behind her bravado. Black crows wings of hair sweep her face. I smile at her all-too-real expression and then pull the other photograph toward me.

This one is taken inside. At first, I'm not sure where. I am not in it. My mother holds Mummy Rabbit in one hand - a hand wearing one of the red kidskin driving gloves; the leather is creased, showing the tension of her grasp on the stuffed toy. The other gloved hand rests on the shoulder of a man. I peer closely at his face. Square with uneven lips, strangely gentle looking eyes, and a thick nose.

Is he or isn't he? I start to feel the splitting thing in my head and then, of a sudden, realize that it doesn't matter. It really doesn't matter.

I smell the soft talc, Chanel No.5 and lavender scent of my mother and feel the white-feathered, horse-sized wings lifting me upwards.

## *GUINEVERE'S GIFT*

Three nights ago, I dreamed of the King. His gentle eyes bore the same love he always showed me in life despite all that happened between us. In my dream, he told me that he forgave me. In my dream, he gave me the freedom to love whomsoever I willed and the freedom to give up my guilt. I bowed before him; kissed the blood-red ruby on his ring and thanked him.

Since then, I have felt, at times, a sense of peace; yes, even I have been allowed to feel peace. Like now, on this early summer's day, seeing the swallows pirouette in the pristine blue square of sky which these walls contain. Their flight is like calligraphy, yet without a record of the words. I wonder what their text would read, were their pointed wings infused with ink. The Abbess says such thoughts are blasphemous; but then she considers me to be cursed – a creation of the devil.

When I came here, the women watched me with the cruelty of wolves, yellow eyes following me, their self-righteous smiles widening as my long, long hair fell to the cold stone in curls, coils and chestnut threads. They thought I wept for the loss of my tresses – and so could condemn me for my vanity, as well as for everything else they claimed I had done. But I wept for love, for lost love, and for the two men who loved me; yes, I wept for both of them.

What do these women, who preach it, really know of love?

One day, sitting by the pond, where the pike prowl in search of prey – their own young will do, they are so voracious – I chanced to look upon the lavender in the borders circling the water. I think the scent must have risen in the dusty air and its sweetness was a balm to me. The steel-blue spears of the flowers reminded me of jousts, and of those two men, Knight and King, who had protected my honour.

According to the chivalric code, my husband could not defend me, so always it was Lancelot fighting for my favour. And yet, watching him perform on his silver horse under the sun's harsh disc, I felt forgotten, a glove upon the ground, over which men battled, but which they trampled in their blindness. I don't know, I don't know… the past plays tricks on me in my solitude, my solitary waiting for death.

Nowhere on earth could I feel so alone as I do here, incarcerated with women who loathe me. It is no exaggeration. These prowling nuns feel that I contaminate their haven. It hurts me; and yet, how can I, a Queen, let their small-mindedness touch me? Why should I consider their sensibilities when they love to see me break, as I do every few weeks or months. The days when to stand up is agony because each inch of my body reminds me of my men; the face they kissed, the breasts they touched, the legs they stroked with such awe, the arms that draped around their shoulders, the lips that met their own. My body carries memory like a burden and a blessing; but some days the weight is just too much.

I remember so well the first time I saw Lancelot. I was a child bride really – in the days when I still wore my hair loose and wild. The men were sitting around the table, debating the future of this green-hilled land. I stood in the gallery overlooking the tapestried hall, seeking to see but not to be seen – a young girl playing hide and seek. I had escaped my ladies and wished to watch my new husband in his proud role. He sat, regal as a lion, in the vast engraved chair where I had, the previous night, laughed upon his knee. I smiled to see him and then the golden fire of a newcomer's presence attracted my eyes, as a moth flies to the moon. Our eyes met and the sound was like oak fracturing after a lightning strike. The blue fire from him seared me. I felt blistered for days. He told me later it was the same for him.

I ran away. That day I ran from the gallery like a doe from the hounds. And then for the rest of the year I tried to run from my heart. In May, when the petals of the hawthorn confettied the fields, I stumbled through tangled grass in meadows smelling of sex. The river bubbled, toying with me, roiling and coiling as sensuous and sensual as bodies wrapped together. I was a child! I knew nothing of love. The King had taught me little; I was his precious, not his partner.

That whole summer, I hid from myself. They were away. The King was stitching his land into a bridal gown for me. The King with his sword and his sorcerer, both so grave and warlike; the King with his knights, prancing across the nation subduing princes and barons. Treaties and pacts were the threads that created this patchwork nation. God has blessed him, they tell me. He is with God. I am sure he is.

In autumn, I wept with uncertainty. Not knowing when they'd be back. Not knowing what my young soul was feeling. Not knowing what was right. Something died inside me – I think it was innocence – and something else went into hibernation. And that was my conscience, I now believe.

When the winter's short days came, I changed. Instead of fleeing what I wanted, I sought it. I wore red and danced with the skeletons of trees, making patterns in the snow. This was my witchcraft – more feminine than Arthur's wizard; more subtle than the witch Morgana. Yet it worked.

Months earlier than the rest, he came.

In dreams, we had joined; there was no first time for us. We had shared the same imaginings; both had felt the other's body in long nights alone. I was so happy then; I pretended that my lover was my husband and the King just some beloved brother, absent often and distant when he was there. Of course, I am not proud of what I have done, but I would not have given up those days and nights we shared for anything... even for a future in which they both lived and the land survived undivided. Is that wrong of me? Is that so wrong? Perhaps. The Abbess says it is. But then, she says all I feel is wrong.

I know that my jealousy was wrong, the foul suspicions I so often harboured. For all maidens loved Lancelot and sought his protection. I was so afraid of being only one of many. I, the Queen! I had to be first in his heart. Alas. Alas for the times I spoke harshly; alas for the times I shunned him; alas for my cold, heavy-lidded grey eyes. Yes, I repent all of that, when my stumbling soul tells me that I should repent my adulterous love. But how could I repent what was dearest ever to my heart. How could anyone.

Instead, when I am sitting in the chapel, counting the clacking beads to keep the female wolves at bay, the colours of the stained glass windows seem to transport me back to my fire-lit tower. Yes, blasphemous though it sounds, the Lord with His halo and scars, dapples me with jewels of light – sapphires, emeralds, rubies – and I feel as if I am once again decked in kisses in the queenly rooms I used to inhabit. Velvet, silk and damask - the colours rich as the stones on my necklaces, bracelets and rings. In summer, fine drapes let in breezes scented with meadow grass; in winter the flames painted the light with honey and mead.

How different my life is now! The soldiers brought me here while Arthur and Lancelot prepared for the final battle. So I'd be safe, they said. Here in the nunnery, I have a small white room, bare walls and a window that lets the cold in during the months of frost and snow, but holds the heat in summer. My bed is hard, not the layered goose down I once enjoyed. The blankets are rough and thin. I suffer as the rest suffer; and I suffer more because of the loss of what I used to have.

My mind, like a hound I cannot call away from the kill, keeps on tracking back to the last time I saw them. The day they each took their leave; the day of the Final Battle.

The King came up to my rooms in the castle before dawn. I was not asleep; I knew that the world was at a turning point. I could feel the mechanisms of our lives grinding out of synchronicity. The stars let out only cold metallic light – their magic was lost in the force of fate. So when he knocked on the door, I was up to greet him. He took my hands in his, kissed them and bade me farewell, telling me that he held me at the core of his heart; that his love and respect for me was the same as the day we met, when he was still almost-young, and I was loose-haired and long-limbed. I wept and clung to his arm as he left, as he gently shook me from him, his smile so sad that it further broke me.

When Lancelot came, I was crying still. My love, my love, my one true love. Oh the pain and the beauty of that embrace. My eyes filled with new tears, tears yet more deeply sourced in my soul and I could hear the stretching stitches of this patchwork nation springing apart. The fabric was left with open wounds; and the old oak table cracked, with a sound like bereavement.

Is it my fault? Is it really my fault? Can the future blame me for love?

They left me, both of them left me.

And I was brought here.

When I was shut in amongst these yellow-eyed women. I turned hollow. I ruptured, loins stinging like childbirth; as though they'd sliced me with the sword, the gall of loneliness poured out of the aching void of me.

And all I was is gone. And all I am is pain.

But I must retain this new gratitude that gives me some peace – I must recall the grace I felt when I dreamed of Arthur, and his forgiveness. Only this gives me cause to praise, and I thank My Lady Mary. I thank Her with honesty, with a soul almost as pure as it was when I first knew the King, as a willowy, grey-eyed girl.

I did see Lancelot one more time. He came here to tell me of my husband's death. His face was white as sculpted snow and I felt the chill of his grief, though all the while I knew that he felt the same love for me – despite it all, despite it all, he still loved me, I could see it in his sea-sparkling eyes. And so I did the only good deed of my life: I told him to let go of me; I told him to give his soul to God. I would never be able to evict him from my heart, but my white knight possessed perfectibility. I gave him the chance to attain it.

So now, I click the beads, look up to the gentle face of our martyred Lord, and feel His calm love encircle me like swaddling clothes. And then – is this madness or miracle? Blasphemy or blessing? – his features form before me and his hand reaches out. Love. As pure as the sweet azure sky. I know that I can go – I know that at last I have served my time. I step away from the cold pew and rise to take his hand. His embrace is as clean as summer rain; his touch is a breath of breeze on hot skin; his kiss is sunshine on the crown of my head. I am with him at last – without guilt. I can be with him, uncondemned, at last.

## *TWITCHES*

The streets in around Kings Cross were nearly empty. The only people about at the almost midnight darkness were drunken teenagers and the occasional homeless person. The sight of them always shocked Susannah into guilt and even as she ran to the station, she jostled her bag in front of her and tried to feel for pound coins amongst the miscellaneous objects within, surprising herself as she touched a New Zealand tiki given to her by her nephew. She gave up her attempt at generosity after almost dropping her car keys and instead pushed on harder, knowing Kings Cross was just a few hundred yards away.

Her body was accustomed to running, though not in heeled boots; it wasn't the effort so much as the awkwardness that hampered her. She felt her breath coming in deep, even draughts; her heart beating strongly, efficiently; already the endorphins were boosting her mood.

'Hey, lady, what you running from?' shouted a young man from the other side of the road.

But she ignored him, her attention drawn to a large car just ahead of her that was stopped at the traffic lights in front of the station.

A dark figure ran from the pavement to the passenger side and opened the door. Susannah heard a shout and the car started to move, the lights now glaring green. She ran on, watching the car. It stopped and now a second dark figure was at the driver's door.

'What are you doing?' she shouted, her boots clattering on the pavement. One of the dark figures turned towards her and she saw a flash of steel. The other was dragging the driver out of the front of the car. He was screaming, a high, terrified sound, like a beaten dog.

'Hurry up, man,' said one of the figures, as the driver lay, curled into a shell on the road.

'What about this bitch running at us? She see me, man!' His face, starkly white under the orange streetlights, turned back to her again. The other man was shadow; the driver was whimpering.

'Get in the fucking car and drive!'

The white man got in and the engine squealed as he pulled away from the lights and the figure on the tarmac... and Susannah, who had come to a flying stop and was now kneeling beside the man who was still whining and foetus-like, his pride and masculinity taken with the car.

'It's ok,' she said to him, touching him with hands sure and gentle, 'they've gone. You're all right.'

He seemed unaware of her; she felt a twitch of irritation. 'Help me get you on to the pavement. You don't want to stay here in the road. Come on.' She stood and pulled at his shoulders and felt the dead weight of him, like gravity, dragging her back to earth; just like the feeling when you run and suddenly the energy dies and instead of flying, you drag your flesh-bound weight with each struggling step.

'Come on! This is crazy. You have to get off the street.'

His head now turned to her; she saw his face for the first time - his mouth pulled down at one side as if by a wire, the muscles in his cheek twitching and his left eye blinking. She put a hand to his skin, feeling the flesh jump under her fingers. She stroked as you stroke the face of a child. The muscular movements seemed to slow. She knelt down again, next to him: one hand still stroking his face, the other holding his hand, as he grasped on to her with the unconscious force of a baby.

She knew her train was gone, the last train. She thought of calling the man she'd had dinner with - but had it been convenient to him, he would had tried to persuade her to stay. As he had not, she assumed that for some reason he could not have her with him in his flat that night. He was married and in this, the second year of their relationship, he showed as little interest in leaving his wife as at any point previously. Susannah thought sometimes that she loved him; at others that she was a fool; but never did she even try to pretend that he had felt anything like love for her.

The man on the road was becoming calmer. The tic continued

to slow. As she watched him, Susannah wondered if it hurt him, to have his muscles pull his features so forcefully. She got to her feet and now could help him rise. He stood with her, favouring one foot and, as she helped him step toward the pavement, she saw that his left leg was bent unnaturally inward.

'Your leg, is it injured?'

He turned to her and spoke for the first time, 'That's just how it is.'

'I'm sorry.' She blushed, but the red from the traffic lights disguised her shame. 'Shall I call the police? Did they hurt you?'

'I think I have my phone.' He put a hand, trembling, into his pocket and brought out a mobile. 'Thank you. You've been very kind.'

'I've just done what I'd hope anyone would do for me.'

He looked directly at her for the first time, and said, 'You were running for the train?'

'Yes... I was...'

'And now you've missed the last one?'

'Yes... How did you-'

'It's my job. Really. I predict things from the evidence in front of me.'

'Really? People running for trains?'

'No, usually the performance of stocks and shares. I predict ways to make money.'

'Are you good at it?'

He shrugged, smiling his broken smile, 'Tomorrow I can buy another car like that - it was a Bentley - and not really notice.'

'Goodness.' She rubbed down her trousers. 'Well, let's get you a taxi - I think you'll feel the shock sooner rather than later.'

'And you?'

'What of me?'

'Do you have somewhere to stay?'

She flicked a look at him, she had started to move toward the station, but he still stood, 'I'll sort something out.'

'I have a large house... many spare rooms...'

'No, I couldn't.'

'In that case, may I pay for you to stay in a hotel - there's one just up the road, by Euston, a Hilton.'

'There's no need.'

'As a thank you?'

He was walking alongside her now, his strides uneven and seeming uncomfortable. She wanted to ask how it felt to lack control over your limbs. He saw her glance at his left foot, swinging inward, and gave that broken smile again, 'It is awkward, frustrating, but it's a frustration I live with - and often forget... though there's always this residual irritation when I walk.'

'I'm sorry-'

'Please don't apologise. That's even more irritating, really, and people feeling pity.'

'I am sorry.'

He laughed and she smiled slightly, hanging her head and holding her bag against her waist.

He said, 'Please, come with me to the hotel - or the house - you can trust me, I'm not exactly blessed with great strength - have a drink and a bed for the night. You can help me with the shock; I can help you with somewhere to stay.'

She looked at him, then nodded, 'OK, thank you. The hotel, please.'

They walked. It wasn't far, but his uncomfortable strides meant that Susannah had to hold back her pace. He told her that his name was Anthony Forsyth and that he lived in Holland Park; he told her that he was passionate about his work and loved making money for his clients. When she turned to him, he said, 'That it makes money for me too is, of course, a wonderful bonus.' His broken smile had more honesty and less complexity at that point than any smile she'd ever seen before. Susannah felt her lips mirror his and the feeling traveled up to her eyes - those muscles around the eyes, which only contract when a smile is genuine.

The bar of the hotel was still busy. It was candlelit and filled with music from a piano in the corner, where a sad-faced man sat dreaming of Mahler while playing Chopin.

Susannah wanted to tell Anthony to sit down while she ordered at the bar - but he waved her into a seat. She watched him, wondering how he would carry two glasses. One of his fists was held with unnatural tension.

She leant back, eyes closed, feeling the emotions of the night flood through her like drugs you have taken and later regret. Her phone buzzed in her bag. A text from her lover, asking if she had got home safely; saying he missed her and wanted to feel her sleek body alongside his. She felt a tightness at the core of her, desire or disdain, she wasn't sure which.

Susannah switched the phone off and looked up to see a waiter walking over to her with a bottle of champagne on a silver tray, while Anthony limped behind him. The waiter, looked at Susannah too deeply, so that she felt that twitching tightness again inside her. He put the two flutes on the table as Anthony sat down with his broken smile now more sharply defined. She didn't know where to look. The *pffft* of the cork broke the crisp atmosphere around them and the waiter poured two perfect glasses. Now the waiter was smiling into Susannah's lips like a kiss and she found herself opening her mouth slightly against her will, then turning away from him sharply.

'To you, Susannah, with thanks.' Anthony raised his glass, his left eye flinching as though from an expected blow.

She raised hers, they clicked together and she sipped. The dry, biscuity flavour of it; the glass damp with condensation and, louder than the Chopin or the chatter from the other tables, was the fizz of the rising bubbles.

'So, do you work in London?'

'No, I am home based... I'm a writer... Feature articles.'

'Oh, how interesting. Do you specialise?'

'Yes, I suppose, women's lifestyle stuff, really. It's not very highbrow, I'm afraid. I'm trying to...' She was going to say, 'I'm trying to write a novel' but she hadn't told her friends or agent yet. She seldom felt the need to build up her credentials. Instead, she said, 'I'm trying to earn enough to own a horse.' She laughed, awkwardly; the mention of money with a rich man seemed indelicate.

'They are expensive, I suppose. Though perhaps less so than a Bentley.'

She wanted to change the subject, 'Had you been out tonight?'

'Yes, I went to Sadler's Wells with a client and then took him back to his place. He asked me in for a whiskey but I wanted to get back home. I have an appointment tomorrow-'

'Oh, then please, don't feel-'

'I shall be cancelling it, Susannah; I would prefer to be here now. With you.' He sought her eyes, but she could not meet his. She saw the waiter looking at her again. His face was expressionless, as though he did not see her, then the waiter winked and she felt it like an electric shot, starting in her seat, the champagne in her glass turbulent for a moment. Anthony's cheek shot up, the distortion like the reflection in glass at an amusement park, where you turn and turn again only to see what is incongruent. 'I'm sorry,' he said, the word slurred as though he spoke drunkenly, 'I think I am in some shock.'

She put a hand on his knee, and saw how his eyes softened. The tension inside her seemed to release too; she put down the glass and held her other palm to his cheek, which relaxed under her touch.

'You are better than medicine, Susannah.'

The music stopped. She turned to the piano player who glanced at her and licked his lips. She flicked her eyes away and he opened a new score and resumed playing. Susannah closed her eyes, and saw in her mind her lover grasping her hand and holding it between his legs. 'You think I don't want you? Feel. Of course I do, but it's not that simple.' He had never loved her. He would never love her. She felt Anthony's touch, light, on the linen of her trousers.

'Susannah?' he said, 'Susannah? Are you ok?'

She shook her head. 'No, I'm not,' she said. She closed her eyes, feeling nausea rise. The shock of awareness, like a series of twitches running through her nervous system. Anthony was speaking, his voice calm and quiet, the bass notes reverberating through his arm, his hand, and echoing into her body as she felt her breathing slow down.

For the past year, people had been telling her not to be a fool about her lover. Why, tonight, did she feel like listening? She lifted her head and opened her eyes again, to see the room bright and clear before her. The piano player looked incapable of flirtation; the waiter was distant and efficient. She felt as though she too had been in shock.

She turned to Anthony and he smiled at her, lifting a finger to stroke the hair from her face.

'Feeling better now?' he asked.

'Yes,' she said, returning the smile, 'better than I have for ages.'

# THE RETREAT

'Ah, Poppy! I was so pleased to get your call. How is Jonah? And your brother?'

'Robert is well enough, but he can't write - not since Kaj moved out.'

'Ah, now that is sad, such wonderful poems he writes. I especially loved the *Sanctity Cycle*, of course.' Father Sebastian was the closest thing to family Poppy and Robert had left. They'd grown up in a house a few hundred yards from the Abbey, using its grounds as their private playground. Ever since their parents had died more than 15 years back, it was Sebastian who had welcomed them back to their childhood hometown with affection, wisdom and tonic wine. The damp room where he worked in the block behind the monastic living quarters was - just as it had been on her first visit 40 years ago - piled high with sheet music, leaving space only for a piano, a stool and two canvas chairs. It's chill earthy smell was, in Poppy's mind, the scent of sanctuary.

The yard was silent, apart from their footsteps echoing between the golden stone of the Abbey and the brick walls of the workshops where, during the periods set aside for work, all the monks would be busy at their trades. The tonic wine was made there, as well as honey, pottery and stained glass.

'And Jonah, how is he?'

Poppy felt the words she wanted to saywhip away from her like silvery fish, too fast and slippery to catch. Sebastian turned to her, the National Health glasses hiding his expression.

'Ah, well. All in God's time.'

In Sebastian's room she listened to scratchy cassettes of his latest recordings and drank the sickly wine - improved by a splash of tonic water. He smoked and asked no more about Jonah. She told him about the visit to her distracted brother in Sweden. Unable to sleep, she had walked to the frozen river at dawn and seen the most delicate of pastels sweep the sky at sunrise, while beneath her the water sang of its own rebirth under the snow-covered surface. Where it flowed into the lake, the ice was breaking up and the movement of the waves created a kind of glockenspiel sound - the voice of the thaw. Sebastian listened; imagining, he told her, the notes, the instruments, which would translate into music the sounds of spring in the cold north.

When they had finished the bottle, he led her to the Retreat. The old Mill had been converted three years previously into rooms for guests. They were simple and basic. Poppy hoped that in this peaceful place she could find the calmness she needed. She watched as Sebastian walked back towards the door of the Abbey Church. The hunch of his shoulders was more apparent now, and she saw that he was limping. There was a fragility about him she had never noticed. She had come searching spirituality, but it was mortality, again, which she found.

Since the nightmares started, she had dreaded the hours of darkness and now slept only in snatches. As she lay in the narrow, white room, she thought of Jonah. Her heart, in spite of herself, had turned against him. This antagonism began around the time that Kaj had walked out of Robert's home and life; when she saw how broken her brother was. She had wanted to talk to Jonah about it - but instead felt herself gradually freezing into speechlessness, the words she might have said fleeing like migrating birds. She continued to do all the things she would normally have done with him but now she did them alone: things like attending the launch party for the paperback edition of her latest book; visiting her doctor about the new, yet familiar, pain in her stomach; and traveling to Sweden to see Robert.

As the days stretched into weeks, it got to the point where finally she was saying nothing at all to him; Jonah spoke into silence. Poppy had retreated into herself. Jonah became angry; he shouted at her, even shook her; but still she couldn't find the words to say to him. Inside, her heart was ice.

A few weeks later, the bad dreams began. In some, Jonah died; and she woke screaming. In others, she found him with another woman - and the detail of it, the smile curled like a cat on the lips of his mistress; the sounds he made; the way her mind capsized as she fled the scene, to wake washed up and weeping on white pillows, with Jonah beside her asking why. And she couldn't tell him, but hated him for deserting her in her sleep.

The previous week, in the kitchen of the house they had shared for 15 years, he had, one last time, tried to talk to her. He started quietly, as though trying to calm a frightened animal, but his patience had become too strained for this tactic to last. Within minutes his frustration surfaced.

'For God's sake, Poppy, this has to change. I can't live like this. You're behaving as though I've done something wrong. Please. You must tell me.'

His face had the passion it showed during sex and she was flung back in time to a holiday some 13 years back. Each year they celebrated their wedding anniversary in a different European city; that year it had been Amsterdam and she recalled so clearly the pale wooden floors, the clouds of white curtains and Jonah, cupping her face in his hands like a chalice and loving her like salvation. In that room, where the dank breath of the canals breezed through the open windows, she was lost in him. Now, in their bright kitchen, she felt lost to him. She turned away, as their neighbour's tractor made its roaring afternoon trip along the lane. The engine noise hushed the birds and when the tractor had passed the silence rushed back to envelop the afternoon, a silence of such intensity that Poppy felt weighed down by it, as if the heaviness of soundlessness could smother her.

Jonah thumped his fist on the scratched wooden work surface, 'Do you even know I'm here?'

She looked at him, loving each line on his face. But she still couldn't say what she wanted to say.

The sun broke through the clouds. It should have been a benediction, but instead a ray of light shone like a barrier between them, lighting the dust motes into solidity. It pooled, warm and honeyed, on the floor - as though through delicacy, not touching either of them.

Jonah had picked up his car keys and left. He came back late at night, and slept in the spare room.

While he was away, she had gone back to work. Even during this crisis, she worked. Every day, from ten until one and from three until seven, she wrote. Her books had paid for the house, the scratched kitchen surfaces, the wilderness of garden, the car in which he had driven away. Their mutual decision not to have children - how much easier it had been for her, with her books like babies she'd created, out of her own mind, like Jupiter with Minerva. Her success was a daily reminder that he'd never sold even a single sculpture.

Even if his pride were hurt, he had still taken pleasure in her success. Yet Poppy knew, nonetheless, that she had caused him far more pain than he had ever caused her. He had always been the more expressive, the more vocal in their private world. At times, it must have seemed one-way traffic. And now she punished him for his devotion with this total inability to tell him even the simplest of things.

The cool interior of the Abbey Church was gentle to her sleepless eyes. On the hard pew, the muscles of her buttocks ached. The monks' voices, as they sang their love to a listening God, were beautiful to her and the Latin of the prayers were like a gift of new words for passion, for fidelity, for hope.

During these visits, after the service was over, she'd often talk to Sebastian, confessing to him all that she could not tell Jonah. His quiet kindness soothed her; though his doctrine did not. Trying to imagine herself, without Jonah, and yet in a state of bliss... well, it was inconceivable.

Sometimes, like today, she stayed sitting alone in the Church, looking at the senseless eyes of the tortured Christ, the open arms of his Mother and the pure colours of stained glass. The air was cool and scented with incense, wax and the cold library-smell of prayer books.

Today, Poppy felt calmness descend, like a peaceful dove. Inside her, the block of ice melted, releasing precious words, like petals, so fragile that they would be crushed by anything but the most tender of touches. Poppy carried them, with the care of a mother for her first-born God-given child, to the telephone in the Retreat. As she dialed, she prayed; as the phone rang, 200 miles away, above a scratched kitchen surface, she closed her eyes, concentrating on the delicate structure of words.

His deep, rich voice; alongside the bass notes of warm earth, she heard the glockenspiel song of melting ice.

'Jonah, my love, I never ever wanted to leave you.'

'Poppy? Poppy, where are you?'

'I'm at the Abbey. I needed to find the words.'

'You're leaving me?' His voice cracked.

'Not of my own will. I didn't know how to tell you. Jonah, I know it's so damn selfish of me, so bloody selfish, but I hate the thought of you having a life with someone else when I've gone. I went to the specialist. It's come back; the cancer has come back.'

Words. She had found them, but now Jonah could not.

## STAINED GLASS

The waitress's skirt was shorter than a one-night stand. Simon watched her thighs kissing against each other as she came over to ask if he wanted anything. Had he not been waiting for Amélie, he'd have said something about wearing her legs as a scarf - and he'd probably get away with it. Instead he grinned, eyes and teeth doing the flirting, and asked for a Sol. She was walking back to the bar when he called to her, just to see the veil of dead straight blond hair spin like metal as she turned back, head slightly tilted.

'Hey - I don't need a glass.'

He didn't want to see Amélie. Their relationship had ended a month previously. They had argued and she'd gone out. After she'd left and Simon was alone, he called his mother and then his brothers. Then, he held his head in his hands. And, surprising himself, he wept. At eleven he decided to go to bed. Amélie had probably gone to a club; she could be hours yet. He considered going home but he'd drunk a couple of tumblers from a bottle of whiskey he'd found in a kitchen cupboard. As he was stripping off, he heard a knock at the front door. Amélie must have forgotten her keys and returned early. In his unbuttoned jeans, he hurried to the door and pulled it open like a child with an advent calendar window. Not Amélie, but Francesca, who lived upstairs.

'Well, hi, Si! You're looking mighty fine, where's Millie?' She was already in the room, sniffing the tumbler, 'Whiskey, eh? Someone's seriously celebrating or drowning some pretty huge sorrows.'

He retreated to the kitchen, 'Sorrows, Fran, and do you mind leaving me to them? I was just going to bed.'

'You're alone?'

'I was until you barged in on me.'

'I'm... I'm...sorry.... I needed to talk to someone....' Her face crumpled like a tissue and he found himself doing the nice guy act, walking towards her, hugging her and apologising. She'd had a disastrous day - finding your fiancé with another woman has to count high on the Richter scale of personal disaster. So, they comforted each other. As Simon would swear until he wondered why he was bothering, nothing happened, except sleep in the hurt presence of another fallible human.

Amélie, of course, found them. Francesca flew out of the flat, in tears. Amélie slapped him, screamed at him and accused him of infidelity.

'I wish, Amélie, I wish. Instead, no, I didn't fuck her. But, what does it matter? We're over; this is over. I'd've had to end it before I went. So what, it's two weeks earlier than I planned.'

And he'd left; she'd watched from the door of her flat - expressionless - and he had bounded down the stairs, only glancing back at her once.

Now he wanted to forget her and get on with sorting out the rest of his life. There was a 'to do' list longer than the waitress's legs. Packing wasn't even on it yet. Aside from the clothes and cold weather equipment he had yet to buy, he still had to sell his car; rent out his flat; and clear all his cupboards, putting into boxes what he couldn't get rid of or take with him in the hope that one of his friends would volunteer space in a loft or spare room.

Simon sipped his beer; she was always late. She worked to her own clock – Amélie-time. He sighed, looking round the bar. It was a converted chapel, with another level of seating where the altar and choir stalls used to be. A circular stained glass window was lit from outside and above, so that multi coloured light pooled in the empty centre of the space. The waitress walked through it, turning from monochrome to blood red and brilliant green, her blond hair, for a split second, blue as a benediction. Simon finished his beer.

On the other side of the bar, he saw a group of young men elbowing each other and pointing to the door. Thus was Amélie heralded wherever she went. A proclamation of male appreciation announcing her arrival. If it wasn't her height and figure that drew their eyes, it was the way she shook out her long black hair whenever she entered a room. When Simon had realised that what seemed charmingly unselfconscious was cultivated, he had mocked her; she had shrugged.

If he was honest with himself, her vanity didn't bother him. After all, he appreciated beauty - and he wasn't without narcissism himself. It wasn't this that ended the attraction he felt for her. The loosening of the bond had happened gradually: starting when he began to mock her snobbery, her lack of punctuality, and her inability to return a book let alone a favour.

But the real reason he'd split up with her was a single incident a month earlier. They were going out for dinner with two of Amélie's friends - an actor and his model girlfriend. Simon had been for a run along the river and returned hot and satisfied, the endorphins released by the exercise adding to the pleasure he always felt at seeing the city across the dispassionate breadth of the Thames. She was preparing for an audition, curled like a long-legged cat on the sofa, her yellow eyes flashing. She had pointed with an impatient gesture at a bottle of red wine open on the breakfast bar. He filled her glass and poured one for himself. She continued reading; he went for a shower.

Later, when she was standing at the mirror, in bra and knickers so small that Simon wondered at their purpose, holding her hair up in different styles, she said, 'Oh, there was a call on your mobile. That bloody ring tone - I answered it to shut it up.'

He pulled a cashmere sweater over his head, 'Who was it?'

'A hospital in Belfast. They said your father is unwell.'

He looked at her reflection, 'Unwell?'

'A few hours, at most. Sorry.'

'Sorry? For what? For forthcoming bereavement or for forgetting to tell me? For Christ's sake, Amélie... where's the sodding phone?' His footsteps were heavy on the wooden floorboards as he searched for his mobile. 'How long ago? What's the number? Did you write it down?'

She was now pinning the heavy curls to her head, 'It's in the drawing room somewhere.' He hated, he had always hated, the term she used to describe her sitting room, her lounge. She said, 'Look, you told me you weren't close. You haven't seen him since you were a little boy. I didn't think you'd fuss so much.'

'Fuss?' He'd stood in the doorway of her bedroom, looking at her, his face dark, a frown forcing his dark brows together. 'Fuss? This is my father. He's dying. You only get one, Amélie.'

The eyes across the bar watched her, and shot green envy at him, as she walked through the darkness towards the kaleidoscopic light from the window. She sauntered to his table and sat down, pulling off her jacket to reveal her sleek shoulders and back, down which her hair poured, like a blue-black waterfall.

She wore very little make-up - she didn't need it - just crimson lip-gloss and black mascara. He used to watch her in the mornings, or in the evenings before they went out. She would stand at the mirror to brush out her hair, tenderly examining her face, her profile, the curve from cheek to neck, the dips - clavicles - at her shoulders. They had, at first, shared this time. It had become a ritual: on Sunday mornings as the bells rang out, they rose from their sheets to worship her beauty. She enjoyed following with her eyes the hands that he ran over her skin. She had inhaled sharply to see the white marks his fingers made in her flesh when he squeezed; or the red marks his mouth made when he bit her. They had been, both of them, eager to adore her.

Over time, he had less and less often watched her with that early intensity. For him, her beauty became simply a part of her, like her slightly rough voice or her fondness for Gentleman's Relish. Now here he was, looking again at the mathematical planes of her cheekbones and the sculptured shape of her perfect skull under hair dark as mystery, heavy as lies.

'See, I didn't even make you kiss me.'

She put him at a disadvantage, his reluctance to see her appearing at once graceless.

'Amélie, come on, you know I'm busy.'

'Yes, and me. I've been busy too.'

'How did the audition go?' He had no idea if she was talented, but she had the looks to succeed, if looks mattered as much as they said.

'Oh, that. I was too upset. I cancelled.'

'What?'

'Later. What shall we drink?'

She picked up the menu. He looked away from her, at the repeated arches of the beams above them, leading the eye to the apex, to the far end of the old chapel, and the raised area where the priest would have stood, where the faithful would kneel for their sip of wine and papery wafer. Simon's mother was a Catholic, and though not brought up in the faith, he had sympathy for it.

'Call the girl.'

He gestured to the waitress; she looked at him differently now, with studied neutrality. He would have liked to run his hand along the firm muscles of her thigh. 'It's always there,' he thought, 'it never goes.'

'One vodka martini for me, with an olive and some of the brine from the olives. And a bottle of mineral water, sparkling; unless it's Perrier, in which case, still. Simon?'

'Another Sol, please,' he smiled at the blond girl. She tipped her head slightly, her eyes widening just enough to notice.

'Quickly, please, I'm thirsty,' Amélie's voice was raised, on the ragged edge of temper. The waitress left. Simon stared across the table. She was fiddling with a little vase holding a tightly bound bundle of lavender, her long fingers twitching. She had such beautiful hands, delicate, golden skinned, those miraculously tapered fingers, which he had kissed with a feeling he'd come close to regarding as love. Her eyes, caramel with a strange brightness about them, a light within, like the eyes of a big cat, narrowed and her lips tightened.

'What's the matter?' he asked. 'You look annoyed.'

'Do you have to be flirt with every single woman you meet?'

'I didn't realise you cared, darling.'

'Don't be a fool - I don't, I just pity you.'

She had seemed, briefly, to pity him that night when the hospital had called.

'Oh, Si, oh baby, I'm sorry,' she embraced him, her face a picture of compassion. He leant down, smelling the perfume she sprayed into her hair, his face cushioned in fragrant blackness. She said, 'I didn't mean to underplay your feelings. It was a genuine mistake - I thought you hated him, resented him for leaving. It was wrong of me.' She pushed him away, holding his shoulders and looking into his face, 'Now, I'm going to get dressed, you make your phone call, then we can go out and drink away your sorrows, ok?'

'I'm not sure I'll want to go out.'

'Oh come on. You don't know what's happened, yet. Make the call.'

He turned away and saw the phone lying by the kitchen sink. Last call, a Belfast number, an hour and a half ago. He pushed at the buttons and listened to the ring tone. A voice, Northern Irish, answered. He gave his name, spoke excuses, asked the question. Received condolences. Heartfelt. A nurse with a feeling heart. Slowly, he'd lowered the phone and disconnected the call.

He rubbed his hands over his eyes, feeling in his body the urge to move, to get away from this bar, from the memories and not be stuck here in the circle of her antagonism. 'You wanted to see me, I came. Do you mind if we get to the point?'

'You hurt me a great deal.'

'So you've told me - though I find it hard to believe that beneath your manufactured exterior and solipsistic world view there is anything there which can feel pain. Amélie, tell me, does plastic have feelings?'

'You bastard.'

'Come on; let's not pretend any longer that you are the poor duped innocent, cruelly dropped by a hard-hearted monster. I was understandably irritated by your behaviour - oh, irritated, what am I saying? Amélie, it was unforgivable.'

'So you go and sleep with my best friend as revenge, is that right?'

'No. I didn't sleep with her - for Christ's sake we've been through all this enough times,' he rose, pulling his leather jacket from the back of the chair. 'I'm not sitting here listening to you justify yourself again.'

'Sit down.' He shook his head and was about to turn, when she spoke more loudly, again with that rawness, 'Sit down, or, as God is my witness, I shall scream this place down.'

He sat, lounging back, his sprawled legs nonchalant, his chair scraped back from the table, his arms folded. The light from the circular window poured to the floor behind her, and he focussed on the golden beams amongst the colours, his chest still heaving. The bar was dark, with a slight sepulchral chill rising from the stone floor.

Amélie was staring at him. He avoided her eyes, though he noticed them dart to the returning waitress, who, without a word, put the glasses and bottles on the table. She left, not acknowledging either of them, although Simon tried to thank her, his voice sounding unfamiliar, echoing around the silence between himself and Amélie.

Then she shattered it, 'I'm pregnant.'

'Mine?'

'Unless it's the Second Coming, yes. Although, wait - I don't think I had the first, did I? Of course it's yours, you shit.' She poured water into a tumbler and sipped it, her eyes burning into his.

What does it feel like; now, what does it feel like? The emotions flood in like strangers. How can you withstand the loss of that connection with your past? His father, alcoholic, bowler-hatted, orange-sashed and marching, had marched out of their lives when he was eleven. The eldest of the three boys, Simon was the new patriarch. A child reborn as a father. As he had grown, so had the hatred for the man who had left them. And yet, it was his father. It was his blood. It was the man who could answer, why am I like this? Why have I, too, set my heart on leaving? For Simon - friend, lover, brother, son - was breaking all connections to go South, to the Antarctic, for as long as the British Antarctic Survey would have him.

A voice from the bedroom, 'Si? Are you all right? Bring the wine in, will you?'

'Amélie, give me a break, will you - my father's dead.'

'Oh, sweetheart, come on, you said he was a horrible man. You told me you never wanted to see him.'

'It's different when it happens.'

'I'm sure - but try to keep it in perspective. Fill my glass, hmm?'

There was only an inch or so left in the bottle. He poured it for her. She was wearing a dress of black silk, open at the back, precipitously low, the skirt clinging to her like a lover. She curled black tendrils, snakes of hair, around her finger and turned to him with a smile, and a shift of her dancer's hips, 'I feel good tonight, baby, I feel really good tonight.' She stepped towards him and he felt bile rise.

'Amélie, I don't want to go out.'

'Yes, you do... what's the time?' Lip-gloss, mascara.

'It's eight. Past eight.'

'Then we're late.'

'I'm not going.'

She spun to face him, all black, crimson and gold, a cobra angered, 'Oh yes you are. Mescadero's is meant to be excellent.' Then she hesitated, looking at him, 'You don't look great.'

'I feel like shit.' He knew she wouldn't stay.

'I didn't make this kind of row when I was orphaned as a teenager, for goodness' sake. Necklace or no necklace?'

In the old choir stalls, a group of girls squealed and smoke rose to the stained glass window. Simon imagined the devotions of choristers rising like incense into the rafters. Now their place was filled with the rabid self-interest of jacketed men and women in black dresses. He felt that familiar whiff of disgust, as if he'd trodden in something; the disgust which was leading him to leave his highly paid job in London to work as a dogsbody in the Antarctic. But now, could he still go?

Amélie's downcast eyes were hidden in a mesh of eyelashes like spider's legs; her perfectly carved lips were compressed. He looked at her and his heart told him nothing.

'An abortion, Amélie?'

She looked up at him abruptly, 'I never expected you to be so fucking cowardly.'

'You don't want a child, surely?'

'I'm Catholic!'

The rays of coloured light seemed to shimmer behind her. His mother's voice spoke in his ears, 'Life is precious, Simon, life is sacred.'

'I don't believe in abortion, Simon, it's against my religion,' Amélie said, her low voice husky.

'No way, I can't. I can't stay for you.'

'You selfish bastard! You'd leave me to have it alone?'

He snorted, 'You'd never go through with it. Stretch-marks, Amélie, sagging tits.'

She glared at him, drinking her water, the cocktail untasted. He watched the movements of her fine throat, and the crimson stain on the glass. An actress, ever the actress, her eyelids fluttered while her jaw clenched.

Her parents had died, both of them, in a car crash in Tangiers, while they celebrated their twentieth wedding anniversary. Amélie, at seventeen, was alone in the world. He wondered if his bereavement could be bringing back her memories and her grief. 'Why don't you go out without me?'

'Well, ok, if you're sure. I'll have my phone if you want me.'

She walked to the door, stopped, turned back, 'Simon? I am sorry, really. I think I'm hardened to loss. I know I don't deal with it well.'

He had nodded, his expression softening.

She raised her eyes from the bunched lavender on the table, 'I can't kill our baby, Simon.'

Around them, the chill air of sanctity and the damp stone scent of the sacrament. In his mind, his mother's fragile china blue eyes and the papery texture of her hands, which touched him, always, with the infinite tenderness of maternal love.

He stood up, 'I think you'll have to, Amélie.'

His face as hard as that of an exterminating angel, he walked away, not once turning back.

# *BOBS AND THE YO*

Roberta Beauchamp ('Beechum, dear, Beechum!') once competed in the Horse of the Year Show at Wembley. She rode a gelding bred by her father, now sadly passed on - the father that is, not the horse - though he too may well have gone to the green pastures in the sky. Roberta and Beauchamp Beau ('Beechum Bow') had three refusals at the wall and there ended, for both of them, what had never appeared destined to be particularly promising careers.

With the competitive life out of her league, Roberta satisfied herself with taking instructors exams and dedicating herself to teaching children - and the occasional adult - how to ride. She had thick, dark tresses - usually held in a low ponytail - very much like the coarse hair of her mounts. Her voice was deep and plummy with the occasional hoarse break into a higher register when she shouted. Like so many horsy women before - and after - her, she had heavy thighs and a face and lower arms always tanned, or, perhaps more accurately, coarsened, by the sun; those arms, by the way, were muscular and toned, from carrying hay and straw, mucking out, and dragging along unwilling ponies. On her rare evenings out, she dressed with the brashness of a colour-blind gypsy queen, with gold jewellery, spangled hair ribbons, creatively applied eye make-up and immensely high shoes. Roberta looked much better, even with her generous thighs, in jodhpurs and a jumper.

Because she so perfectly looked the part of a riding instructor, she was popular amongst the parents of her charges. Since their expectations were totally fulfilled, they felt sure they were getting their money's worth and indeed that she would be good at her job, which in fact she was. Despite their conviction of her skill, though, the parents would nonetheless mock Roberta - or 'Bobs', as she encouraged everyone to call her - because they thought her little more than a stereotype.

That, of course, is a foolish supposition - for there is no one, however conventional they appear, however hackneyed their language or second-hand their opinions, who is without a sprinkling of originality and a splash of the unique. We are all of us individuals; and there is little so true in life as the admission that humanity is infinitely various.

As for Roberta, she had psychic powers. That's what she would tell you, straight-faced as a Roman statue, if you asked her. She would then relate tales of seeing ghosts as a child; turning fate her way on a daily basis through the power of thought (she could, for example, always find a parking place in the centre of the busy market town of Stamford); reading the minds of troubled horses; and healing pains and diseases with the laying on of her hands.

These claims made the parents nervous, so they would, as a rule, write it off as imaginative eccentricity. Horse owners, more inclined, strangely, to superstition - at least when the powers seemed to promise a greater understanding of their precious equines - often asked her to treat their animals. They all swore, wide-eyed and innocent, that whatever she had done 'had worked wonders for Darkling Dove' or whoever the patient happened to be.

Bobs lived in a modern house in a village north of Peterborough with her life's partner, Yolanda Rowland. Yolanda, a tall, lean character of 40, was a farm machinery salesperson. She travelled around East Anglia with brochures full of boiled sweet coloured tractors and combine harvesters, tempting salivating farmers to sign on for 15 years of high interest hire purchase.

'The Yo', as Bobs called her, earned a decent salary and, though she had little interest in horses herself, was inclined to humour her partner's passion. Behind the square house, painted the pale orange of worn terracotta, was a pair of stables, a little paddock and a small indoor riding school. The expense had been more than they could sensibly afford. Yolanda extended her hours - her salary being based on commission. In her turn, Roberta helped pay back some of the cost of the building work by supplementing her earnings from the riding school 12 miles away with private lessons given at home on one of her own horses or at the homes of her clients. She tried to restrict her extra work to the times when Yolanda was away in her Peugeot estate, counting down the miles to Saffron Waldon or Ipswich.

Even with the pressure of financial worries and long working hours, Bobs and The Yo were a contented and self-sufficient couple. They entertained each other with their own brand of wit and desired little of life that they did not already have. The only thing that could possibly improve their existence was a hefty sum of money. Not an uncommon wish. Just like so many others, they did the lottery every week.

One of Roberta's private clients was the daughter of the local baron. Lady Clarinda Gilbert-Maier had her lessons on her pony Prince Rudolf at Courtenay Hall - a rambling and ancient structure, kept in some degree of habitability by grants from English Heritage. The house was open to the public three days a week and the outbuildings were rented out as 'craft workshops'. The lady of the house, the Baroness, had started an antiques business, which Roberta suspected was a front to sell off, quite literally, the family silver. She and The Yo often commented on the hilarity of the situation - that the nobility, like them, also hung the promise of their future on the dubious hook of the National Lottery.

Money always has the potential to be a motive in any crime; but most of the time, the need for it is not so intense that moral quibbles can be overcome. That changed for Bobs and The Yo when Yolanda became ill. It came on suddenly, with a dramatic loss of weight - which her lean frame could not sustain - and an equally rapid loss of energy. She hid the pain and some of the exhaustion from Roberta, feeling a peculiar shame about her weakness. Roberta was sharp-eyed and shrewd enough to see the decline in her beloved's health, yet she did not want to wound Yolanda's pride by stamping clumsily on her obvious desire to keep her illness to herself.

Finally, the deep bruise-coloured stains around Yolanda's eyes made pretence an impossibility.

'Bobs, I'm not quite right, you know.'

'I realised, dear, that you weren't 100 per cent, but I didn't want to pry.'

'I didn't want to worry you.'

'You are a silly thing, Yo.'

'I know, I know, Bobs. We've been so happy; I don't want it to end.'

Roberta, clasping Yolanda's hands in her own, felt her eyes moisten as she said, 'My own darling girl. You've always made me happy, from the very first day we met.'

The two women sat in silence for a moment - both recalling that long ago afternoon at the Country and Game Fayre at Otterley House. The Yo had been manning the farm machinery stall, while Bobs walked around, slightly tipsy, in one of her glaringly brash outfits. They had spent that evening drinking whiskey at a nearby pub and gradually realising that they shared more than a fondness for country life.

Their relationship had developed with glacier-like sloth, but at length all potential problems and embarrassments between them had been smoothed away like moraine, and they moved into a tropical realm of warm, moist passions - which neither could ever speak about, even to the other.

Bobs looked up from their clasped hands, 'Will you let me try to heal you?'

Yolanda had always remained sceptical about Roberta's powers, not that she vocalised her doubts - knowing that would cause severe offence to her dearest friend. And now it seemed singularly inappropriate to refuse, although she said she would, the following day, also make an appointment to see their aging doctor - whom neither had found reason to visit more than a handful of times in their 20 years together.

Over the next few months, Roberta laid her hands over Yolanda's concave stomach twice a day. Meanwhile, conventional medicine informed her that it was too late for an operation, so she was also subjected to the harsh unpleasantness of chemotherapy. The Yo lost her hair - though, as she pointed out, it was so short that the loss of it was hardly a calamity - and remained tired and weak. Even so, whether it was the chemotherapy or Bobs's healing hands, the noticeable shrinking of the tumour, which they had not been optimistic enough to predict, delighted the medics.

If The Yo's health was encouraging, however, unfortunately, their financial situation was the reverse. Yolanda's company paid a miserably short four weeks of sick leave and then hired another salesperson to cover her patch. In addition, Bobs's nursing duties limited the hours she could spend teaching - and horse-riding instructors scarcely earn more than the minimum wage at the best of times. All of this meant that red letters were arriving daily and the bank was refusing to honour their cheques.

Life had become desperate.

Roberta, when not working or tending to The Yo, would spend minutes at a time in deep contemplation, trying to 'think' herself wealthy enough to care for her dear friend here at their home without the constant threat of bailiffs and bankruptcy.

And it seemed that her prayers were answered.

Roberta had driven in her old Cavalier to Courtenay Hall one evening to give Clarinda her weekly lesson. When she pulled up and parked in the yard, surrounded by craft workshops now empty and locked up for the night, she saw that one of the doors was open - the door to the storeroom used by the Baroness for her little antiques business. Roberta, curious as to what the family were selling, looked around quickly to see that no one was watching, and then slipped as inconspicuously as possible for a generously proportioned middle-aged woman in jodhpurs, into the gloom. Once her eyes adjusted, she made out piles of oriental rugs and tapestries, some folded, some rolled, others just dumped. There were a couple of large boxes containing pitchers, copper pans, porcelain figurines, Chinese vases and silver teapots. Against the wall, ten or so paintings were stacked. Bobs went over to them and saw, with a shock of recognition, the Turner from the dining room at the Hall. Now, she didn't have any specialist knowledge of paintings. She only knew this one because one Sunday she and Yolanda had done the tour of the house and both had admired this painting which was said to be 'priceless'. Bobs was law abiding and honest, yet she felt that fate was handing her a lifeline. If she didn't take it, the powers that had aided her through life would perhaps abandon her. Besides, she reasoned, however needy the Gilbert-Maiers might be, they were highly unlikely to have greater need than The Yo.

Once the painting, with some shoving and grunting, was safely swaddled in horse blankets in the boot of the Cavalier, she trotted up to the kitchen door of the Hall to find Clarinda - and suggested to the girl that she tell her mother the door to her storeroom was wide open.

Bobs could scarcely concentrate on the lesson and poor Clarinda, who was not a natural equestrian, had more trouble than usual following her commands. Both were relieved when the hour was up. Clarinda gave Bobs two scruffy, creased ten-pound notes and waved her off.

'Same time next week?' she called, as the car pulled away.

'What? Oh - yes, yes!' The car kicked up gravel as Bobs accelerated away. Once on the open road, she shouted out in exultation, burying her shame under relief that The Yo would get the treatment she needed.

Back at the pale orange house in the village, Roberta jumped out of the car and scrambled through the door without taking her boots off, 'Yo! Yo! I come bearing glad tidings! Yo!'

Yolanda, dozing in front of Master Chef, pushed herself upright in the reclining chair, disturbing the snores, though not the sleep, of the Jack Russell terrier on her lap, 'Well, dearest girl, out with it!'

'I know this is wicked and dreadful, but, really, Yo, my Guardian Angel has been on the lookout for us.' She told Yolanda the story and then ran, heavy thighs squashing against each other, back to the car to collect the painting. She leant it against the television stand and the two women sat, holding hands, and staring at it.

Yolanda broke the silence, 'What do you plan to do with it?'

'Well, take it to Sotheby's, I suppose.'

'But perhaps they are already expecting it, perhaps that's what the Baroness planned to do with it - they'll wonder why you are selling it not her... And if the Baroness reports that it's stolen, well, we can't sell it anywhere without getting into serious hot water.'

'Oh, Yo! I've been a fool, haven't I?' said Bobs, all her eager excitement evaporating, her face now as taut and drawn as ever it had been over the past hard months.

'Wait, wait, wait - don't give up just yet, dear, we can still sell it another way,' said Yolanda.

Bobs turned to her, the light in her eyes switched back on, 'How?'

'Through illicit channels.'

'But we don't know any illicit channels!'

'I do!'

'What, Yo, you know someone who sells stolen paintings?'

'You betcha! Or at least, I know a man who knows a man who I'm sure knows a man who sells stolen paintings!'

In her many years travelling round East Anglia, Yolanda had met all sorts of people. Because she was a friendly woman with a certain mannish charm, she'd made friends in roadside cafes and grimy windowed B&Bs. Some of these people lived sordid, underground lives. Yolanda wasn't one to judge, but she had never really wanted to involve Bobs with such folk. In The Yo's mind, Bobs was her 'lovely, innocent darling' and not to be sullied by contact with the low or the criminal.

She made a few phone calls and by the next afternoon had a plan. 'Right, Bobs, here's what we have to do. We're to meet a lad called Lee Favell at the boarded up petrol station on the A11 near Wymondham at 11:30 tomorrow night.'

'All right,' said Bobs, looking a little pale.

'Favell will be in a blue van. Whichever one of us gets there first will lift up the bonnet when the other appears, so's to look as if we've broken down.

'Right.'

'He'll have with him some old boy who knows a bit about art to check over the painting, that it's not a fake and then, hey presto, we get the cash.'

The sun slanted in through the window, and Bobs appeared to be watching, with great interest, the dust motes dancing in the light, 'What's it worth, do you think?'

'Well, my pal Arctic Tony, he...'
'Arctic Tony?'
'Yes... he...'
'That sounds like a horse's name.'
'I assure you he's a man. Anyway, he says Favell won't totally con us, but he's not exactly trustworthy so he suggested we find out a little more about the painting - you know, what it's worth, and so on, before the meeting.'
'How will I do that?'
'I suggest you go to the library and look on the Internet.'

Bobs was not computer literate, but thanks to Andrea Buck, who had taken riding lessons for a year or so until she discovered a preference for men over horses, she managed to find a few facts. The key fact being that the painting, worth two and a half million pounds, had been reported stolen from Courtenay Hall.

'What that means,' said The Yo, 'is that we get less for it. But even so, a couple of hundred thou will certainly help.'

Bobs nodded. Aside from growing guilt, she had another gnawing worry. How exactly could they explain away a deposit of 200 thousand pounds in their bank account? When she voiced this concern, she was startled to discover that Yolanda hadn't just thought about this, she'd conceived a workable scheme - to do with false-paper trails, invoices and shadowy accounting. That night they went to bed in silence: Yolanda thinking about the end of their destitution; Roberta considering the end of their age of innocence.

At nine o'clock the following evening, Bobs had wrapped up both the painting and her beloved Yo in blankets. The car was loaded - with the Turner, a flask of tea, a hip flask of whiskey and a half packet of Milk Chocolate Digestives (their usual fare for a long drive). The Jack Russell, Timothy, was trotting around in excitement, sensing adventure, and the night was clear and star-filled - as though promising salvation.

Bobs sat at the kitchen table, trying to distract herself by writing a shopping list for the next day. 'Decaf, bacon, free-range eggs... Free? Will we still be free having committed theft and larceny!

Handling stolen goods... Oh dear...Stop! Pull yourself together, Bobs!' she said to herself, 'this is for The Yo. Right... eggs, dog food... Whatever will happen to Timmy!' With a sniff and a long, controlled inhalation, she calmed herself again. She finished the list, added up the total - she had always been a diligent housewife - and went to the china dog to check their cash situation. In it, she found two scruffy, creased ten pound notes. Roberta started to cry.

The Yo, who was having 40 winks in the reclining chair, heard her and came in, holding the slightly doggy blanket around her shoulders, 'My dear girl, whatever is it?'

'I can't do this, Yolanda,' her use of the full name stressed her urgency. 'We have to take it back.'

'What?'

'I can't do it! I can't steal from the Gilbert-Maiers. For 11 years now they've paid me well to teach their poor useless girl to ride - she never improves, you know, Yo, whatever I do. Yet, every week they have me back. They have so little for themselves, once they've poured money into keeping that stupid house going, yet they have never once been late in paying me, never once. We must take this back.'

Yolanda put her cold hands to Roberta's face and wiped away the tears. She bent forward and kissed both her salty cheeks, 'Dearest Bobs, I should never have expected you to do this. I am proud of you - my good, innocent darling. I'm so sorry to have tried to lead you astray.'

'But, Yo, I stole the painting. Don't blame yourself at all. We've just got to put it right.'

'Of course, but we can't just give it back, "Baroness, we've got something that belongs to you." We'd definitely end up in the clink.'

'No, you're quite right. I plan to take it back now and leave it by the door of the storeroom.'

And that is what they did. As they had already, on Arctic Tony's advice, wiped the painting clear of fingerprints, they drove straight to Courtenay Hall. The Gilbert-Maiers had not been able to afford security cameras or even lighting, so it was a simple task to go through the deserted lanes, up the servants' drive and park a few 100 yards short of the yard. Roberta, wearing black, tiptoed along the track, in almost complete darkness, and once in the yard felt her gloved hands around the doors until she came to the storeroom. She left the painting - now wrapped in greaseproof paper (to protect it from the damp) - and hurried back to the car.

On the way home, the two women sang along to their Dirty Dancing cassette and had a couple of celebratory swigs from the hip flask.

The next morning, the Baroness discovered, wrapped up like a sandwich, the priceless Turner that she had already told her insurers was stolen. She was expecting, in a few weeks, after the necessary investigations, a rather large cheque to pop through Courtenay Hall's letterbox.

'Ah, well,' she thought, 'I'll have to set them right.'

She was halfway up the path back to the kitchen door when another idea crossed her mind. Her visits to small auction houses round the country had widened her acquaintance and somewhere she was sure she had the number of a man who might be able to help... What was the name? Winter Pete? Snowy Joe? No, Arctic Tony! That was the man!

A few weeks later, the Gilbert-Maiers invested in 20 thousand pounds worth of CCTV and security lighting.

'You can never be too careful these days,' said the Baroness to Bobs.

As for Roberta, well, in the days following the return of the Turner, she felt lighter of spirit than she had since before The Yo got ill. Yet, their financial situation was still a disaster. And, in the quiet mornings after she had seen to the horses, while The Yo slept in, and Bobs fed the dog and made breakfast, she considered her powers. Clearly, she had misread the message from the heavens - this was about temptation and integrity. She had proven herself noble and deserving. Thus did she explain away a story that might have suggested that her psychic ability was on the wane.

Which is why Roberta Beauchamp was not in the least surprised that her numbers came up in the lottery the very next week. Not a massive win, but enough to pay off the building costs and keep herself and Yolanda, frugally, for as long as they both had left.

And, by the way, whether through chemotherapy or healing hands, the tumour went into remission and, as far as I know, Bobs and The Yo still live in the pale-orange house in a village north of Peterborough.

## *PIKE*

Pike. Voracious and sleek with sharp inward pointing teeth.
 One morning, walking in the thin dawn light, Ted Hughes finds two dead pike on a riverbank. A predator – a cannibal - has suffocated trying to swallow its prey. The murderous looks and violent greed, the ferocity and the self-destruction of the fish both inspire and unnerve him.
 Despite his fear, he is determined to catch one of the legendary, immense pike from the deep, ancient pool on the grounds of a destroyed monastery. The pool is near his family home in the Yorkshire town of Mexborough. What attracts him, what makes him want to catch the pike, is the dangerous, uncompromising life force of the creature.
 Hughes draws energy from the natural world, such as the pike's fierce vibrancy, and weaves it into his verse. This is what makes his poems so alive. Yet he isn't only concerned with capturing nature on the page; no – in person as much as in poetry he retains the instincts of a predator.

   \*   \*   \*

Move on a decade or so, travelling from Yorkshire to Cambridge and imagine Hughes casting earth at a window… He doesn't even know if it really is the window of the woman who's enthralled him.
 He remembers kissing her neck at the St Botolph's party: the metallic, knife-blade danger of the kiss. She bit his cheek until the blood flowed. The salty taste of his blood and the wax of her crimson lipstick. Something in him seeks something in her. Isn't that always how it happens? It's inexplicable - except that it's in your nature, just

177

as it's in the nature of the thrush to bounce, stab and kill some writhing creature; just as it's in the nature of a salmon to return, at price of death, to where it was spawned.

So, he throws earth at her window – at a window – he wants to see if he can catch something ferocious with the bait. Or perhaps it is she who has already hooked him.

Whichever one of them has snared the other, neither is willing... or, perhaps more accurately, neither is *able*... to let the other one go without pain.

The woman is the poet, Sylvia Plath

\*       \*       \*

A dream in 1956: a dream of pike deep down in a pool, huge and mysterious. He's afraid, too afraid to cast, and yet he casts because he has to, his heart dictates that he does so. He senses beneath the water the predatory eyes and the prehistoric shape of the beast. Hughes is predator and prey. Will he be killed by his need to embrace that which he fears? Will he kill that which he needs to power his wild creativity?

The dream haunts him.

The following morning, he marries Sylvia. They go on honeymoon to Paris. In a photograph taken on that holiday, her white wool sweater emits a mysterious glow. Her face glows too, with pride that she has, as she had planned, ensnared that handsome bear of a man in half shadow beside her. Ted appears as the dark setting for Sylvia's brilliant stone. His wedding ring shines in the radiance of his dangerous, endangered wife.

Such hope. Such potential.

Their brilliance does explode through their marriage. It is, while they hold the balance between them, productive - almost miraculous. Both grow as poets. Yet, it is inevitable, perhaps, that they should pull from the deep pools of each other's personalities something more threatening too.

\*       \*       \*

*A sultry day in May 1962. Devon. They've been married for six years. Their second child - a son, Nicholas, a brother for little Freya - was born the previous winter but their relationship is fracturing. They strike against each other like flint.*

*A matter of days earlier, a couple visited them – David and Assia Wevill. Hughes has started to pursue sensuous, black-haired Assia. Does Sylvia know? Nothing suggests she does, except her mood. She appears inflammable and yet constrained, a spark ready to explode into flame. To combat the threat of fire and the claustrophobia of a small mid-Devon town, she plans to drive with the children to the coast. She and Ted argue as Sylvia is bundling the children into the car.*

Hughes thinks, 'She'll do something crazy.' So, as she makes to drive off, he jumps in too and they head for the coast, the family together but disunited. The journey passes in a blur under the early summer sun – the parents tense in the front, the children quiet in the back of the car.

When they come close to the sea, they struggle to find a path out to the cliffs. Sylvia is furious about the English determination to fence everything off; her temper frays yet further. Eventually, they find a track, which crosses a meadow and leads them into gorse and sea wind.

Sylvia feels as if the wind is gagging her with her own hair, tearing away her words. The spikes of gorse seem like torture instruments. They are walking down a narrow path into an airless hollow – and that is where they find the snares. As soon as Sylvia sees them, she feels the agony of birth pangs, hears the shrieks… To her, it is as though the screams make holes in the hot sky…

She starts to tear them from the ground and throw them into the trees, screaming, 'Murderers!'

Hughes is shocked – as a countryman, he regards her act as desecration. For the rural poor, a rabbit caught in a trap keeps hunger pangs at bay – to him, that's what it's about, not birth pangs. As Ted watches Sylvia tear the snares from the sweet, damp earth, he feels as though she is shutting herself, and her hysteria, in that airless bell jar. He sees in his wife the spirit of destruction. He is reminded of the dangerous, voracious pike.

She too senses the predator close by. She feels the wires between him and her, between husband and wife; the pegs pushed so deep into the earth that she cannot pull them out. She feels his mind, his interpretation of her behaviour, like a ring, closing round her… the constriction killing her… Perhaps she has seen something nocturnal, something dangerous, in him that he is not aware of, something that threatens her. Or perhaps she sees her own self-destruction.

Both are trapped in their natures, in their fate.

Hughes, looking back, realises that she was right, in a way, about those birth pangs; but it was her poems that were being born.

Between that May and her death the following February, Sylvia's typewriter scarcely stops its clattering production line of powerful poetry. She writes poems rich with the fierce life force that Hughes recommended she direct into verse.

As for Hughes himself, beneath concern for the rural poor, 'something nocturnal' in him has set its sights on new prey… Assia.

They separate. Sylvia moves to a flat in London with the children. Ted pursues his relationship with Assia.

\*  \*  \*

Ten years on… Sylvia, Assia, and Shura, Ted and Assia's daughter, all, all three, have died. The two women committed suicide; Assia took her child too. Ted has grieved; has married again and now farms Devon's blue hills.

It's early spring, so early it's almost still winter, and every few hours, Hughes walks the fields to check the sheep. He's looking for ewes or lambs in trouble. The cawing presence of crows or ravens might suggest simply the red-blue tangle of placenta from a successful birth – or it might signify that a mother has lost her newborn.

The spring comes that little bit earlier here in Devon than in his native Yorkshire, but the almond-like scent of moorland peat, the sharp tang of newly sprouting bracken and the sheepish look of clouds so fleecy that the breeze itself seems to bleat – all that is the same.

If he sees a ewe struggling, he has enough knowledge to help. Hughes has learned the skills of a sheep farmer. Yet, even with his assistance, births on these damp hills can still end in deaths.

Early morning, and, having climbed through a sunrise of violent orange and red, listening to the curlew's call tearing the sky, and watching the frost evaporate into steam, he sees a young ewe straining to heave her lamb from its warm haven onto the chill of the heather-bruised pasture. The lamb's hard white head juts out, its tongue blue and swollen. The ewe is pushing, her groans grounding the morning, pulling focus from the delicate sky to the heaving earth, but the lamb is stuck fast.

Hughes tries to aid the delivery, but he cannot push his hand far enough inside. Lambs should come forelegs first, as if to tiptoe onto land. But this one is tangled up – head pushing through too eagerly before the legs were ready, paw-soft hooves now caught up inside the mother's aching womb.

Creation can be murderous. For Hughes, listening to sheep bleating and crows cawing, nature, birth, death and predation are all deeply connected to his poetry - and, to his life. When he looks at the cumulus stacking above Dartmoor's tors to the south and the high cirrus to the east gleaming in the rosy gold of the climbing sun, perhaps he considers what has been created and what has been lost.

\*         \*         \*

Imagine: darkness comes, the mysterious water is miles deep; somewhere below the surface, ferocious pike glide. Are you brave or fierce enough not to shy away? If you cast, what will you catch? Something to love or something to destroy? Or, perhaps, something nocturnal with the power to destroy you.

## VINCE, PETE AND VALERIE

I suppose my life changed the night Indian Joe came round with that poor bloody dog torn to pieces and asked me to look after it. He knew I loved dogs - but I'd always had boxers, not those damn Pit Bulls. That's what this was - and it'd been in a pit by the looks of it.

I gestured him to come in and be quick about it, the dog's blood was dripping on the step. Looking back, it gives me a shiver to think how close I was to slamming the door in his face. I wasn't the friendliest of neighbours in those days. But Indian was a nice enough lad and that dog - it fair broke me inside to see it suffering like that.

'What the bloody 'ell's 'appened 'ere, then, Indian?' I led him through to the kitchen. I had some old newspapers by the bin and I put them on the table, nodding at him to put the dog down.

'Oh, 'e got hurt, Pete, and I need you to look after 'im, mate. I can't take 'im home like this - Suzy would have a fit and it'd scare Lauren half to death. Please, take him. He's a good dog. No messing in the house or nothing.'

I didn't want to. I don't like dogs that are bred to fight. As for this one, maybe it was my dislike of the breed, but I'd always thought he looked at me funny. Now here he was on my kitchen table, with his face and neck a mess of scratches, tears and bites, his ears in shreds and one of his back legs looking not like it should do. The blood warm as roasted chestnuts and red as holly berries in the winter. The iron smell of it was close to making me gag.

'You've gotta take 'im to the vet, Indian. He needs stitches and antibiotics and God knows what else.'

Indian's eyes showed round and pale in his perma-tanned face, 'No way, no way - there's no fuckin' - sorry, Pete - no way I can take him to the vet.'

'What have you been doing, you blinding idiot?'

I could see Indian's defences fail; like I say, he's a decent lad, just he keeps on getting caught up in the wrong crowd.

'Well, you know Lee Favell?'

I nodded. Everyone on this estate knew Favell. He was a scumbag of the first water in my reckoning. Scrawny as a shaved whippet and mean as a cornered rottweiler. The man was a GBH waiting to happen. His hair was like a badly mowed lawn - all tufts and uneven, and patches without growth. Green, too, of course. I could never work out if it was some fashion or he was trying to disguise alopecia.

'Well, he gave me the dog last year and I thought it was like a pet for Lauren or whatever.' Trust Indian to think the best, anyone else would smell a rat. 'But then he says, after I've had the dog in the house with me and Lauren and Suze for a few months, he says, "IJ, you may be looking after it, but it's my dog and it's gonna earn me some money."'

IJ. Bloody Favell, thinks he's too PC to call Indian Joe by his full name - well, his full nickname at any rate. When Indian moved here, he and Suzy had just come back from Ibiza or some such place, where they'd apparently been doing that dance and drugs thing you hear about on Channel 4 at three o'clock in the morning when you can't sleep. So, anyway, Indian was brown as, well, brown as an Indian and as his name was Joe, he became Indian Joe and it's stuck. I can't remember who gave him that name - but it's not racist, mind - even Mr Gupta in the bank calls him Indian. But then I think he's from Pakistan so maybe he feels differently.

'So then Favell starts telling me how to train the dog. I have to take it out twice a day - swimming down in the canal and then going out on my bike with the dog running and then play tug of war with him and all this stuff.'

I remembered seeing him cycling round the estate with the dog following behind. I used to wonder at the creature's devotion. If I'd been the dog, I'd've waved the bike farewell and sat on my arse. But then, I'm a fat old bloke, and the dog's fit as they come. Or had been - it was looking very sorry for itself now. I knew what'd happened. I'm not a complete fool. Dog fighting. I'd heard some of the lads on the estate were up to it and had considered that Indian was spending a bit too much time with his mutt. If I hadn't been tied up in my own problems, perhaps I'd've taken more notice. Though it was hard to believe a softie like Indian could really get involved with those scummy little bastards.

While he was speaking, I filled a bowl with warm water and started looking for the salt. Since Val passed away, I've moved everything round. She was very determined about what went where and putting things in the right place. When she'd gone, every time I opened one of the doors, I'd feel like someone had kicked me in the gut. So, I jumbled things up. Now I can't find anything without searching every damn cupboard, accompanied by falling tins, curses and slamming doors. But at least I don't feel like jumping off a bridge.

Indian carried on talking, 'He told me to starve Tyson from last Friday and I had a hell of a job to stop Lauren from giving it her toast and that. Then he came round and took me and the dog down to the old warehouses.'

He meant those empty industrial units a mile or so away. It used to be, when Val and I moved here, that people would have a little business that maybe didn't earn much but meant they had some self-respect and kept their money clean. Nowadays, people live on the social and get their cash by drugs or guns or, it seems, dog fighting, and all the units have been abandoned.

'So we leave Tyson in the car, and there's all this cheering and shouting and, oh God, Pete, the dogs, growling and panting. You could hear their teeth snap and the sound, like in a butcher's when they cut through the chops, when the dogs bit each other - even above the noise the men were making. And blood - it stank of piss and blood - Favell had just pushed through to the front and pulled me with him. Pete, if I'd been able to, I'd've left. I nearly puked. And Favell was watching, all eager as these two fucking - sorry, Pete - these two dogs, tore each other to bits.'

I'd found some rags in a drawer and was starting to clean up the dog's wounds. Tears in his tan hide, but I didn't think there were any deep puncture wounds. The white patch on his broad chest was a mess of blood and flesh. I was worried about that leg, too. He'd lost a bit of his left ear - and nearly all the right one. That was an ugly wound - I was just glad there wasn't anything hanging off that I'd have to cut.

Indian was talking as if the words pouring out were carrying with them the poisonous images - like he was now puking, a sort of psychological puke, if you get my gist.

'And then one of the dogs sort of yelped and just, well, it just gave up. The other was growling, its teeth, its mouth stained red by the blood, and lunging forward, snapping. Then it got the dying dog by the skin of its ear and face. And just kept on yanking. The weaker dog, oh Pete, its paws sort of jerked, but that was it. And the owner was right there, shouting at it, pleading sometimes and threatening other times, "Come on, Mickey, don't give up! Come on Mickey, get him, Mickey." Then the other dog grabbed Mickey's throat... the blood, Pete, and the sound. I'll never forget it if I live to be a hundred. Fuckin' 'ell - sorry Pete - but it was horrendous.'

'So why, in God's name, did you let them put your dog in there, you idiot?'

'It was Favell. I went back to the car, I'm saying, "No way, no way, Favell," but he grabbed my arm and just like shouted in my face - he said, it's his dog and he'll do what he likes and if I try anything, I'm fucked - and Suzy too.'

Sounded like Favell. Val was a dinner lady at his primary school and he'd been a little bastard all his life - punching, hitting, bullying, he'd even bitten some kid's arm so hard he'd drawn blood. And it sounded like Indian to give in as soon as Suzy was involved. She's a beautiful girl, Suzy, and Indian's as doolally about her as a man's ever been. Val always said it wasn't surprising - she said Indian was lucky to have her and knew it. Suzy was the daughter Val never had. When she and Indian first came here, Suzy was pregnant, just starting to show, and she didn't have any family. So, she and Val got close. Especially when Suzy lost that first baby. Val was over there every day - she'd retired by then. And no one was happier than Val when Suzy fell pregnant again and had Lauren. That little lass may as well have been a grandchild to us, we babysat that often. Suzy still liked to paint the town a vibrant shade of pink, as she put it. And then she was doing the courses, so's she could work at Val's school. Val loved the time with Lauren. And when she got ill, Suzy and Lauren visited every day while I was walking Max, to keep Val company.

So Vince had Indian round his little finger and he fair dragged him and the dog through the crowds and into the ring. Then he shouted:

'Tyson, nine month old dog. He'll take on anyone. Who's stepping forward?'

The men, and boys - there were kids in that crowd, eleven or twelve years old and there with their dads or their brothers watching dogs rip each other to bloody pulps - they didn't seem too impressed by Tyson. He wasn't the nicest looking creature, but he didn't exactly instill fear with his physique. Some of them laughed. And that was the worst thing to do around Favell. Indian said he could see Lee's jaw muscles clench and that fixed expression came into his eyes as the veins in his neck jumped under the white skin. His head shot forward, chin out.

'Which one of you fuckers is laughing?'

He jerked the dog's chain and Tyson growled.

'Alright, you mad fuck,' said a greasy haired pikey in faded jeans, which hung in folds where they should be shaped around the curves of buttocks and thighs. 'I'll give your pup a go with Herakles. This should be a laugh.'

Herakles was a full ten kilos, at least, heavier than Tyson, according to Indian's reckoning. In Indian's words, he looked ugly as a bulldog licking spit off a nettle. Mean too. Indian was stroking Tyson, saying goodbye, he figured that'd be the last time he'd touch the dog alive. It'd die in the ring most likely, or Favell, with his pathetic pride at stake, would kick it to death, if it lost, as a spectacle for the crowd.

I'd finished bathing the dog's wounds and I felt sick to the stomach with what Indian was telling me. But there's something inside all of us as wants to know all the details, however gruesome. That part of us that rubbernecks at road accidents; watches horror films; listens to news about serial killers with particular interest. Don't you deny it;

you know it's in your nature too.

I put the dog in an old bed I had left from Max, my last boxer. I hadn't the heart to throw it out. He was put down six months after Valerie's passing. It was like tearing apart all those unhealed wounds to go through him dying. I tried to make that Pit Bull as comfortable as he could be while Indian carried on telling me how he'd managed to get the dog out of that hellhole alive.

Once the money had changed hands, Favell held back Tyson on one side of the ring, while the pikey held Herakles on the other. They would throw a lump of meat in the middle and the two starving dogs would fight over that - as if their natural aggression and man-made desperation weren't motivation enough.

'Just want to warn you,' said the pikey, 'This dog's so game his parents had to be muzzled, yeah, muzzled, when they shagged so's they didn't kill each other - kill each other - as they shagged. And he's more game'n either of 'em. You still want to put that weasel in the ring with him?'

Favell just gave Tyson a kick in the balls to piss him off. Not that he wasn't already more than a little upset. Imagine it - famished, surrounded by screaming idiots, smelling the scent of blood and death and faced with Herakles who clearly wanted to decorate the gore stained concrete with his entrails.

Someone threw the lump of meat and bone between them, the animals strained at their leads, the pikey screamed, 'NOW!' and the dogs launched into each other. Indian told me how it happened. It was like he had to get rid of the pictures in his head. Tyson, well, I guess he was in part lucky, in part canny. He wounded the bigger dog in the chest early on and then kept on going for the same place. The other dog dripping blood like a tap turned on halfway. Then Herakles got hold of Tyson's leg, and Tyson was chewing on his head to get him off. Finally he managed to get hold of that wound again. The other dog died. The dog died there in front of Indian, who was retching, having already emptied his stomach amongst the seething crowd of men too focussed on this foul fight to notice a bloke puking on their stinking trainers.

Favell was doing high fives in the van all the way back to the estate, his pockets full of filthy tenners. Indian Joe was too shocked to think straight and the dog was whimpering quietly in the back. At every corner, it was sliding across the slick metal in the back of the van, opening its wounds. The van smelt worse than a butcher's backyard. Indian's mind kept on playing and replaying the fight.

'Sick fucks. Sick fucks - sorry, Pete, but that's what I was muttering under me breath in the van and then I thought, "If Favell hears me, it'll be even worse." I don't know how I got me and Tyson out the van without Favell coming in for a beer or what. So anyway, I came here.'

The sound of his phone ringing made both of us start. 'It's Suzy,' he said, 'I gotta go. What the fuck am I going to tell her about the dog?'

Val's voice in my head, 'You must look after Suzy.' To Indian Joe, I said, 'Tell her the dog got run over. You didn't want to scare Lauren, so I'm looking after it. Tell Lauren he's on holiday at the seaside.'

'Thanks, mate, you're a brick. Oh, listen, Suzy's always saying as we should have you over for dinner, like - but she reckons you've been hiding away.'

'Just as well, since I've got to keep this dog hidden away.'

'Yeah, right. You're a diamond, Pete.'

'Indian, get rid of that jumper before you go home. You're drenched in claret.'

He stripped off, and when he started looking vaguely for somewhere to ditch the jumper, I took it off him. 'I knew I could count on you, Pete.' And with that, he left the dog and me together.

I gave Tyson a bowl of water and he lapped at it. I stoked the patch of uninjured tan fur between his ears. He'd killed. But he was just a dog. I couldn't hold him guilty. He'd been treated cruelly and he'd done what he could to survive. I'm a firm believer that you can train any dog to be obedient, or to be aggressive. Tyson was still a young dog and I felt this eagerness inside me to turn his life around. There's a peculiar bond comes when you nurse something. Take me and Val; I never looked at another woman from the day I met her in 1956 at St

John's Market here in Liverpool. Our eyes met over my dad's carrots and turnips and that was it. Even so, after forty years and more of loving each other and being together, we reached another level when she was ill and I was looking after her. Everything you do for a child, feeding, drinking, dressing, undressing, washing - and the bathroom stuff.

In a way, I'm glad we had that time together. That intimacy. And the gallows humour too. Did I mention Val was funny? She had the old Scouse wit by the bucket load, she did. Oh and she was as funny as hell when she was dying. 'I'll die laughing if I'm to die at all,' she said. Of course, it wasn't quite like that. But we still managed a lot of laughter in those last weeks.

Tyson wasn't going to die though. I could see it in him, that strong life spirit. When I saw he'd held the water, I offered him some chicken I had in the fridge. Warmed it up in the microwave to make it smell good to him. Just a little, mind, and I was careful too - a starving dog will be a snapping dog - as those bastard dog fighters know all too well. But he was gentle as a lamb, looking up at me like I was god hisself.

It was like that for the next week or so. Food and water, little and often, him licking my fingers and fair doting on me. Saline washes to keep those wounds clean. That leg I was worried about, the back left one - it wasn't broken, just sprained and badly bruised. It took a while for the swelling to go down, but in time it did. His ears were always going to be a mess, but we can't all be oil paintings, I told him, as he smiled up at me with that dear doggy face of his, wagging his tail fit to fall over.

As a name 'Tyson' didn't seem quite right any more. So I thought about it and decided on Vincent, after Vincent Van Gogh, what with the lost ear. And that was it. The beginning of Vince and Pete.

With him in the house, I had a reason to get up in the mornings. Not that I'd been lazing in bed since Valerie passed away. I'd wake up at six, get up at seven, and wonder what on earth for. I wasn't depressed or anything, just, I couldn't get any enthusiasm for life. It started when her cancer was diagnosed: I'd felt myself crumbling inside, but on the outside it's all stiff upper lip and put a brave face on it. Besides, I had Val to think of.

Do you know, when she died more than a hundred people came to her funeral? And it's not like either of us had much in the way of family left. All the other dinner ladies, the teachers too; her hairdresser and her dentist and Mr Gupta; the lady GP and even the bloody vet; half the local constabulary and most of the estate. I never realised she knew all those people. Suzy read a poem and Val's old friend from when she was on that typing course, Rose Cooke, spoke about Val's sense of humour and her love of life. She did it well, too, Rose; she always did have the gift of the gab, mind. Everyone crying - except me. The only times I cried was out on the Rec when Suzy and Lauren were with Valerie. Poor old Max, chasing the Frisbee and trying to encourage his tired old legs to share the enthusiasm of his young at heart mind. Lovely dog, he was. Anyways, I'm not ashamed to admit I shed a few tears there, with the brisk autumn wind chilling them as they rolled down my face. No one ever saw me though and I kept upbeat for Val.

All those people at the funeral - and I've scarcely shared a good morning with any of them since. After Max died, I had no real reason to go outside much. And of course, no one has much reason to call on me.

I learnt how to do all the housework to Val's specifications when she was ill. She'd be calling me from the bedroom to dust this or vacuum that; clean the bath; mop the floor. She used to do it when I was at the wholesale veg market early in the morning stocking up my stall and I never realised how much there was to do, even in a little place like ours with just the two of us. Anyway, I kept it all up when there was just the one of me. A little on the obsessive side perhaps. I suppose it kept me busy and I thought of her reading her magazine in bed while I did it. So the house always smelt of bleach and Pledge. The only thing different was the insides of the cupboards.

Vince changed everything. Once he had the run of the house, he'd wake me up, bouncing onto the bed and pawing at the covers. He'd squirm down under the sheet and lick my toes. I challenge anyone not to laugh when a dog's licking your feet and you're kicking out because it tickles so much and you can feel his strong tail bashing against your shins. I can't remember the last time I woke with laughter.

I'd get up and take him out into the garden for his ablutions. Then I'd make us some breakfast - dog food and the lean meat off a bit of bacon for Vince; a bacon and egg sarnie for me and a mug of tea. By then, the newspaper would have come, so we'd have a bit of a doze over the sports news and the quick crossword - his head heavy and warm through my slippers. A bit later, I'd do a few chores round the house, Vince chasing the head of the vacuum, crouching down, making little yappy barks, tail going fourteen to the dozen. Before lunch, we'd go for a stroll, up to the Rec or the longer walk to the woods via Redland Road and North Western Avenue.

You might mock me for it, but I told that dog everything - about how I missed Val, about how life was black and white without her kaleidoscopic mind turning everything Technicolor. I told Vince about how much she'd cried when we realised we couldn't have children. And about us deciding that we didn't want to adopt. So, instead of sticking to the secretarial side of things where Val could have gone a long way, she went into school catering, so's she could hear the laughter of children every day, she said.

She was a good woman, my Valerie, and she was the world to me.

Vince, head on one side, ragged ears cocked, seemed to sympathise. Whether he did or no, just saying it all out loud seemed to help. 'You're better than Sigmund Freud,' I told him. Vince tilted his head even further; a quizzical expression on his scarred face, and gave something of a questioning sweep of his tail.

This was on a fresh October day, coming up two-ish, I suppose. I'd be late back for lunch but the woods had seemed especially lovely with the red and gold leaves crinkling on the paths. It was sunny enough to encourage an old man and his dog to stay outside. So we were walking back to the estate later than usual.

I suppose everyone has routines. Mine usually has me back indoors by half past one on a week day. So I wasn't usually around when teenage mum Nikki Lawson at number 48 North Western Avenue took her toddler out to the kiddies' Play Group; or when Dick Spencer at the corner of North Western and Redland Drive left his bruised wife in tears after lunch and headed back to the snooker club; or when Paddy McCabe drove his disabled daughter to her physical therapy classes; or when Lee Favell spied his way through the streets looking for someone to bully.

Today that someone was me. Vince and me.

The van braked abruptly, the choking engine stalling after coughing out a final cloud of black diesel fumes. The rattling slam of a door that's seen better days, and Favell was in front of me. All 5'6" of him: small and thin he might be, but that wiry little arsehole had more venom than an angry rattlesnake and more aggression than a pricked bull in a ring.

'I recognise that dog, old man,' he hissed, lip curled over pointed yellowish teeth, 'and it's mine. If I were you and had any sense at all in my ugly old head, I'd hand it over now.'

'Fuck off, Favell.' Oh very bright, I thought as I started walking off, very bright, Peter, piss him off, why don't you. I was trying to look confident and dignified, but I'd already walked a long way and my hip was causing me grief.

Two or three strides, and despite his small stature, he was in front of me again. His skin had the white sheen of the unhealthy, but his eyes had the reptilian brightness of a killer.

'Come on, granddad, I'll give you one more chance not to make a big mistake. Give us the lead.'

My hands were trembling. I almost did as he asked.

'You're out of your league, you ancient, piss-smelling idiot - the dog's a Pit Bull - it's illegal. Do yourself a big favour and hand it over, before I tell the police you got it.'

All the time, Vince had been silent, walking to heel as I'd taught him over the past month or so that he'd been living with me. He's a smart dog, my Vince, and it hadn't taken me long to train him in all the basics. Now I wished I'd trained him to run away on command. I dropped the lead, hoping that I could communicate with him psychically or something.

That was when Favell grabbed my shirt collar with one hand and punched me in the left cheek with the other. He was leaning towards me, must've been on tiptoes, the shortarse. He was about to shout in my face - I was flinching, blinking, trying to pull away. I knew his breath would have that rotten smell of uncleaned teeth and I was screwing my face up, when suddenly he yelped like a pup and went down. I teetered, nearly following him, but somehow found my balance. Vince had a grip on his ankle with jaws that can snap a man's tibia, fibula or neck without any effort.

So Favell's writhing on the ground, shouting at me and the dog; the dog's growling and sort of looking between me and its victim as if to say, 'What now, boss?'; and I'm standing there all six foot and fifteen and a half stone of me, blinded in one eye and no bloody use to anyone.

Two thoughts come to me. Firstly, it'd be just my luck if the community copper, who I last saw when Methuselah was a kid, turned up now. He'd take Vince and shoot him. Secondly, I realise Favell's going to be mad as hell. It'll be better if he can't walk well enough to chase me.

So, I counted to ten, then called Vince sharply and trotted off down the street to my house as fast as my aching hip would take me. I only just managed to get the key in the lock and once we were on the other side of the door, and I'd bolted it, I started crying like a child. I slid down the wall and wailed, holding Vince as he licked the snot and tears from my face.

I knew that Vince and I couldn't risk Favell meeting up with us again. But, by God, I'm nearly seventy years old. I've never broken a law - well, not one that mattered. I've never hurt anyone or threatened anyone. Yet all of a sudden my life's a mess. I couldn't go to the police because Vince had bitten the bastard and because Indian Joe might get in trouble. But I couldn't be a prisoner in my own house - which was the only alternative... Apart from hiring an assassin. I'm sure there are plenty of them in Huyton, but I didn't have their bloody mobile telephone numbers.

That was when the glass above me smashed. I cradled my head and Vince as the sharp shards cut the air around us an settled on the doormat - along with half a brick with a piece of paper folded round it.

As soon as I could control my hands, I took the paper and squinted down at it with my one good eye.

'Granddad, u no Ill win. I want the Dog by tommorrow nite - or Im telling the Polise it attacked Me. Its bye bye Doggie one way or the other.'

I was clutching hold of Vince like a drowning man to a life jacket. The dog seemed the only thing that could keep me afloat in this world without Val.

Maybe it was the grief or the fear; maybe it was a lack of food; whatever, it was like I sort of passed out there, hiccoughing and weeping, holding my dog and smelling his rich scent above the clean odour of this sterile house.

When I was conscious enough to listen to myself, I realised I was crying for Valerie. Asking her why she'd died and left me; telling her how much I loved and missed her; claiming that without her my life wasn't worth living so Favell may as well do his worst. I was like an hysterical toddler, when you see them in the supermarket, purple faces, the tears leaping out of their eyes as though shot from a water pistol, hands beating the floor, so small and yet so totally uncontrollable. The mothers stand there, embarrassed, saying the angry words, the impatient words, the loving words, the gentle words until finally the child listens. And for me, all of sudden, amongst the despair and the fear; the concern about the dog and the longing for my dear wife; in my head I heard her gentle voice. Just saying one word, so calmly, such a small voice amidst the storm of my emotions, she said, 'Suzy'. That was it, just 'Suzy'.

Val had always said that Suzy had more sense than the whole road put together, and more brains than the entire estate. If anyone could think a way round this, it'd be Suzy.

I crawled to the kitchen. Suzy and Indian's number was up there on the message board above the phone from when Val was ill. She knew Suzy's number by heart, of course, but neither of them trusted me to remember it or look it up in Val's phone book when the time came. They both insisted I call Suzy first when Val passed. And I did. She'd come through the front door five minutes after I rang her, though it was half past four in the morning. She took over everything, arranged everything. I just sat there, my cardigan on over my pajamas and listened to her clear voice sorting things out.

Now I wanted to hear her clear voice again.

It took me a couple of attempts to get the numbers in the right order. Then the phone was ringing and I was praying she'd pick up - I didn't want Indian - or little Lauren - hearing me like this.

'Hello?' Her voice.

'Suzy...'

'Pete? Is that you? Give me five minutes to get Lauren organised and I'll be there.'

I was spluttering and trying to pull myself together when I heard the door rattle against the bolt. I started. Vince, pushing his body against my legs, let out a low growl.

'Pete? I can't get in!'

Suzy. It was Suzy. I climbed to my feet and stumbled down the hall, clumsily unbolting the door. She came in and took me in her arms, speaking to Lauren at the same time, 'Mind the glass, sweetie. Why don't you go and watch TV in the sitting room? Your programme's on BBC1 in ten minutes, anyway.'

She led me to the kitchen and sat me down, then crouched in front of me, holding my hands. 'Who did that, Pete? What's happened?'

I was crying again. Never once in all our life together had I cried in front of Val. I was there to look after her, to be the strong one - and now I was falling apart in front of this little chit of a girl, who took my ugly old face between her cool brown hands and stroked the swelling skin around my eye as a mother soothes a child.

'Pete, Val told me to keep an eye on you - and I did try, but you made it so hard - shutting yourself away. She always said you could be a curmudgeonly old bugger, but I didn't expect you ever to hang up on me. Lauren's missed you too. Pete, you used to pop in nearly every day with a lollipop or some sweets from Mr Gupta's.'

She was right. I used to love the little girl and it was returned. Now she scarcely recognised me. 'I'm sorry, Suzy.'

'I'm sorry too, Pete, but all that can wait. Tell me what's

happened.'

She and Vince were the only two creatures on God's earth to have shown me any affection since Val died, and though I'd done all right by the dog, I had treated Suzy badly. Truth was, I couldn't think of her without imagining her and Val together in those last days, foreheads touching, rocking backwards and forwards, Val moaning with the pain and sweet Suzy soothing her like a daughter. I'd been jealous, I think, that Suzy could show her love while I was stiff as a board in the face of the one thing in my life that mattered. What I should have done was to hold Val to my heart and tell her, while she still lived and breathed, that she was my everything, my Koh-I-Noor, the only woman who ever touched me. I should have told her that she was etched through me like the letters in a pink stick of Blackpool Rock, that my very blood beat with joy just to see her face. I should have said it all and more. But I never did. Instead, the only creature to know how I felt was a damned dog.

I looked into Suzy's wide caramel eyes, fringed with such thick black lashes, and said, 'Su... Suzy, love, did Val know... did she know that... that I...'

'That you loved her with all your heart from the day you met? Yes, Pete, she knew, everyone knew. Don't worry for a moment about that,' she paused, thoughtful, before continuing, 'She said to me - more than once - that no woman was as blessed in her husband - and that the only reason she didn't tell me to walk away from Joe was that she saw the same kind of devotion in his eyes for me. What she said was that no man with that kind of love could fail to make his woman happy. There might not be much money, or fancy clothes and posh holidays, but there was a love and a loyalty that counted more than diamonds, more than riches, more than anything princes can buy. She knew, Pete, she knew.'

I'm not sure how much longer I wept, and she, with such simple grace, held my hands in hers. I know her knees got stiff and she stood up and dragged the other chair closer to mine. She didn't say anything, didn't rush me to explain about the broken glass. She gave me time. I'd already had two years, but I'd wasted them in hiding from the world and from myself.

Finally, I regained some control. It helped to concentrate on the neat rows of tiny plaits on her head, their regularity as soothing as the lines in the ploughed fields of my childhood, with the sunlight reflecting off the sheer cuts of damp earth. I wondered how the hairdresser managed such miniscule perfection, just as I had wondered how the old farmers kept their roaring tractors straight in the fields. I felt like a child now - and like a cloud blocking the sun, a shadow of humiliation swept over me.

Suzy must have caught the look in my eyes. 'Pete, this is ok, you know. You are allowed to grieve. Don't you dare feel ashamed or embarrassed. You've been better than a father to me. Please - I don't want to lose you again.'

Val was right, she's a smart cookie that girl. It so easily could have been that I'd never have felt comfortable with her again. Instead, I accepted what she said. And I thanked her with all my heart for being so good to Val and so good to me.

And then she asked me about the glass. So I told her the whole story. She knew what Indian Joe was like - a good boy, but easily led - it would never change her feelings for him to know his failings and I had been a fool not to see that before. I told her about the blood and the dogfight and Favell. I told her about nursing the dog and coming to love him. I told her about my black eye and the brick. I told her that I couldn't bear to lose Vince.

He, while all this was going on, was lying against my feet, warm and comforting as a scarf in winter. Suzy leant down to stroke his scarred face and his torn ears. She asked practical questions and listened to every word. It was reassuring just to tell her the whole story of me and Vince - a story that, please God, could not end with me alone and him killed.

'I wondered what had really happened to Tyson - Vincent. It did cross my mind. I always try to think the best of Joe, but sometimes the best is a little off the scale of reality. Right,' she looked thoughtful, still caressing Vince, who was giving her his most appealing doggy grin. 'Right, I have a plan.'

Suzy's plan was a straightforward and simple as Val's always were. Val often said I couldn't see the wood for the trees.

Indian - or Joe, as Suzy insisted I now call him, she didn't hold with that Indian Joe malarkey - was to phone Favell and say that I, terrified by the brick, had given Joe the dog and he'd hand it over the next night. Suzy reckoned that the reason Favell was so set on getting the dog back the following day was because a fight had been planned. Favell would come to their house - Suzy and Lauren would be back here with me - and no doubt he'd boast to Joe about how much they'd win. Then Suzy's mates in the local constabulary would follow the two men in the blue van to wherever the fight was to be held. And that would be that.

'What about Ind ... Joe? Won't he be arrested too? And what if it goes wrong and they put Vince in the ring again?'

'Pete, the coppers are friends - well, actually they're Val's friends. Like Val, I don't like this estate much - but knowing the police and having them on my side makes it bearable, just as it did for Val. Remember how quickly the graffiti at her bowls club was sorted out? And how fast that problem of handbags being stolen from the cars outside the Play Group was sorted? Val was a wonderful woman - you know that, but so did a lot of other people. These coppers came to her funeral - and I've just continued to maintain the contact.'

'But won't they have to take Vince. These Pit Bulls are illegal, Favell said, they'll have to take him and put him down.'

Fire flashed in her golden eyes, 'They'll have to put me down first. "He's a Staffy,"' she said in a posh version of her voice. '"I should know, got him as a pet for my neighbour who's been lonely since he was made a widower. These scars are from when he was attacked by a Rotty on the Rec - the police should be chasing that owner - he's a liability. Bloody hoody."'

She seemed to have covered all bases, but, but, but, I was so afraid of losing Vince.

'It'll work, Pete, I promise it'll work. It's about time Favell had his comeuppance and that those bastards pay for what they're doing. You know, at school,' Suzy is a teaching assistant, 'One of the kids snapped a leg off the classroom hamster. I was shocked, then I realised it was Dick Saunders' boy. Doesn't make it any less evil but the kid's screwed up seeing his mother beaten up each day or so. It's a horrible world, Pete, but by doing our bit maybe we can make it a little better. That's what Val used to say.'

She was right. She has such a clear vision of life, how it is and how it should be, and she has the strength of will to affect how it is, making it more as it should be.

It all happened as Suzy had planned it. Favell has been locked up; he'll serve a couple of years. The police somehow discovered a few other bits and pieces, which Favell couldn't deny once they had the evidence. A handful of other arrests and eight dogs seized. I feel sorry for those dogs, the Huyton Eight, I call them, who paid with their lives; but surely a lethal injection is better than being torn to death in the ring or being covered in petrol and set alight because they lost. They couldn't be rehomed, so twisted and aggressive they'd become thanks to the sheer wickedness of the men who bred and trained them.

Vince was lucky. Just the one bad night in his life. He may have killed once, but he won't get the chance again, even in self-defense. I mostly keep him on the lead and never leave him with Lauren, just in case.

My life has changed so much. I eat dinner with Joe, Suzy and Lauren twice a week. I baby-sit Lauren on Friday nights when Suzy and Joe go to their antenatal classes - yes, they're expecting again. I've started helping out two mornings a week on the old fruit and veg stall, my dad's business as was, which I gave up when Val was ill.

Those cupboards in my kitchen, the tins and jars are once again stacked with almost neurotic neatness. When I open them and see the orderliness Val loved, it's not a stab of pain I feel, but a caress. And the dog too, Vincent, every time I look at him it makes me chuckle. Anyone who sees us together would know in an instant that his love for me is deep and constant – it's almost as obvious as my undying love for Valerie.

## *THE PERFORMANCE*

Claire woke to daylight, not sunshine: daylight, dripping through the curtains like dishwater. She was stiff-necked and sore eyed. In the bed next to the reclining chair, her mother slept on. The chemical smell of the hospital and the seeping scents of death filled Claire's nostrils. As she stretched, the thin blanket slid down to her waist, and without it she felt chilled, though the plain white room was warm as ever. It must be tiredness. This, after all, was her seventh morning waking from interrupted sleep on an unsuitable bed.

Claire had flown back to England from Australia to be with her mother during what appeared to be her last weeks. The illness had been diagnosed some seven years back and Anna had been admitted to hospital for radiotherapy and chemotherapy at various points since. Claire had never previously felt able to return. This was in part due to her work. Her career was taking off – or at least, it kept promising to take off - and she couldn't risk being away when the offer of a succulent part came her way. She was an actress - a skill she'd developed at boarding school. Only her ability to play the part of a down to earth, happy go lucky girl had given her the strength to get through those years at Broadhayes. Not that she disliked the school – it was more that she was afraid of the suspicions which had started to grow in her adolescent mind after she'd heard her parents talking deep into one sultry summer night. She had once called home, weeping, begging to talk to her father about her fears. Her mother had answered the phone and Claire improvised, saying she was suffering from nightmares and headaches.

'You'll grow out of it, Claire,' her mother had said, 'or at least, learn to deal with it.'

She looked down at the dying woman. Thin strands of greasy

looking hair were matted over a skull as delicate as a baby's, even without the unsealed fontanelle. In sleep, the pained lines of her forehead eased, but were still evident, as was the tension in her lips; lips that Claire remembered as a broad red gash, but which now were pale and thin. Her cheeks had sunk into hollows over the past seven days, since she had refused food. The doctors were not tube feeding her, even though Claire's brother Andrew had tried to persuade them to do it.

Each evening, when he came in after work, Andrew sat on the side of their mother's bed. Her knotted hands fluttered like captive birds and he embraced her fragility. Supported by his large hands, she leaned towards him, their foreheads touching and they rocked gently backwards and forwards. Andrew crooned to her, a soft wordless hum, and her frequent pained moans slowed and ceased until, after ten minutes, her hunched shoulders relaxed and he lay her back on plumped up pillows, more peaceful than she had been all day. Claire watched.

She and her brother had been close as little children; that intimacy ended when she went to Broadhayes. He was the easy-going one, allowed to stay at home. Anna explained that his epilepsy made it difficult for him to be away from a familiar environment. That explanation didn't wash with Claire – it hadn't when she was a long-legged straggly-haired 11 year old and it didn't now. Her interpretation was simpler: her mother didn't like her.

Under the covers, Anna's bones seemed as delicate as a bird's. Her talc-soft skin was loose, the muscles beneath having disappeared, leaving the remaining flesh to move uneasily over the tendons and bones. The tight mound, which might have been a stomach, housed a tumour the size of a grapefruit. The surgeon had told Claire this, with airy ambivalence, the first day she'd come in, jet-lagged, straight from the airport.

She had organised the trip, the flight, the hire car, all of it, online from her rented apartment in Sydney, where, each morning, she drank black coffee on the balcony overlooking the sea and where, each evening, when she was not working, she tried to teach her English heart the open honesty of the Antipodes. She was there, staring sightlessly at a seersucker sea when Andrew had called her, telling her that their mother had developed a blood clot and had been admitted to hospital. His voice, coming halfway round the world in a split second, echoed emptily, as though it had absorbed the blankness of space on its way. She had expressed shock, concern, sympathy. He had done what none of the family had done before - he had asked her to come home.

She had stood at her window, suddenly registering a night of startling beauty. The clouds floated majestically between the milky light of the moon and the silvered surface of the becalmed sea. They were semi-transparent and amazingly, visibly, three- dimensional, thanks to the effect of the moonlight upon them. Claire hesitated a moment as she watched the clouds scud, blue-veined, across the indigo horizon. Then she span back into the room, facing her reflection in the mirror. The Claire in the mirror always slightly unnerved her - both too familiar and far too strange - but on this occasion, as the two Claires nodded in synchronicity, the reflection bore the same emotional detail as the heart that beat within the woman herself.

From Sydney to Singapore, she watched - twice - an Australian film by a director she admired. At Changi Airport she showered and had a massage. Then, on the long flight to London, Claire, fortunate to have four seats at the back of the plane to herself, had lain down, wrapped in the purple blankets, to be rocked by turbulence as a baby is rocked in its cradle by a mother.

Coming in to London, the plane had dropped through dense cloud, into thick fog. None of the passengers had realized they were so close to the ground and 400 people gasped as the wheels lightly took the impact of 400 thousand kilograms descending from 30 thousand feet at 240 kilometres per hour. For Claire, the sudden shock of the return to earth seemed appropriate. On the aircraft, she had been in a state of preparation, of rehearsal. Now, for the performance.

On the rough hospital cotton, her mother was waking. She groaned a little as her eyes started to open - a process which came later and took longer each day, as though only unwillingly did she return to some form of consciousness.

When Claire had first seen her mother, a week ago, Anna had

looked just as she had expected. She had aged, of course, in the eight years that Claire had been away, and she had suffered too. Claire's stepfather had died three years previously. It had been unexpected, a heart attack. No warning. No suggestion of high blood pressure or aneurysms. Claire was reminded of the death of her father, in the January of her second year at Broadhayes. He had been getting weaker and weaker. Each time she went home, he looked smaller and less capable. But no one told her. No one warned her. All she had was the suspicion that her mother wished him dead and the half-remembered conversation she had overheard before she had started school.

'Anna, I'm sorry.'

'You bastard'

'Stop this, Anna. Please. I don't have long; we don't have long; our children don't have long with a mother and a father. Please, try to...'

'How can I? You disgust me! As if the whores weren't bad enough – this–'

'Please, Anna, the children, please.'

Claire could forgive, she felt, her father's infidelities – who could stay faithful to a bitch like her mother. What she could not forgive was being kept at school, away from her father while he sickened and died. Nor could she forgive her mother's easy transfer of affections to Jasper – the family friend (ha!) who supported Anna in her trials. The hypocrisy repulsed Claire. She felt her father had been maligned and forgotten. So, when she heard of Jasper's death, she said goodbye to him in her own way: driving the Great Ocean Road with the emotions passing through her and out of her, into the warm wind. The money she would have spent on the airfare to attend the funeral, she spent on a dress for the premiere of *Electric*, a reworking of Sophocles' *Electra*, in which she played the female lead. She sent the celebrity magazine in which she featured to her mother.

At last, the rain cloud-grey eyes, with pupils always far too big or too small for the situation, sought an object on which to fix. On this day, as for every one of the last six, Claire was there. She wanted the first sight her mother saw upon waking to be the evidence of her feelings; this was her last chance to show her mother exactly how she felt. Words would never be able to express what Claire needed to say. And so, though she might have missed the first few years of her mother's illness, but she was not going to miss any of the end.

Her mother's eyes floated uncertainly for a few moments, then locked on to her daughter's features. Claire smiled, an actress, she was able to put every last remnant of the bolts of feeling for her mother into her expressive face.

The older woman screamed. Hands - now claw-like, thin with sharp nails that wouldn't even stop growing when she died - scratched at her daughter's face. Claire stepped back and then came closer again, speaking to her mother in her soft voice, telling her about the memories she had clasped to her bosom for years, telling her how much she wanted to be here with her now. The screams continued. Claire saw real fear in her mother's face.

A nurse, rushing in on silent rubber feet, swept to the head of the bed and held the dying woman's arms, bending in close to coo and soothe.

'Please leave,' she said to Claire.

'What? I'm her daughter.'

'I know, Miss Vassell, but you're upsetting her. Please. Leave.'

Claire, letting her posture break like a puppet whose strings have been dropped and allowing the scars of grief to mark her smooth face, stepped slowly backwards out of the room, the nurse watching her. She felt the heat and the rush of tears.

She went to the hospital canteen. The grey tables always housed a few clusters of strained relatives, their skin often as pallid as that of the patients they visited. She had sat here with Andrew on the day she had landed. Before she met him, Claire had carefully removed much of her make-up leaving only a fine layer of pale foundation. For the past eight years she had watched the make-up artists as they created her mask and she felt she had needed some help for this reunion. Pale faced and pony-tailed, she had shown him a look of shame, affection and shy eagerness. She was satisfied with the response: softhearted Andrew had wept and hugged her.

'Andy, I'm going to stay here with Mum. Is that ok with you?'

she'd asked.

'I'm glad. I know she was hard on you-' Claire flinched, feeling the coldness and the fear '-but she regrets it. So much. You two have missed too many years - of course, you need to be together, to forgive each other.'

'Yes, I do want time alone with her.'

'She told me that you wrote to her about Dad...'

'I think she was a bitch to him, Andy.'

'She had her reasons.'

'Nothing can excuse the way she behaved!'

'I was there, Claire, I was with them. I saw them. She cared for him at the end.'

'Cared? Really? She's cold as ice!'

Andrew took her hand across the table, 'He had AIDS. She was scared-'

'What?' Claire felt the confusion of flush and chill on her cheeks.

'HIV, Claire. I don't know how... Mum didn't know then what we know now...'

Claire pulled her hand away. 'No one told me!'

'You weren't around to tell. It's not something for a phone call. She only told me after Jasper died. She was in a state, anti-depressants and vodka and she told me...'

'I can't... Does it change anything? I don't know...'

His eyes jerked up to meet hers, 'She's dying now, Claire. Stop punishing her.'

'She made me what I am, Andy.'

When she went back to her mother's cell, as she thought of it, the doctor stopped her at the door. He said that her mother did not recognize people now. He wanted to reassure Claire, tell her that she should not be devastated by this turn. The quantities of morphine and other drugs had affected the dying woman's mind. She would no longer be consoled by her daughter's presence, having now - in her mortal confusion - associated her daughter's face with some terror.

'So what should I do?' Claire looked up at him, all filial duty.

'We have your number, Miss Vassell.'

'I came back from Australia to be with her.'

'I'm so sorry - but now, it would be kinder if you were to stay away. It won't be long. You have shown great devotion. I'm sure that in some sense she is aware of that.'

Claire wondered how long it had taken her mother to see the artfully constructed emotions on her face - the resentment, the fierce antagonism, the dislike. She considered herself capable of becoming a great actress and this dying woman had, without doubt, read the anger in her expression and form. She just hoped her mother had read the apology too.

'I didn't want to miss the end,' she said to the doctor, and to herself, 'I didn't want this to be the end.'

## THE KEY

'Here, take it. It's yours.' Richard handed her the key; cool black metal, an ornate decorative top and the shaft unscratched. It had never been turned in a lock.

Lara took it, surprised at how heavy it was, and put it in her bag, before looking up and smiling, 'I'll keep it because, for some crazy reason, it seems to matter to you. But I still don't understand what it does.'

'I suppose you could describe it as an aid to meditation.'

'That's not really my thing, Richie.'

He put his head on one side, clasped his hand in a gesture of pleading, 'Please? For me?'

Lara rolled her eyes and said, 'So, what do I do?'

'You just hold it and sort of empty your mind. It's like you're in a really peaceful garden and … it helps you see who you really are, what you really want.'

'I know that already.'

'Well, I don't think you do. So, as a favour to me, please, use it.'

'Richie, I'm fine.' She spoke quietly. Her voice was always quiet, calm. He noticed this anew every time he was with her, that sense of leaning toward her to hear, that sense of wanting to be close.

'I don't think you are, Lara. I'm worried about you.'

'I can't spend the rest of my life looking back.'

He nodded and stroked her hand. She smiled again. The smile never entirely left her face; in the crinkles around her eyes and the tilted lilt of her lips, it was always there, carrying with it the potential for happiness.

'Hey, I'd better get a move on,' he said.

They stood, the flimsy café table scraping on the tiled floor, and walked arm in arm to the departures area. Richard went through, waving, wearing his hybrid grin, the one bred for times when he wasn't confident of his feelings.

Lara left the airport and drove back to her farm. It took a couple of hours and, as the July sun was at its highest, the air conditioning of her old Shogun struggled and failed to keep the heat at bay. She felt sweat between her breasts, prickling the back of her neck and down her spine. Richie's visit had brought a similar prickling sensation, making her question her decisions, her existence.

Back at the stables, she spent a few hours on her accounts. The Spanish tax system hijacked her mind, leaving her stranded in wastelands of hypothetical percentages. In the cool of the evening, she schooled two of the horses before showering and heading into Tobarra to meet Juanmi. He was in Los Torros with his friends. When she entered, the bubbling tide of Spanish ebbed into silence. Juanmi rose and went to her; one hand possessively in the small of her back, he directed her to the table. She sat and the young men welcomed her with florid flattery before ignoring her and carrying on their conversation about Pablo Hermoso de Mendoza, the *rejoneador* currently being feted in Jerez.

Lara had only once been to a bullfight and had been shocked to find herself attracted by the balletic arrogance of horse and rider. She remembered their grace more clearly than the bewildered aggression of the taunted bull. The stench of blood rose, metallic as anger, choking her, and something visceral was born inside her, something she didn't know she wanted but realized then that she needed.

As the men talked, Juanmi's hand on her knee, then her thigh, Lara thought about Richie. He was an old friend, a friend from university. He knew why she'd moved from Cornwall to breed and train horses in rural Spain. A broken heart; lost hope; the chance of – what else? – another chance. God help her, this time she needed it to work. Richie didn't believe it would and had come over 'to check up on her' on behalf of their mutual friends. She'd evaded his questions and instead they'd talked about what she loved (art), what he did (poetry), and then had drunk enough red wine to forget both.

Juanmi had been unwilling to spend languid hours listening to *el ingles* reading Lorca in an appalling accent. Instead, he'd exercised Lara's horses, frowning at Richie whenever he passed.

'He's rather young for you, Lara,' Richie had said.

She'd shrugged, 'He's old enough.'

'You're a wicked woman.'

'No, just a lucky one.'

'Well, yes, but wouldn't a brain be nice to go with the brawn?'

She laughed, but the laughter was raw edged and he knew her well enough to sense the change of mood; he went on anyway, 'Lara, we all worry about you. You've had such a bloody tough time and I can't help wondering how much of this Hemingway style escape to Spain and the thing with the kid isn't all some big reaction – and a dangerous one too – you stand to make a real fool-'

'Leave it, Richie.' Even with a threat in her voice she spoke quietly and he deferred to her.

The sun smashed down like a cymbal, heating the silence into a peal of vibrations.

Finally she said, 'You and I, Richie - that was a mistake. And yes, you're right: I haven't forgotten him; Ash and I were together for nine years, of course he's still in my mind. I haven't "got over" him. But I have to try, don't I?'

'Yes,' he said, 'yes.'

That was when he'd told her about the key. It was something he'd tried, which had worked for him: a key to the idea of a garden. Just touching the metal, he claimed, was enough to sense dappled sunlight passing through the tender leaves of young oak trees.

In the bar, Juanmi played with his Zippo as he spoke. Lara listened to the click of the lid; the grind and crunch of the lighter's mechanism. She heard, despite the music and the talk, the delicate 'ppffutt' as the wick burst into incandescence. She knew that the scuffed brass, kept in the pocket of his breeches or jeans, was warm as his blood. Sometimes she wanted to snatch the lighter from him and click it into life; yet feared that if she opened it, like a defective mechanical flower, it would perversely refuse to bloom.

The other two boys got up to greet their girlfriends, girls who seemed like children. Lara blushed, feeling, for that moment, too old, while Juanmi's hand caressed her. He asked where she wanted to eat; she named a restaurant and they went, alone, the two of them - like a couple.

When they'd ordered – *gambas al ajillo, imperador, pimientos* – Juanmi left her and went to speak to his uncle, who was in the bar next door. The Zippo lay on the table and she picked it up, sniffed the petrol scent, and slowly opened the lid. That click: like a gun going off in a distant dream. She didn't try to light it – just in case. Instead, she opened her bag and lifted out the key. She held the heavy, cool metal in her hand and felt the green thoughts and the green shade.

While Juanmi's rapid Spanish engulfed a table on the other side of the square, the slow growth of an English summer surrounded the plates and glasses in front of Lara. A garden in the midst of woods or moorland... lark song, just at the edge of hearing, tearing the sky like tin; the mews of a buzzard and the intoxicating scent of sun-warmed grass, damp with newly fallen rain.

Lara, in a bar in Castilla la Mancha, sensed the coolness, the damp, the quiet sounds of home; a garden protected by stone walls; a fox's yellow eyes watching; a lawn, green as artifice and mown to taut perfection... All that she had once wanted; the sort of life; the sort of man, even, that she had once wanted. The idea of a garden, a contained manicured space, was closely bound to memories of her past. For Richie, the past was still the ideal: what he desired for himself. And for her.

Lara snapped open her eyes and put the key in her bag. She picked up the Zippo again and, breathing quickly, struck the flint, hearing, in a desperate beat, the whoosh of the flame. She felt Juanmi's hand on her back, between her shoulder blades, a gesture of grace, not possession. As she turned to him, smiling, the warmth of his touch unlocked the possibility of a future.

## THE SOUND OF BEES

Everything was so green and the valleys were so deep that as we drove down the narrow lanes I felt as though we were diving into and out of a fish tank.

James said, 'The air is damp.'

But I don't know if he really understood what I was signing and it was hard for him to reply. That's what I hate about car journeys. There could be no easy communication between us.

The light is different here. I noticed that on the very first day. It has a richness to it. I call it honey light. To me it's as though there's more than just air in the atmosphere. When the sun shines, this land is bathed in gold. Perhaps because it's a peninsula. Perhaps. Or perhaps there is some strange magic here.

The farm's driveway was overgrown on either side with knee-deep grass and out-of-control shrubs. In the back of the car, Shulie woke up and started to cry. James tapped my arm and pointed back at her before parking in front of what I assumed was to be our cottage, a small stone house across the yard from the main farmhouse.

James worked for the Apiculture and Social Insect Laboratory at Sheffield University. His team was studying Colony Collapse Disorder, a new disease affecting bees in North America which European beekeepers feared would cross the Atlantic. Researchers were being posted around the U.K., to survey the situation and find out ways to prevent the disease. Or at least to try. We were both pleased that James had been assigned to Devon. This site was the most desirable for us as it included a cottage.

I climbed out, stiff from the journey. James stretched, his hair-encircled navel showing, his arms reaching up to the china blue of the Devon sky, his neck arched back. I poked his belly and he folded forwards like a crash test dummy and he stuck his tongue out at me, gesturing to Shulie. Her face was crumpled and red. He'd often said that I was lucky not to be able to hear her screams. He opened the door and I reached in and undid the buckles holding her in the child seat and scooped her up into my arms.

Every time I touch her, even after a break as short as a minute, I still feel the same overflow of emotion as I did when I first held her in the hospital; I feel as though my cup really does runneth over. She was 19 months old when we moved to the farm. Walking and starting to talk. And to sign.

I could feel the tension in her muscles as she screamed and then the gradual relaxing. I could feel the sobs and hiccups as her tears subsided. I rocked her and stroked the tender skin at the back of her neck, just as I comfort James when the depression gets too bad.

I was lost in Shulie when James tapped my arm. I span round and saw him standing with a woman, the woman who owned the farm.

He was speaking to her – telling her my name and the baby's. When he turned back to me he signed and spoke – I am good at lip reading, but it's better to have both. 'This is Mrs Amory, our hostess. She welcomes us to Trehill and hopes we are happy here.'

He raised his eyebrows at the word 'happy' and I smiled at him and then at the woman.

She was slim with hair of silvery white. It was full and curling, more in the style of a younger woman. She wore white jeans and a white silky blouse and her smile was wide and also white.

She spoke to me as though I could hear her. I caught some of it, as she seemed to be mouthing the words especially clearly. She said Trehill was a special place and that she was sure we would come to love it.

It was only when Mrs Amory had finished talking that I realised Shulie had been watching her too. My daughter had turned in my arms and was now reaching out to the woman and bouncing in my embrace the way she does when she wants to get down. I tried to contain her but Mrs Amory stepped forward and bowed her head to me, saying, 'May I?' I could read the words as clearly as printed text. I nodded and she took Shulie from me.

She talked to the child, who was stroking Mrs Armory's hair and chuckling, I could tell by the shape of Shulie's mouth. I knew how her body juddered and shook when she giggled. It was like the bubble and dance of boiling water.

Afterwards, when James and I were alone in the cottage, he asked me if I'd understood what she said.

I nodded, though of course I hadn't caught everything. I didn't really care. I wanted James to hold me, not have to sit looking at each other trying to explain. That's what frustrates me about not hearing: you have to pay so much attention to communicating. You can't have a conversation while you iron or put your make up on or dig a garden or paint a wall. It's the one thing or the other. Pillow talk. How I'd love pillow talk...

He was starting to sign, to tell me more about her conversation, but I moved towards him, trying to end the talk. He laughed, and kissed me, then pushed me back and asked, 'Do you think we'll be happy?'

He didn't mean 'we'. Or at least, not simply 'we'. He meant 'I'. He meant himself. For James, happiness is a troubling concept: something that he grapples towards, occasionally grasps hold of and then feels the desperate fear of its loss – and that fear, it seems to me, precipitates his descent into depression. If he did not fear the absence of happiness so much, perhaps he would be more content with life.

The bees arrived in their special transporter a few days after we had settled in. James flustered around them like an inefficient nanny. At least being busy (as the proverbial bee) kept his mind from obsessing on his mood.

That first evening, I walked out through the old apple trees, carrying a sleepy Shulie in my arms. My husband, in his white astronaut's suit, was standing between the five hives, with the bees buzzing silently around his head. The tilt of his shoulders told me that he was tired, but when he turned to me, I saw that his eyes were full of energy. The lilt in my own heart in response reminded me how anxious I always was in case I saw despair instead.

The bees themselves were sunlight and shade in motion. I did not want to move any closer, but the gold of their stripes and the glinting whirr of wings tempted me. Yes, those wings glinted and shone like love, wild with life. Only Shulie's perfect face kept me away. I motioned to James and he came over, put his arm around me and squeezed. I felt real hope then.

'What kind of noise do the bees make?' I asked him.

When I had asked him about birdsong, he had said that it was like seeing light playing on the surface of a swiftly running stream that flowed over golden glimmering sand. I loved that. The sound of the bees seemed more difficult for him to explain.

He paused before signing, 'Gentle, soothing, soft. Like velvet.' I must have frowned, shown my incomprehension, for he signed, 'If you felt them, held them, you would understand.'

'But they sting!'

'Maybe the sting is worth it to get a sense of their sound.' He looked down into my eyes and smiled.

The evening light shone golden around us. The wispy strands of Shulie's hair gleamed like a halo around her fair head and James was smiling. He had pulled off his mask and rubbed a hand through his sweat-dampened hair. I jogged Shulie on my hip and she bubbled with giggles.

'She is at home here already,' James signed.

I nodded and kissed her sweet skin. She smelt of milk and honey. James reached out and took her from me. She raised her hands to his face and he pretended to eat her fingers before starting to walk back towards the gate.

It was like this for a fortnight. I remember it as though each day was lit with that honey light; each day was yellow and gold and the evenings were rich with amber. James worked with the bees; made his notes; put his entries in the computer and spoke, occasionally, to his Head of Department. I wrote and tended to Shulie. And I got to know Mrs Amory.

She had lived alone on the farm ever since her husband died in a road accident when she was only in her 30s. 'This place is magical,' she told me, writing the words on paper as I made a pot of tea in her kitchen, where two cats curled on the rug by the Aga, and a spaniel twitched in his dreams under the wooden table. 'It has given me so much. Happiness and serenity. I think these blessings give one a sort of power.' I looked over her shoulder as I put the milk back in the fridge and I felt a shiver run down my neck, my back. She carried on writing. 'It enables you to have an influence. I mean, to help others.'

I handed her a mug and placed a plate of biscuits on the table and checked on Shulie, who was having her afternoon nap on a dog-haired sofa in the next room. Then I shuffled between pew and table to sit next to Mrs Amory.

I took the pad from her and wrote, 'What do you mean?'

She smiled again, 'I feel that I can...' She stopped. I waited. The next words were, 'Shulie is awake.'

I went into the other room and picked her up. She was dreamy and confused, her body soft as overproofed dough, yet when I brought her into the kitchen she grinned at Mrs Amory.

My questioning eyes asked the woman to continue. She poured orange juice into a plastic tumbler for my child.

She sat down again and wrote, 'I can pull things towards me. Some things.'

I looked between her and Shulie.

Mrs Amory's face coloured, 'No, dear, no! I have not been toying with your child! That is just... her and I, liking each other, I promise. I mean, not people, I would never do that, I mean energy, health, parking places.' She looked up. 'I must sound an old fool.' I smiled at her, shaking my head. I had heard her make such claims before. Then she wrote, 'You have always known how to be happy, haven't you.'

I nodded at her, my lips parted in surprise.

'Thought as much. It's your husband who suffers.'

This time I could not nod. Her knowledge unnerved me. Although perhaps James's distant eyes made his tendency for depression obvious. Perhaps.

She seemed to have caught my thoughts for she wrote, 'James lives too much in his head and too little in the moment.'

I took the pen from her, 'Except when he is with his bees.'

That evening I cooked risotto for James and me. The rhythm of stirring matched my contemplative mood. I remembered the early days of our relationship when James started to learn sign language. His commitment was endearing. He was a fast learner. He is able to focus on a task so completely that nothing else can touch him then– not even his own dark imagination. While his hands were busy, his mind was too and we had the most light-hearted time of our lives, both of us.

That sun was low by the time he came in. Shulie was in bed and the risotto was losing its freshness. I had been putting my shoes on to run across the yard and through to the orchard when I saw James open the gate and walk, round-shouldered, toward me.

I waited at the door of the cottage. My eyes drank in the sight of the man I loved, and with it, the knowledge that his mood had dipped. His arms hung heavily and his eyes focused only on the ground in front of his feet. I would have run to him but I wanted to keep on seeing him. I always feel that if I look at him for long enough I shall find the missing piece of his jigsaw. And so I watched him. I watched my husband stumble in his pain across the cobbles of the courtyard in front of the stables, and my heart hurt.

I held out my arms and he fell against me. In my head, I spoke to him, 'My lover, my beloved, what has happened to you? How has this vampire leached your strength again? How has it got past my watchfulness?' And the guilt flared up.

He pulled away from me and his eyes were bleak. I signed, 'What?'

He replied, 'I'm sure the bees are going.'

'What?'

'There are less of them. The hives are too quiet.'

'Can you be certain?'

'No, but I am afraid.'

The next morning, James seemed a little less fragile. He carried Shulie into our room when she cried and played with her and read to her while I went downstairs to make breakfast. It soothes him to be with her. I felt relief.

He told me that he would stay in the house that morning to work on his computer modelling. And then he said, 'I am sorry that I worry you. I should not let things affect me so much.'

Later, I crossed the yard with Shulie to Mrs Amory's house

I sat on the pew, while she made tea, talking to herself, or singing, or chatting to Shulie perhaps. I stroked a tiger-striped grey cat which lay against my leg, my fingers sinking into silky fur. His body began to vibrate as he started to purr and through my jeans I felt the minute motor in his throat. I smiled. Mrs Amory caught my eye. She leant down and wrote, 'A cat's purr has healing qualities. Something in the vibrations – it's like a monk chanting as he meditates. Your James would know.'

I frowned the question.

'Like bees, like the sound of bees.'

She must have noticed my eyes clouding; when she sat down she wrote, 'What's wrong?'

The spaniel was resting his head on her lap, wagging his stub of a tail. The cat yawned next to me on the pew.

I looked into her calm grey eyes and took the pad. I wrote for what seemed like hours. And she read. She nodded. She took my hand and smiled. I could read her lips when she said, 'It will be all right.' Strangely, the words soothed me.

The following day, when James left to inspect the hives, I sat cross legged on the floor while Shulie watched her Disney video and I tried to let go of my feelings. I had my eyes closed, so when he shook me, I cried out, I felt the sharp catch of the air in my voice box.

He was speaking, the words tumbling like water from his lips, and as silent as the picture of a river.

I caught at his hands, held them up. He stopped, looked at our joined hands and realisation struck him.

'Bees have gone. All gone. Except one queen and some workers. A grub. No bodies. The colony has collapsed.'

'Impossible!'

'They've gone. They've gone. It's here. I'm destroyed.'

He slumped onto a chair, leaning his elbows on the kitchen table.

'It's not your fault.'

'It's my life. I've failed. I am nothing.'

I shook my head, fierce with hurt, and went to him, slipped onto his lap so that he was forced to enfold me, support me. I signed, leaning away so that he could see, 'You are the love of my life. You are the father of our child. These are the successes that matter.'

He held me, but I knew it gave him little comfort. When the pain stole over him, he could see only the shadows, not the light. I'm sure in that mood even his bees would lose their gleaming beauty and appear all black to him. And be blind to their bars of gold.

'I'm afraid,' he said. 'I feel myself falling apart. I can't hold on to the pieces.'

He pushed me from him and stood up, passing through the living room and running up the stairs. I lifted Shulie from the sofa and held her warm struggling body to me, breathing in the unique scent of her. When I pulled my head away from my child, I saw James coming back down.

He was carrying a bag with entrails of shirt, socks, crumpled trousers escaping. He handed me a piece of paper and walked through the kitchen and out the still open door.

He'd written, 'I need space.'

I followed him. Watched as he got into our car, throwing the bag onto the back seat. In silence, the car door closed and the engine started. He turned around and drove out of the farm yard.

Mrs Amory watched from her kitchen window. I backed into the house and shut the door. My legs felt weak. I rested against the door frame, breathing deeply, my vision blurring and my face wet. I scrubbed a hand over my cheeks and tried to stand up straight. The time passed.

I don't know how long he was gone, but it was dark when he got back.

He came through the door, his eyes ringed with shadows and his steps heavy. He collapsed next to me and held me. I smelt the fumes of petrol and grief on his skin and his unshaven chin scratched my shoulder through my T-shirt. Finally, I stood up, pulled him to his feet and pointed upstairs. He nodded and obeyed. I got into bed next to him and we slept.

I dreamed of him driving away: just as it had happened, I saw the car pull away, I wept at the door. In the dream, Shulie must have climbed off the sofa. I felt her hands at my thighs, warm, soft, insistent. I looked down at her face. The child was smiling. She raised her hands to me and I bent down, picked her up, stepped back sharply as I nearly lost balance with her weight on my unsteady legs. She pointed at the door. I turned, wanting to take her upstairs, to hold her sweetness to me, but she bounced and struggled, pointing back at the door and beating her fists on my shoulders when I ignored her and walked on.

I stopped when she leaned against my arms and signed in front of my face, 'Bees. Go bees.'

I shook my head, feeling the tears again, but she repeated the signs and then, 'Please.'

Our child. I followed her command and walked back to the door, outside, across the yard and through the gate into the orchard. We followed the path around the back of the old stables, the long grass catching at my legs and the breath of early summer surrounding us.

As I climbed the slight rise and passed the first of the old, gnarled apple trees, grey and green with lichen and small fruit, I saw a figure in white by the six hives, her arms raised to the pristine blue of the sky.

She was too close to the hives - James had said there were some bees left – enough to hurt an elderly lady. I fell into a clumsy jog towards her, Shulie bouncing on my hip, the gold of her hair as precious as sunlight. I was still 50 yards from the woman and the hives when I realised that my little girl was trying to attract my attention, wanting to stop. I thought I had hurt her, crushing her tender body against my body, but as soon as I stopped she was at peace, watching.

I turned from Shulie to Mrs Amory and saw a dark column had formed, was being funnelled, between her upraised arms. A shadow of vibration. A cloud narrowing to tunnel through the woman's embrace and then separating into six thin lines, each streaming into one of the hives.

Shulie bubbled in my grasp and strained to the right. I followed the angle of her body and saw my husband walking through the glittering grass, now running towards us and towards the bees.

He stopped beside us, put his arms around us. But neither he nor I could look away from the dance between silver white Mrs Amory and the black gold of the returning bees.

It was early when I woke. James slept on. I watched him for a moment. His skin shone, unwashed, in the morning light and his eyelids jerked in dreams. I stroked his cheek and he moved his head as though to nuzzle the hand that touched him. I felt myself smile and was surprised to feel pleasure.

Shulie was standing at the bars of her bed. She bounced on the mattress and her eyes were as blue as a summer sky. I picked her up and felt her curls at my neck.

In the kitchen, she was still restless in her chair, not interested in water, juice or food. I signed, 'What?' And she replied, 'Bees.' My heart thudded in my chest like a fist and I jumped to feel James's hand on my shoulder.

'I had a dream about the bees,' he signed. 'Maybe she did too.'

I stared at him and asked, 'Dream?'

'Yes. Strange. That the woman – Mrs Amory -'

I didn't give him time to stop, but instead grabbed Shulie from the chair. James watched, the frown deepening, then followed me as I slipped on sandals and left the cottage. He tugged me to a halt halfway across the courtyard and said, his lips easy to read, 'What are you doing?'

I passed him our daughter so I could sign, 'The dream. Me too.'

His mouth opened and, holding Shulie in one arm, he caught me by the other hand, and pulled me along, only letting go to open the gate.

I was breathing heavily by the time we got close to the hives. At the place where I had stopped in my dream, James told me to stay, and he moved closer. As though in slow motion, he lifted the lid of the nearest hive and I saw a dark blur rise. He turned back to me and his expression was all wonder.

Shulie jumped in my arms, as she had in the dream, reaching out to my right. I followed her gaze and saw that Mrs Amory had appeared at the gateway and was now stepping through the grass. James must have seen her too. She smiled to him and then looked across to me… and she winked.

REFERENCES FOR 'PIKE':

Feinstein, E. (2002) [2001] *Ted Hughes: The Life of a Poet*, London: Phoenix.
Obsession with fishing and pike as a child pp.5-23; 'The Rabbit Catcher' poems pp. 265-6; farming and the writing of *Moortown Diary* pp221-2

Hughes, T. (1998) *Birthday Letters*, London: Faber and Faber.
Notably: 'St Botolph's', 'Visit', 'Your Paris' and 'The Rabbit Catcher'

Hughes, T. (1986) [1984] *Selected Poems 1957-1981*, London: Faber and Faber.
Notably: 'Pike', 'The Horses', 'Thrushes', 'An October Salmon', 'Ravens' and 'February 17th'

Middlebrook, D. (2004) [2003] *Her Husband: Ted Hughes and Sylvia Plath – A Marriage*, New York: Penguin.
The dream which inspired 'Pike' pp. 54-55: 'The Rabbit Catcher' poems pp.166-176; importance of fishing/water pp. 281-2

Plath, S. (1989) [1981] *Collected Poems*, London: Faber and Faber.
    'The Rabbit Catcher'

With great thanks to Mandy Kasafir – firstly for the one-on-one creativity session which opened my mind to writing and my eyes to the richness of colour; secondly for the painting 'Nananlia' which hangs above my desk; and thirdly for 'Caneldra', the front cover of this book.

You can see more of Mandy's work at www.mandykasafir.com

Many thanks also to Elly-Elaine, for hours spent proofreading and making wonderful suggestions, for encouragement and affection; to Issi for providing Antarctica for White and the photograph for the back cover; to Mehran for help with Violet; to Kath for helping with Black and Green; and to my father for being who he is.

Printed in the United Kingdom by
Lightning Source UK Ltd., Milton Keynes
138832UK00002B/112/P